# Reckless Lies

Ivy Hale

Published by Ivy Hale, 2024.

RECKLESS LIES

**First edition. October 30, 2024.**

ISBN: 979-8227671592

Written by Ivy Hale.

# Chapter 1: Fateful Encounter

The evening sky drapes a rich indigo over Chicago as I step out of the art gallery, the faint buzz of conversation swirling behind me. My heart races, not from the thrill of the vibrant paintings I've just admired but from the unexpected presence of Jonah Harrington, the very man I've clashed with at every charity event for the past year. His sharp wit and piercing green eyes have always managed to unnerve me, and tonight, they hold a dangerous glint. He stands leaning against a sleek black car, his silhouette outlined by the streetlights, an aura of confidence that makes my pulse quicken.

"Didn't think you'd make it out of the gallery without a security escort," he quips, a smirk dancing on his lips. The air between us simmers with unspoken challenges, our usual verbal sparring warming up like a prelude to a storm. I lean against the gallery's doorframe, crossing my arms to mask the rush of adrenaline that comes with his presence.

"I didn't realize you were such a connoisseur of the arts, Jonah. I assumed you were too busy counting your stocks and updating your social media to appreciate anything more profound than your reflection," I shoot back, the words tumbling out sharper than I intended. Yet there's a thrill in the exchange, an electric connection that has always simmered beneath our feuds.

He raises an eyebrow, his expression one of feigned innocence. "Touché. But art, like life, is all about perception. Maybe I'm just here for the free hors d'oeuvres. I hear the brie is to die for."

"Or maybe it's because you enjoy making other people's lives a little more... difficult," I retort, my voice a playful lilt. My stomach twists, not entirely from irritation but from the way his laughter rolls like velvet through the night air.

"Maybe I enjoy watching you squirm," he counters, his tone light but laden with a sincerity that catches me off guard. I glance away, pretending to admire a nearby street vendor setting up for the evening rush, while inside, my thoughts whirl. Jonah Harrington, the man whose every glance feels like an invitation to a duel, somehow keeps finding a way to invade my mind.

"Do you ever tire of the same old games?" I ask, a hint of genuine curiosity weaving through my bravado.

"Not when the stakes are this high," he replies, pushing off from the car to step closer, the scent of his cologne—a warm, woodsy aroma—mingling with the crisp evening air. I can't help but notice how the low light plays off his chiseled features, casting him in a glow that feels too intimate for our banter.

We stand mere inches apart now, the world around us fading to a dull hum. There's a pause, a stillness that feels charged, as if the city itself holds its breath. My heartbeat thrums in my ears, a wild drum echoing the anticipation crackling between us.

"So, what's next? A dance-off in the middle of the street?" I jest, trying to break the tension but suddenly wishing for something far less frivolous.

"Only if you promise to lose spectacularly," he shoots back, his grin widening, and for a moment, I consider the impossibility of sharing an actual dance with him—my heart and mind colliding in a frenzy of conflicting emotions.

As if on cue, a group of rowdy pedestrians bursts into laughter nearby, jolting me from my reverie. I take a step back, needing space to regain my composure. "Look, Jonah, as much as I relish our delightful exchanges, I have plans for the evening that don't involve you or your attempts at wooing me with your charm."

"Oh, come now. It's not like you could resist me if you tried," he retorts, an undeniable gleam in his eyes.

I scoff, unable to help the grin tugging at the corners of my mouth. "Confidence is a good look on you, but it won't work tonight."

"Challenge accepted," he replies, his tone suddenly serious, a dark edge creeping into his words. "But let's make it interesting. I'll let you pick the stakes."

Before I can process the implications of his challenge, a siren wails in the distance, shattering the moment. I glance over my shoulder, noticing a couple of friends from the gallery strolling out, their chatter mingling with the city's night life. It strikes me then—how easily we slipped into this back-and-forth, how quickly the world beyond us faded.

"Okay, fine," I say, a mixture of excitement and trepidation coursing through me. "If I win, you have to donate a hefty sum to the local art program."

"And if I win?" he asks, his voice low and intriguing, sending shivers up my spine.

"Then... I'll let you buy me a drink," I concede, the challenge now feeling thrillingly precarious. The very thought of sharing a drink with him stirs something deeper, a temptation I can't quite shake.

He extends his hand, an invitation to seal our bargain. "Deal."

The moment our hands clasp, I feel the shock of connection—a jolt that sends warmth through my fingertips and flutters in my chest. I let go quickly, the heat lingering like a ghost between us. "Well, then. I suppose I should warn you—I don't intend to lose."

"Neither do I," he replies, a wicked grin forming.

With that, we part ways, the night air still crackling with tension, my heart racing not just from the thrill of our bet but from the knowledge that, somehow, this encounter is only the beginning of something much more complicated. As I walk away, a smile breaks through my earlier bravado, echoing with the promise of what's to come.

The tension lingers in the air like the fading scent of expensive cologne as I navigate the city streets, my mind buzzing with thoughts of Jonah. Each step I take seems to resonate with the spark of our earlier encounter, the thrill of our banter still dancing in my veins. I pull my scarf tighter around my neck, the cool wind of the evening whispering secrets I can't quite grasp. The city lights flicker above, their reflections shimmering in the puddles left from an earlier rain, painting the asphalt with a glistening, chaotic beauty that mirrors my thoughts.

It's a Saturday night in Chicago, and the energy pulsates around me. Laughter spills from nearby cafés, and couples stroll hand-in-hand, their faces illuminated by the soft glow of street lamps. I push the distractions aside, focusing on the cocktail bar just a few blocks ahead. It's a place I often visit, a small haven where the bartender knows my favorite drink—the fiery ginger mule, with just the right amount of kick. The thought of that familiar warmth settles me as I navigate through the throng of people.

As I arrive, the door swings open to reveal the lively interior. The bar is bustling, filled with familiar faces and new ones, laughter and chatter blending into a melodic hum. I squeeze through the crowd, making my way to the bar, where my refuge awaits. The bartender, a burly man with a welcoming grin, nods at me. "The usual?"

"Absolutely," I reply, a smile breaking across my face. As he starts mixing, I scan the room, searching for a quiet corner where I can gather my thoughts.

But as fate would have it, Jonah appears from the shadows, weaving through the crowd with an effortless grace that could only come from someone used to commanding attention. He catches my eye, and the warmth of the ginger mule I had been anticipating suddenly feels distant and cold. "Fancy seeing you here," he says, his tone light but his gaze intense.

"Do you follow me everywhere?" I counter, pretending to be annoyed, but my heart beats a little faster.

He shrugs, that familiar smirk returning. "Only to places that serve overpriced cocktails and feature stunning women."

"Charming," I reply dryly, though the compliment lingers in the air between us like the scent of a particularly alluring perfume.

"Why, thank you. It's a gift," he quips, leaning against the bar beside me, our elbows almost touching. The warmth of his presence radiates through the air, and I force myself to concentrate on the bartender, who slides my drink across the counter with a flourish.

I take a sip, the sharp ginger dancing on my tongue, and glance at Jonah, whose expression is now decidedly serious. "So, about that bet..." he starts, his voice lowered, as if the mere mention of our challenge could ignite some hidden flame.

"Right. My art program needs your deep pockets," I say, adopting a mock-serious tone. "How do you plan to fulfill your end of the deal?"

"Let's make it interesting," he replies, eyes glimmering with mischief. "How about I take you to see some art—real art? None of this pretentious gallery nonsense."

I blink, taken aback. "And by 'real art,' you mean what? A warehouse full of graffiti?"

"Precisely. There's a new exhibit in a converted loft space down by the river. I promise, it's not what you think."

"And what makes you think I'd willingly follow you into a place full of spray paint and questionable hygiene?" I challenge, my curiosity piqued despite myself.

"Because you're just as curious as I am." His voice is low, coaxing. "And let's face it, it's more entertaining than the stuffy event circuit we've been trapped in."

"You've got a point," I admit, my own curiosity battling with the wariness creeping into my thoughts. I can almost feel the thrum of excitement in my veins at the idea of exploring something new, something unexpected with him.

"I'll even let you pick the time and place," he adds, raising an eyebrow. "I promise to behave."

"Right. Your version of 'behaving' is like a tiger promising not to bite."

"Touché. But I like to think of myself as a rehabilitated tiger," he quips, flashing a grin that is both charming and infuriating.

Before I can respond, I catch sight of a familiar face across the room. Claire, my best friend, is waving enthusiastically, her blonde curls bouncing as she pushes her way through the crowd. She approaches us, her eyes alight with mischief. "Well, well! If it isn't the fierce competitors. What are you two plotting now?"

"Just discussing art," I say, trying to sound casual as I sip my drink.

"Oh, please. You two are practically glowing," she replies, a knowing smile spreading across her face. "And if I didn't know better, I'd say there's a bit of chemistry sparking in the air."

"Chemistry? Hardly," I protest, but the heat rising in my cheeks gives me away.

"Of course not. Just a delightful tension, then?" Jonah interjects, his gaze steady on me, and I suddenly wish for a witty retort. Instead, I feel flustered, caught in the spotlight of their banter.

"Should I be worried?" Claire asks, her voice dripping with playful concern as she eyes Jonah.

"Only if you value your sanity," I say quickly, shooting Jonah a look that dares him to tease me further.

"I'll take that as a compliment," he replies, amusement dancing in his eyes.

As Claire grabs my arm, pulling me aside for a moment, she whispers, "What's going on with you two? This feels different."

"It's not. It's just... a bet. A little competition," I murmur, unsure how to articulate the sudden flurry of emotions that swirl within me.

"Sure, a bet. But he's been looking at you like you're the most interesting person in the room," she whispers, glancing back at Jonah, who is now animatedly discussing something with a stranger.

I shake my head, trying to dismiss her words. "It's just banter, Claire. Nothing more."

"Just banter that makes you blush? You're kidding yourself."

"Let's just see how the bet plays out," I say, turning my attention back to Jonah, who catches my eye and winks. The world around me fades once more, leaving only the heady mix of laughter, music, and the promise of something unforeseen waiting just around the corner.

In that moment, I can't help but feel that this encounter, woven into the tapestry of our prior confrontations, is about to unravel into a narrative much richer and more unpredictable than I had ever anticipated.

The warmth of the ginger mule lingers on my tongue as I watch Jonah from a distance, his laughter blending seamlessly with the upbeat tempo of the bar. Claire's teasing comment about the chemistry between us loops in my mind like a catchy song, one I can't quite shake. But as I observe him effortlessly navigate the crowd, charming everyone in his path, I can't help but wonder how much of this playful rivalry is just that—playful.

"Hey," Claire nudges me, her bright eyes alight with mischief. "What's the deal with that guy? You've been trading barbs for so long, I'd swear you two were vying for a reality show."

"Funny, isn't it?" I reply, forcing a casualness into my tone. "It's all just banter. The thrill of competition. Nothing more."

"Right," she scoffs, arching an eyebrow. "Next, you'll tell me that the way you glare at him is just a friendly gesture."

I roll my eyes but can't stifle the smile creeping across my lips. Jonah catches my gaze from across the room and flashes that infuriatingly handsome grin, his expression a mix of challenge and curiosity. I swallow hard, a rush of warmth flooding my cheeks. "Okay, maybe there's a bit of tension," I admit, unable to deny the electric charge that flares up every time he's near.

"Just a bit?" she teases, nudging my shoulder playfully. "Why don't you go talk to him? It's not like you to back down from a challenge."

The thought of walking over to him sends a bolt of nerves through me. What if I trip over my words, or worse, he sees the way my heart races at the mere thought of him? But Claire's challenge lingers in the air, a spark that ignites a sense of daring I didn't know I possessed.

Before I can second-guess myself, I push away from the bar and stride toward Jonah, who is now engrossed in conversation with a tall, willowy woman dressed in a sleek black dress that clings to her every curve. My stomach twists as I approach, but I shake off the fleeting insecurity. It's just Jonah.

"Ah, the art aficionado returns," he calls out, a teasing lilt in his voice that sends a shiver of anticipation down my spine. "Decided to abandon your safe haven for the wild world of real art?"

"Only if you promise not to lead me into any sketchy alleyways," I counter, my bravado growing with every step closer. The woman beside him raises an eyebrow, and I catch a flicker of something akin to amusement in her expression.

"Trust me, if I were going to drag you into danger, I'd at least ensure it was artfully done," Jonah replies, leaning in slightly, the heat of his presence wrapping around me like a warm blanket.

I laugh, my nerves easing as we slip back into our familiar rhythm. "Artfully done, huh? That's a generous way to describe your antics."

"Generous? Perhaps I'm just trying to win you over," he says, his voice dropping to a conspiratorial whisper that sends a thrill racing through me.

"And how exactly do you plan to accomplish that?" I challenge, raising an eyebrow.

"By taking you to that exhibit I mentioned. But you'll have to trust me," he replies, his tone surprisingly sincere.

"Trust you? The man who revels in tossing verbal grenades at every opportunity?"

"That's the beauty of it," he insists, his eyes sparkling with mischief. "You're already invested in this game. Why not see where it takes us?"

There's something enticing about the way he proposes the adventure, a blend of danger and intrigue that feels undeniably magnetic. Just then, Claire reappears at my side, her eyes dancing between us.

"Did you two miss me? Because it looks like you were about to elope," she quips, causing Jonah to chuckle and me to roll my eyes yet again.

"Oh, you know how it is," Jonah responds with an exaggerated sigh, "the art world is fraught with unexpected temptations."

"Right," I interject, unable to suppress my smile. "And I'm sure it's all purely professional."

Claire leans closer to me, a conspiratorial whisper escaping her lips. "What are you waiting for? Go for it!"

As tempting as it is to accept Jonah's invitation, something deeper tugs at my hesitation. It feels like stepping off a precipice into the unknown. "I'll think about it," I say, trying to keep my voice steady despite the flutter of anxiety stirring in my chest.

"Just think quickly. You know how fast this city moves," Jonah interjects, his gaze locking onto mine with an intensity that feels like a secret shared between just the two of us.

The night wears on, filled with laughter and conversation, but I find myself continually drawn back to Jonah. Each glance exchanged holds the promise of more, a dance of emotions just beneath the surface.

As the bar begins to thin out, I feel a wave of uncertainty wash over me. Jonah watches me with an unwavering gaze, a playful smile lingering on his lips. "So, what's it going to be? Are we doing this or not?"

The challenge lingers, heavy and tantalizing. I glance at Claire, who is watching me with an encouraging nod, and then back at Jonah, whose eyes glint with expectation.

"Fine," I say, gathering every ounce of courage I can muster. "Let's see this 'real art' of yours. But if it involves a spray paint can, I'm out."

He laughs, the sound rich and deep, wrapping around me like a cozy blanket. "Deal. I promise to keep the cans at bay."

As we step out into the cool night air, I'm struck by how easily he navigates the world around him, his confidence infectious. Yet just as the thrill of the moment begins to settle in, a loud crash echoes through the alleyway beside the bar, shattering the vibrant atmosphere.

We both freeze, the night's excitement transforming into an edge of danger. A figure stumbles into view, silhouetted against the neon lights, clutching a package that spills its contents across the pavement. My heart races as adrenaline spikes.

"Stay here," Jonah says, his voice low and commanding.

"Like I'd let you face this alone," I reply, instinctively stepping forward.

As we approach, the figure raises their head, and a chill runs down my spine. The face that emerges from the shadows is all too familiar—a reminder of a past I thought I had left behind.

"Surprise," the stranger smirks, their voice dripping with malice.

In that moment, the world narrows down to just us, a whirlwind of emotions spiraling as I realize this is no longer just a game. What began as a playful rivalry has suddenly turned into something much more perilous, and the stakes have risen beyond my wildest imagination.

# Chapter 2: Unlikely Allies

The scent of linseed oil and aged canvas clung to the air as I stepped into the dimly lit gallery, the walls adorned with the vivid strokes of creativity that seemed to pulsate with life. My heart raced, not from the usual thrill of art's embrace, but from the gnawing anxiety of something gone terribly wrong. The corner where the painting had hung was bare, a ghost of its vibrant colors lingering in my memory, mocking me with its absence. The gallery was my sanctuary, the carefully curated collection a testament to my passion and painstaking effort, now reduced to an empty space that echoed my dread.

I paced in front of the blank wall, every creak of the wooden floorboards beneath my heels a reminder of my failure. The painting, a stunning work by a local artist, had been the crown jewel of our exhibit. Now it felt as if I were standing at the edge of a cliff, teetering dangerously close to a fall that could shatter everything I had built. My phone buzzed insistently in my pocket, a stark contrast to the silence that enveloped me. I fished it out, half-hoping for a miracle in the form of a text or a call that would resolve my crisis. Instead, the screen lit up with a name I had long associated with frustration and irritation: Jonah.

My fingers hovered over the screen, hovering between pressing 'call' and letting it slide into oblivion. Jonah, with his sharp tongue and even sharper suits, was the last person I wanted to deal with right now. But as I glanced again at the empty space on the wall, a reluctant thought crept in. If I wanted to get the painting back, I needed someone with an edge, someone who thrived in the chaotic underbelly of the city. I rolled my eyes, resigned to the inevitable. With a sigh that seemed to carry the weight of the world, I pressed 'call.'

"Fiona," he answered, the cadence of his voice both grating and somehow comforting, like the first sip of coffee on a cold morning. "What do you want?"

"I need your help," I said, forcing the words through clenched teeth. The irony of needing assistance from someone I despised was not lost on me, but desperation had a way of lowering one's pride.

"Is this a joke?" His laughter was a sharp edge against my vulnerability. "You can't be serious."

"I am. The painting—it's gone," I admitted, a part of me bracing for the fallout of admitting my failure.

"Gone? As in... stolen?" His tone shifted, genuine curiosity threading through the skepticism.

"Yes, stolen. And if you want to keep hearing your own voice, you might want to help me figure out who took it."

After a moment of silence, during which I imagined Jonah tapping his fingers against his desk, probably smirking, he finally relented. "Fine. Meet me at The Rusty Nail in an hour. And wear something... discreet."

As I hung up, a mix of irritation and reluctant anticipation coursed through me. The Rusty Nail was the kind of bar where shadows danced and secrets mingled like patrons nursing their drinks. I wasn't keen on venturing into that world, but if Jonah could help me retrieve the painting, I would brave whatever twisted alleyways we needed to explore.

An hour later, I stood at the bar, taking in the eclectic mix of artfully tattooed souls and weary-eyed patrons. The low hum of conversation intermingled with the soft clinking of glasses, creating a soundscape that felt both chaotic and oddly comforting. Jonah appeared moments later, clad in a dark jacket that did nothing to mask his imposing presence. He scanned the room, his expression a mix of bemusement and annoyance.

"There you are," he said, sliding into the seat next to me. "I thought you might've chickened out."

"Not a chance. Let's just get this over with," I replied, narrowing my eyes at him. "What's the plan?"

Jonah leaned closer, his voice dropping to a conspiratorial whisper. "We need to hit the streets, talk to some contacts. There's a rumor about a thief going by the name 'The Raven' who's been hitting galleries around the city. You might have stumbled into their crosshairs."

"The Raven?" I scoffed, half-amused, half-terrified. "Sounds like something out of a bad detective novel."

"Maybe," he shrugged, "but this isn't a novel. It's our lives, and right now, we need to take it seriously."

With a reluctant nod, I finished my drink, the whiskey burning a path down my throat, igniting a sense of courage I hadn't anticipated. As we navigated the dimly lit streets, the night wrapped around us like a shroud, each shadow morphing into potential threats and allies alike. Our banter was laced with a strange familiarity, as if we had danced this dance before, despite the venom that usually colored our exchanges.

"So, tell me, Fiona," he began, glancing sideways at me, "what's the story behind the missing painting? I'm sure it's more than just a pretty canvas."

I paused, surprised at his unexpected curiosity. "It was a gift from my grandmother. She always believed in the power of art to tell stories. Losing it feels like losing a part of her."

Jonah's expression softened for a fleeting moment, and I found myself momentarily disarmed by the vulnerability hidden beneath his brash exterior. "We'll find it, then," he said, his voice more earnest than I had ever heard it. "Just stay close. The streets can be unforgiving."

And with that, our unlikely alliance began to take shape. Each turn and every whispered conversation opened a window into a world I had never wanted to see, filled with complexities and layers that blurred the lines between good and evil. The thrill of the chase electrified the air around us, weaving a narrative that was as much about discovery as it was about danger.

The chill in the air wrapped around us as we navigated the narrow, graffiti-laden streets, the faint glow of streetlights illuminating our path. Jonah led the way, his stride confident, though I could sense the tension coiling between us like a tightly wound spring. Each corner we turned felt like we were stepping deeper into a hidden world, one filled with uncertainty and an edge of danger that crackled like static electricity.

"Keep your eyes peeled," Jonah murmured, glancing over his shoulder as if expecting a shadow to spring to life. "We're looking for any signs of The Raven's crew. They say he has a network of eyes everywhere."

"Great. Just what I wanted," I replied, attempting to mask my unease with bravado. "To be hunted by a mythical thief. Can't we just put a sign in the gallery window saying, 'Missing: One Painting, Reward for Information'?"

His chuckle was low and rich, surprising me. "I'm not sure The Raven takes bribes, but we could give it a shot." He paused, his expression shifting as he pointed ahead. "There's a bar, The Vulture's Nest. We might find some leads there."

The Vulture's Nest was a dive, its neon sign flickering like a warning, yet it pulsated with an energy that drew us in. The door creaked ominously as we entered, revealing a dimly lit interior where smoke curled lazily through the air, mingling with the scent of cheap whiskey and the distant hum of a jazz band. The walls were adorned with an eclectic mix of art—some beautiful, others distinctly disturbing—and I felt an odd sense of kinship with this motley collection.

"Stay close," Jonah whispered, scanning the room. "I'll do the talking."

As we weaved through the crowded space, I couldn't help but marvel at the strange tapestry of humanity that surrounded us. From the grizzled bartender polishing glasses to the couples huddled in corners sharing whispered secrets, everyone seemed to have a story. But Jonah's voice sliced through my reverie, pulling me back into focus.

He approached a man hunched over the bar, his fingers tapping anxiously on the wood. "Eddie," Jonah greeted, his tone light yet commanding. "Heard you might have some information for us."

The man looked up, revealing a face etched with lines of worry and exhaustion. "What kind of information?" he asked, his eyes darting between Jonah and me.

"We're looking for a missing painting," I interjected, summoning all the charm I could muster. "Stolen from my gallery. Maybe you've heard something?"

Eddie took a long sip from his glass, considering my words with the careful deliberation of a chess player contemplating his next move. "You're stepping into dangerous waters, sweetheart. The Raven isn't just a thief; he's a ghost. You won't catch him by looking for leads in bars."

"Maybe not," Jonah replied, leaning closer, his voice dropping. "But we need to know who his buyers are. Someone must know something. You've got ears all over this city."

The tension in the air thickened as Eddie weighed his options. Finally, he sighed, the weight of his decision evident. "There's a rumor that The Raven is working with a dealer named Lila. She's got connections to some serious players. You might want to check her out, but don't say I sent you."

"Thanks, Eddie," I said, relief flooding through me. "We appreciate it."

As we stepped back into the cool night air, the adrenaline surged through me, mingling with excitement and dread. "Lila, huh? Think we can just stroll into her gallery and ask for a chat?" I asked, trying to gauge Jonah's thoughts.

"Not a chance. Lila plays her cards close to her chest," he said, his voice steady. "We'll need to be strategic. I have a plan."

My heart sank a little at the word 'plan.' I had long since learned that Jonah's plans often involved more chaos than I was comfortable with. "What's the plan?"

"Simple," he said, grinning. "We crash her opening tomorrow night. I'll charm my way in, and you'll play the part of my art-savvy girlfriend. We'll gather intel and see if we can catch a glimpse of The Raven's handiwork."

"Art-savvy girlfriend?" I scoffed, a laugh bubbling up unexpectedly. "You must have me confused with someone who enjoys wearing low-cut dresses and flinging compliments around."

"I have complete faith in your ability to pull off both," he shot back, his smile infectious.

The teasing banter hung in the air like a shared secret, an unexpected warmth unfurling within me. Maybe this would work; maybe the thrill of the chase would mask the underlying tension that buzzed between us like a live wire. As we walked side by side, I began to appreciate how his presence shifted the dynamic, turning our shared mission into something more vibrant and alive.

When we reached the gallery the following evening, the atmosphere buzzed with excitement, art lovers milling about like bees in a garden, each one intent on finding their own piece of beauty. Jonah looked remarkably composed, the charm in his demeanor evident as he greeted familiar faces, his confidence drawing me in.

"Remember, play it cool," he whispered, nudging me with a playful smirk. "Act like you belong here."

We moved through the gallery, past vibrant canvases and sculptural forms that beckoned for attention. As Jonah struck up conversations, I took mental notes of everything around me—the paintings, the people, and the understated elegance of the space. I felt a sense of belonging wash over me, even amidst the chaos of our mission.

"Can I offer you a glass of wine?" Jonah asked, catching my eye with a raised brow, the hint of mischief dancing in his gaze.

"Only if you promise not to spill it on my dress," I shot back, laughing despite the tension coiling within me.

Just then, a voice cut through the ambient noise, sharp and smooth like silk. "I see you've brought a date, Jonah."

I turned to see a woman with a striking presence, her dark hair cascading like a waterfall of ink over her shoulders. Lila's gaze flicked between us, assessing, predatory. "And who might you be?"

"Fiona," I said, extending my hand, my heart racing under the weight of her scrutiny. "I'm an art enthusiast. Jonah's told me a lot about your work."

"Has he?" Lila's smile was all sharp edges, but there was an undercurrent of curiosity that flickered behind her dark eyes. "Well, I hope you appreciate the finer things."

As she turned to walk away, a sudden thought struck me. "I'd love to hear about your recent acquisitions," I called after her, pushing my nerves aside. "The buzz around town is incredible!"

Lila paused, her smile freezing for just a second before she recovered. "Perhaps we can chat more privately, then. Follow me."

As we trailed behind her, I exchanged a glance with Jonah, his eyes glinting with both apprehension and excitement. Whatever game we were stepping into, it was clear we were no longer mere spectators. We were players in a dangerous dance, where every move counted, and the stakes were higher than I ever imagined.

The gallery buzzed with the intoxicating energy of art lovers, their laughter and conversation mingling like paint on a canvas, creating a vibrant tapestry of sounds. Jonah and I followed Lila through a corridor adorned with striking pieces, each one whispering secrets of creativity and ambition. The walls shimmered with color, reflecting the ambitions of the artists and the buyers who coveted their work. My heart raced—not just from the thrill of being here but from the precarious tightrope we were walking.

"Here we are," Lila announced, leading us into a small alcove that housed a private collection. The lighting shifted, casting an ethereal glow on the canvases. "These pieces are the newest additions. I'd love your thoughts, Fiona."

I took a breath, forcing my mind to settle amidst the overwhelming sense of intrigue. "They're stunning," I managed, letting the words roll off my tongue. "Each piece tells a story. What's the narrative behind this one?" I gestured toward a large canvas, its colors swirling in chaotic harmony.

"That's an original by Maxine Lorrimer," she replied, her pride evident. "It's inspired by the contrasts of urban life—a blend of chaos and beauty."

Jonah leaned in closer, his posture relaxed yet alert. "Do you often feature local artists?" he asked, his tone deceptively casual.

"Only the best," Lila responded, her smile widening. "And only those who understand the value of discretion."

The implications hung in the air, thickening the atmosphere with unspoken tension. "Discretion?" I echoed, probing for more. "In this business, I imagine it's quite essential."

"Indeed," she said, her gaze shifting toward Jonah, and I sensed a subtle challenge in her demeanor. "And you both seem to be... quite interested in art. Are you collectors?"

"More like enthusiasts," Jonah replied smoothly, his charm apparent as he flashed a disarming smile. "We appreciate the finer things in life, but we also enjoy a good story behind the artwork."

Lila tilted her head, her curiosity piqued. "Is that so? Then you must know about The Raven. He's the kind of story that fascinates and terrifies all at once."

The air crackled with anticipation, and I felt a chill run down my spine. "We've heard whispers," I said carefully, trying to gauge her reaction.

Her eyes sparkled with mischief, as if she were considering how much to reveal. "They say The Raven has an eye for talent and a taste for mischief. Some believe he's more than just a thief; he's a connoisseur, stealing not just art but the very essence of it."

"What does he do with it?" I asked, unable to suppress my curiosity.

Lila leaned closer, the scent of her perfume mingling with the soft musk of the paintings. "That's the million-dollar question, isn't it? Some say he holds it for ransom. Others think he simply revels in the chase. But then there are rumors that he's connected to a black market network that thrives on the hidden art world."

Jonah's expression shifted, his intrigue morphing into something deeper. "And you would know all this because...?"

"I have my sources," she said with a hint of pride. "In this business, information is as valuable as the art itself."

Before I could respond, the gallery door swung open with a dramatic flourish, and a tall figure stepped in, his presence commanding immediate attention. He was impeccably dressed, his tailored suit exuding an air of authority that made everyone's conversation falter. Lila straightened, her playful demeanor evaporating as the newcomer approached.

"Ah, the star of the evening," Lila said, her voice suddenly cool. "Nico, I didn't expect you here so soon."

"Business never sleeps, Lila," Nico replied, his voice smooth like velvet, with an undertone that suggested danger. "I'm here for the same reason everyone else is—this collection is exceptional."

I exchanged a glance with Jonah, whose expression had darkened, and I could feel the tension in the air shift. "Who's this guy?" I whispered under my breath.

"Someone you don't want to cross," Jonah replied quietly, his body language suddenly tense. "Nico's got connections that reach into the darkest corners of this city."

Lila, now fully in control, moved toward him with a calculated grace. "You're just in time to meet some guests. This is Fiona, a rising star in the art scene." Her tone dripped with irony, as if she were toying with me.

Nico's gaze settled on me, and I felt as if I were being dissected under his scrutiny. "A pleasure," he said, his voice low and alluring, yet laden with an unshakeable chill. "So, what brings you into this world, Fiona?"

I forced a smile, battling the urge to retreat. "Just exploring the beauty of art," I replied, trying to keep my voice steady. "Jonah and I are here to appreciate the finer things."

"Fascinating," he mused, his eyes narrowing slightly. "There's beauty in the hunt as well. Are you good at finding what's been lost?"

Before I could respond, Lila interjected, a hint of tension underlying her casual tone. "Fiona has an eye for talent, Nico. She understands the value of art. Perhaps you could use her insights."

Nico's smile widened, but it didn't reach his eyes. "Perhaps," he said, his gaze piercing through me. "But remember, in this world, not everything is what it seems. Keep your friends close and your enemies closer."

As the conversation shifted, Jonah leaned closer, his breath warm against my ear. "We need to find a way out of here," he murmured, urgency threading through his tone. "Nico's not someone to trifle with. We've overstayed our welcome."

But before we could make our escape, the lights flickered, and a sudden commotion erupted outside. The raucous sounds of shattering glass and raised voices filtered through the gallery, sending a wave of panic coursing through the crowd.

"What the hell was that?" I gasped, my heart pounding as chaos ensued around us.

"Stay close," Jonah said, gripping my wrist as we pushed toward the exit.

As we reached the door, a figure burst through, silhouetted against the chaos outside. It was a man clad in dark clothing, his face obscured by a mask, and in his hands, he held a bundle—my missing painting. The room erupted into confusion, screams and gasps filling the air, but all I could see was the masterpiece I had lost, now in the hands of a thief.

"Jonah!" I shouted, panic rising within me. "That's it! That's my painting!"

"Don't move!" Jonah commanded, his voice cutting through the chaos as he pulled me behind him, shielding me from the potential danger.

The masked figure turned, and for a heartbeat, our eyes locked. There was a recognition in those fleeting moments, a jolt of electricity that threatened to consume everything around us.

"Fiona," Jonah breathed, urgency coursing through his words. "We need to go—now!"

But as we turned to flee, the figure lunged forward, the painting clutched tightly under his arm. The chaotic energy of the gallery swirled around us, and just as we stepped into the chaos outside, everything went dark.

# Chapter 3: Dangerous Liaisons

The night air felt charged, electric with possibility and danger as we approached the dilapidated warehouse on the outskirts of the city. It loomed before us like a specter, its broken windows gaping like the hollow eyes of a ghost. The moon hung low, casting silvery shadows that danced across the cracked pavement, while the scent of rust and decay wafted through the air, a reminder of what had been abandoned here. My heart raced, not just from the thrill of the hunt, but from Jonah's presence beside me. His shoulders were broad, his jaw clenched in that familiar way he had when he was determined, but there was something softer in his gaze, an unspoken invitation to draw closer, even in the face of danger.

"Are you sure about this?" I asked, trying to keep my voice steady as we slipped into the darkness of the warehouse. The echo of our footsteps was swallowed by the vast emptiness, swallowed whole by the shadows that enveloped us. I could feel the weight of his protective nature wrapping around me like a cocoon. Jonah was always the one to shield me from harm, but tonight felt different; the air was thick with tension, our bodies too close, our hands brushing against each other as we navigated the debris-strewn floor.

"Yeah," he replied, his voice low and steady, yet laced with an undercurrent of urgency. "We need to find out what's going on. If the tip-off was right, this could be bigger than we thought." He paused, glancing over his shoulder, the tension radiating from him palpable. "Stay close."

I nodded, trying to ignore the shiver that ran down my spine, though it had little to do with fear and everything to do with the thrill of being so near him. Jonah's instincts were razor-sharp; he was the kind of man who could smell trouble before it even knocked on the door. Yet there was a flicker of vulnerability in his stance, a tension that spoke of unguarded moments I wished to explore.

Was it absurd that I found comfort in chaos? That in the heart of darkness, where shadows played tricks and danger lurked, I felt more alive than ever?

As we delved deeper into the cavernous space, the smell of mildew and old wood filled my lungs, and I couldn't help but think how out of place we were, two souls tangled in a web of intrigue, facing an uncertain fate. A scuffle echoed from somewhere within the bowels of the warehouse, a low rumble that sent adrenaline coursing through my veins. Jonah's grip on my arm tightened, our bodies instinctively aligning as if we were two pieces of a puzzle that had been lost for far too long. The moment hung between us, heavy and electric.

"We should move," he whispered, his breath warm against my ear. "We can't let them see us."

We pressed against the wall, hearts racing, each echo of our breath a reminder of how precarious our situation was. Suddenly, a shadow darted across the dimly lit expanse, and Jonah's body stiffened beside mine. I could feel his muscles tense, his instincts firing off like a signal flare. "Get ready," he murmured, eyes scanning the room, a predator locked onto its prey.

In that instant, everything shifted. We barely escaped a confrontation with a gang known for their ruthless dealings. Their voices were rough, the cadence of their words dripping with menace. I could barely make out their silhouettes as they loomed under a flickering light, the dull glint of weapons flashing momentarily before being swallowed by the darkness again. My heart thundered in my chest, a wild animal desperate to escape.

"Follow my lead," Jonah commanded softly, his breath steady despite the chaos around us. With each step we took in the shadows, the world outside felt like a distant memory, the cacophony of sirens and city life muted. We slipped past the gang members, our bodies moving as if choreographed, a silent ballet of evasion and survival.

Once we were safely tucked into the backseat of Jonah's car, the adrenaline rush transformed the air between us. My breath came in shallow gasps, and I was acutely aware of the heat radiating from him, the way his brow furrowed in concentration as he gripped the steering wheel. The engine purred softly, an intimate sound that seemed to vibrate through me, echoing the thrill of our narrow escape.

"Are you okay?" he asked, glancing over at me, his eyes searching mine for signs of fear. Instead, all I saw was a flicker of something deeper, a longing that sparked like kindling ready to ignite.

"Yeah, just a little shaken up," I admitted, though my heart raced for reasons I couldn't entirely comprehend. The reality of what we had faced settled over us like a heavy blanket, and I couldn't help but smile at the absurdity of it all. "I didn't think I'd be running from gangsters tonight."

He chuckled, the sound warm and rich, breaking through the tension. "Well, you definitely know how to keep things interesting."

The vulnerability in his gaze deepened, as if he was opening a door into a part of himself he rarely showed. "You could have gotten hurt back there," he added, his tone serious now, the laughter fading into something softer, more intimate. "I don't want to lose you."

The weight of his words hung between us, a thread of honesty that connected our hearts in a way I never anticipated. It struck me then that perhaps the line between love and hate was far thinner than I had ever imagined, a gossamer web woven from shared danger and vulnerability. My pulse quickened, and as I met his gaze, I felt the walls I had built around my heart begin to crumble.

"Jonah," I whispered, my voice barely a breath, yet it was enough to draw his full attention. In that fleeting moment, we were suspended in time, two souls bound by the chaotic dance of life, teetering on the edge of something beautiful and terrifying all at once.

The air inside the car was thick with unspoken words, the kind that hung around us like a delicate mist. I could feel Jonah's tension simmering beneath the surface, a barely restrained energy that buzzed in the confines of the small space. He stared out the windshield, eyes fixed on the road ahead, but I caught the flicker of concern that danced across his features in the dim light of the dashboard.

"You really scared me back there," he said finally, breaking the silence. His voice was steady, but I could hear the undercurrent of anxiety lacing his words. "You shouldn't take risks like that. It's not worth it."

I turned to face him fully, feeling the weight of his protective instincts pressing down on me like a heavy cloak. "You make it sound like I'm a reckless thrill-seeker," I replied, a teasing smile tugging at my lips. "I didn't exactly plan to tango with a gang tonight. I thought we were just going to find a few clues and head home."

Jonah's expression softened, but there was still a glint of seriousness in his gaze. "It's not just a game, though. Those guys don't play by the rules. You could have gotten hurt. Or worse."

I could see the shadows of past experiences flicker behind his eyes, memories of danger that had forged him into the man sitting beside me. It made my heart twist, both in sympathy and an odd exhilaration. "I know you're looking out for me, and I appreciate it," I said, my tone earnest now. "But I can handle myself. I've dealt with my fair share of trouble."

"Yeah, but this isn't the same," he countered, frustration creeping into his voice. "You're not just dealing with a few petty thieves. This is serious."

I crossed my arms, a playful pout on my lips. "So, what are you saying? That I should stay home, bake cookies, and avoid the big bad world?"

"Maybe just one of those things," he shot back, a hint of amusement breaking through his concern. The corners of his mouth lifted slightly, and the tension in the car seemed to dissipate, if only for a moment.

The banter between us felt like a lifeline, something to cling to amid the chaos of the night. As I studied him, I couldn't help but admire the way his brow furrowed with thought, his lips pursed in concentration. Jonah was undeniably charming, a blend of ruggedness and sincerity that pulled at something deep inside me, stirring feelings I had long buried beneath layers of sarcasm and self-preservation.

The car engine hummed a low melody, and outside, the city lights flickered like stars fallen from the sky, illuminating our shared silence. I had always been a solitary soul, wrapped in my own world, but Jonah had a way of inviting me into his, filling the gaps I hadn't known existed.

"Why do you care so much?" I asked suddenly, the question slipping out before I could rein it in. It was the vulnerability in his eyes that prompted me, the flicker of something deeper simmering just below the surface.

He hesitated, a brief moment of vulnerability passing over his features. "Because you matter to me," he replied, his voice low and earnest. "I don't want anything to happen to you. I can't lose anyone else."

The weight of his words settled over me, heavy yet strangely comforting. It was the first time I truly understood the depth of his feelings, the silent struggle behind his stoic exterior. "You won't lose me," I reassured him, leaning in closer, drawn to the warmth radiating from him. "I'm not going anywhere. Besides, who else would keep you in check?"

He chuckled, the sound rich and warm, and for a fleeting moment, the world outside melted away. Just Jonah and me, tangled in our own private universe. Yet beneath the surface, an undercurrent of tension still bubbled, a reminder that our connection was precarious, as delicate as the web of fate we found ourselves caught in.

"Alright, but you have to promise me something," he said, his eyes locking onto mine with an intensity that made my breath hitch. "If you ever find yourself in a situation like tonight, just...call me. Don't try to be the hero. Let me handle it."

A smile danced on my lips. "You mean to tell me that you want me to call you when I'm in trouble? As if I'm going to risk my life for a little excitement when I can just dial your number?"

He grinned, the warmth of his expression lighting up the dim car interior. "That's the spirit. Let me be the knight in shining armor, or at least the guy who gets you out of sticky situations."

"Knight, huh?" I raised an eyebrow, teasingly. "And here I thought you were more of a brooding rogue type."

Jonah chuckled, shaking his head. "Maybe I'm a bit of both. A rogue who knows how to wield a sword when necessary."

"Just so long as that sword isn't too sharp," I quipped back, the laughter bubbling between us like a spark igniting a flame. The tension was still there, lurking at the edges, but our playful exchange wrapped us in a cocoon of comfort, if only for a moment longer.

As we sat there, laughter dancing in the air around us, the faint sound of footsteps echoed outside the car, bringing with it a cold rush of reality. The laughter faded, replaced by the heavy pulse of dread that settled in the pit of my stomach.

"Jonah..." My voice was barely above a whisper, but he was already shifting, alertness washing over him like a wave.

"I heard it too," he said, scanning the darkness beyond the windshield, his body tense, every muscle coiled like a spring. "Stay low."

My heart raced as I crouched down in my seat, the playful banter forgotten, replaced by the reality of the danger we had just narrowly escaped. The world outside seemed to freeze, a moment suspended in time as we held our breath, waiting for the next move. Shadows flickered across the ground, and I could sense the threat moving closer, the danger becoming tangible.

"Do you think it's them?" I whispered, the uncertainty biting at my insides.

Jonah nodded, his jaw set in determination. "We need to go. Now."

The adrenaline surged once more as he shifted the car into gear, and in that instant, I knew that whatever lay ahead, we were in it together, bound by the unexpected twists of fate that had drawn our paths together.

The car lurched into motion, tires crunching against the gravel as Jonah navigated the back streets with a determined urgency. My heart raced, not only from the thrill of escape but from the unexpected intimacy of the moment. We were cocooned in the confines of his vehicle, the hum of the engine mixing with the thrum of adrenaline coursing through our veins. The world outside blurred into a kaleidoscope of neon lights and shadows, but inside, it was just Jonah and me, two survivors grappling with a dangerous dance of attraction and fear.

"Which way?" I asked, my voice barely above a whisper, the urgency of our situation forcing the banter into the background.

"Just keep an eye out," Jonah replied, his brow furrowed as he focused on the road ahead. "We can't go back to my place just yet. If they're on our tail, we need to lose them first."

I nodded, scanning the shadows that flanked us, a cold knot of anxiety tightening in my stomach. The night had morphed from an adventurous outing into a high-stakes game of cat and mouse. The thrill of danger clung to us like a second skin, igniting something raw and undeniable between us. "I can't believe we almost got caught. It's like something out of a movie," I said, attempting to lighten the mood, though the weight of reality pressed heavily on my chest.

"Yeah, well, most movies don't have a pretty blonde getting dragged into a gang war," he shot back, a hint of a smile breaking through the tension. "You're lucky I was there to save you from becoming a leading lady in a crime drama."

"Lucky?" I arched an eyebrow. "I'd argue it's the other way around. You get to be the brooding hero with a dark past and a soft heart."

He chuckled, the sound rich and warm. "If I'm the brooding hero, what does that make you?"

"Definitely the sassy sidekick who steals the show," I quipped, enjoying the easy banter that momentarily pushed aside the looming threat.

As we turned onto a quieter street, the glow of streetlights painted Jonah's profile in soft light, revealing the contours of his jaw and the determination etched across his features. I couldn't help but marvel at how quickly our lives had intertwined, how the mere brush of our hands had ignited something electric. A thought flickered in the back of my mind: Was it possible that danger had somehow thrown us into each other's arms?

"Do you think they saw us?" I asked, glancing back over my shoulder, half-expecting to see shadows closing in.

Jonah's expression turned serious, the playful glint in his eye replaced by a steely focus. "It's hard to tell. But we need to stay sharp. If they're hunting us, we can't give them a chance to catch up."

My stomach churned as I processed his words. "Great, just what I wanted. A thrilling night out followed by a high-speed chase."

"Could be worse," he replied, turning to shoot me a sideways glance. "We could be stuck in a boring meeting instead."

"I'd take the meeting," I retorted, a mix of laughter and disbelief bubbling up. "At least there'd be coffee."

His laughter echoed in the confined space, a sound that both reassured and stirred something within me. I liked this side of him—the man who could make me laugh in the face of danger, who could lighten the load of a night that had turned dark far too quickly.

Just as I was about to respond, a sudden sound shattered the moment—a loud bang, followed by the unmistakable crunch of gravel beneath tires. Jonah's expression shifted instantly, eyes narrowing as he glanced in the rearview mirror. "Hold on," he warned, his voice steady as he accelerated.

The engine roared to life, but in the distance, I could see headlights barreling toward us, cutting through the darkness like a pair of angry stars. My heart plummeted. "They're coming," I whispered, dread curling in my stomach.

"Keep your head down," Jonah instructed, weaving the car through a maze of side streets. Each turn felt like a gamble, the stakes rising with every passing second. The night outside morphed into a blur of movement, the trees flashing past us like ghosts trying to hold us back.

I gripped the edge of my seat, my pulse racing. "What if they catch up?"

"Then we'll make sure they regret it," he replied with a grim determination. "Just trust me."

The headlights drew closer, illuminating the rear of our car with an ominous glow. I couldn't tell how many vehicles were behind us, but the roar of engines and the adrenaline coursing through my veins told me that we were no longer in control of the narrative. "Jonah, they're right on us!"

"I see them," he said through clenched teeth, his focus unwavering. "Just a little further. There's a shortcut up ahead."

The engine roared louder as Jonah pushed the car to its limits, and I felt the weight of the moment settle in my bones. Each turn sent a shudder of fear through me, but also a strange thrill. This was not how I had envisioned my night, yet here we were, navigating a life-or-death scenario as if we were characters in our own twisted romance.

As we careened around a corner, I caught a glimpse of the pursuers—a black SUV, the headlights glaring like angry eyes, the driver clearly intent on catching us. "We can't let them box us in," Jonah said, the tension in his voice palpable.

"I think they already have a plan," I replied, my heart racing as I spotted another vehicle joining the chase. "There's another one coming from the left!"

"Hold on!" Jonah shouted, veering to the right, tires screeching against asphalt. The sound pierced through the night, a shriek of panic and defiance. The world outside had become a chaotic blur, filled with adrenaline and uncertainty.

With each passing moment, the distance between us and our pursuers narrowed. I could see the driver of the SUV now, a shadowy figure intent on revenge. Jonah's grip on the wheel tightened, knuckles whitening as he fought to maintain control. "Keep your head down!" he urged again, the urgency in his tone cutting through the chaos.

I ducked instinctively, heart hammering, but a wild thought flickered through my mind: What if this wasn't just about escape? What if this was a turning point?

As the SUV closed in, I felt an overwhelming surge of determination wash over me. "Jonah!" I shouted, my voice rising above the roar of the engine. "We can't let them win!"

Before I could think better of it, I reached for the glove compartment, yanking it open. Inside lay a small, silver object—Jonah's old baseball bat. "What are you doing?" he asked, disbelief mingling with concern as I held it up.

"Fighting back," I declared, adrenaline pushing me forward. "If they want to play rough, we'll show them how it's done!"

Before he could respond, I rolled down the window and aimed the bat out at the approaching SUV, adrenaline surging through me. Just then, the world shifted. A sudden jolt, and Jonah swerved to avoid a collision with a lamppost, causing the SUV to swerve as well.

In that moment of chaos, as I swung the bat with all my strength, I felt a jarring impact—a resounding thud echoed in the air, followed by a crunch. My heart raced as I watched the SUV veer off course, but the victory was short-lived. The driver regained control, his vehicle careening back into our lane.

"Hold on!" Jonah shouted, his voice slicing through the confusion as he swerved again, but this time it felt like the weight of fate had shifted. The world spun, chaos engulfing us, and just as I thought we'd lost them for good, a flash of headlights surged forward.

Then, out of the darkness, a shot rang out—sharp, piercing, a warning that cut through the adrenaline-fueled haze. The sound echoed around us, and my heart dropped, time slowing as we faced the oncoming storm.

"Jonah!" I screamed, the panic igniting within me as I braced for the unknown, knowing that whatever happened next would change everything.

# Chapter 4: Secrets Revealed

The quiet hum of my apartment often felt like a lullaby, but tonight it wrapped around me like a suffocating blanket. Papers were strewn across the coffee table, evidence and theories bleeding into one another. The harsh glow of my desk lamp cast long shadows, distorting the familiar contours of my life. I was tangled in a mess of mysteries that seemed to grow by the hour, and Jonah was beside me, his presence both a comfort and a storm.

"Okay, let's review," I said, tapping a pencil against the edge of a file folder, trying to concentrate. "If the piece is a fake, it must be linked to whoever owned it before..." I trailed off, the words falling flat in the air, weighed down by our unspoken tension.

Jonah leaned closer, the warmth of his shoulder brushing against mine, an electric current that made my heart race despite the chaos around us. "They would have had to have an accomplice. Someone who could create a good enough replica." His voice was low, a gravelly timbre that rumbled through me, settling somewhere deep in my chest.

"Right," I replied, almost breathless. I shifted in my seat, glancing up at him. The faint light highlighted the angles of his face—the sharp line of his jaw, the way his hair fell carelessly over his forehead. He caught my eye, and for a moment, the investigation faded into the background.

"What?" he asked, a playful smirk dancing on his lips.

"Just... you have this whole brooding artist vibe going on," I teased, trying to break the weight of the moment, but my heart wasn't in it. Beneath the surface of our banter lay an urgency, a need to push through the layers of the case—and our own tangled emotions.

"Brooding artist, huh?" he mused, raising an eyebrow. "Is that how you see me? I'll take it. Much better than 'rival.'"

I couldn't help but laugh, the sound brightening the dim space around us. "Well, you have a penchant for hanging around my crime scenes uninvited."

"Crime scenes are sexy," he shot back, leaning back in his chair, his arms crossed behind his head. The casual confidence in his posture was almost magnetic. "And they have a way of bringing people together."

"Is that your grand strategy?" I quipped, rolling my eyes but unable to suppress a smile. Yet, as I sat there, I felt the vulnerability beneath his bravado. Jonah was like a complex painting—every layer hid something more profound, and I was starting to peel back the edges.

"Honestly?" He leaned in again, his expression shifting, shadows flickering across his features. "I never thought I'd find myself here, working with you. My dad always said the art world is about connection. He built his career on it. I wanted to escape that legacy." His voice dropped, the lightness evaporating.

"Why would you want to escape?" I asked, intrigued. "Your father's work is incredible."

Jonah sighed, looking away as if the memories stung. "It was never mine. Always his, and I was just his shadow. I wanted to be my own person, but now... I don't know. Maybe I'm just repeating his mistakes, diving into a world of deception."

I felt a pang of empathy, recognizing that our pasts echoed in each other's stories. "You're not repeating mistakes. You're chasing the truth." My voice was steadier than I felt. "That's brave."

He met my gaze, and in that moment, the air thickened with unsaid words and shared secrets. I realized how deeply I wanted him to see me as more than just a competitor, to understand that we were both navigating a landscape littered with treachery and uncharted emotions.

Just as the connection felt like it might solidify into something more, a loud crash echoed from the hall, rattling the fragile bubble we'd created. I jumped, my heart thundering against my ribs. Jonah was instantly on his feet, alert and poised like a cat ready to pounce.

"What was that?" I whispered, a sense of foreboding creeping up my spine.

"Stay here," he commanded, his voice firm as he edged toward the door, every muscle in his body tense with readiness.

"No way, I'm not just sitting back while something's happening," I protested, adrenaline spiking through me. I followed him, moving through the small apartment like a shadow.

The hallway was dimly lit, the glow of the streetlight casting eerie shadows on the walls. Jonah creaked the door open, and we peered into the murky darkness. A sound—muffled voices mixed with the soft shuffle of footsteps—filtered in. My heart raced; this was no ordinary disturbance.

"Stay behind me," he whispered, as if he could sense my urge to leap into action.

We inched forward, the sounds growing louder. The air was thick with tension, each step measured, every breath held. Just as Jonah reached for the doorknob to step out fully, a figure burst into view—tall, cloaked in shadow, face obscured.

"What the hell?" I gasped, frozen in place.

The figure paused, seemingly just as startled, and in that split second, I saw a flash of recognition in Jonah's eyes. "Noah?" he called out, the name heavy with surprise.

The figure stepped into the light, revealing a face I hadn't expected. Noah, Jonah's estranged brother, stood before us, his expression a mixture of urgency and something darker. "We need to talk," he said, his voice low and edged with desperation.

The air crackled with a sudden intensity, and I felt the fragile strands of connection that had begun to weave between Jonah and me snap back like a taut wire. This was more than just a casual visit; this was a revelation that threatened to unravel everything we had started to build. As the three of us stood there, the weight of unspoken truths hung heavily, ready to tip the scales of our entwined fates.

Noah's unexpected arrival turned the air in the room thick with unspoken questions and simmering tension. His features were familiar yet hardened, as if life had drawn deeper lines on his face since the last time I'd seen him—though I couldn't recall that last encounter, the memory dulled by time and the complexities of family ties. Jonah's brother stood there, an intruder in our delicate world, and I couldn't shake the feeling that he had walked in with more than just the weight of a familial burden; he carried secrets.

"What do you mean we need to talk?" Jonah's voice was a mixture of surprise and cautious indignation, echoing the uncertainty that wrapped around us like a fog. "You're not supposed to be here."

Noah glanced around the small apartment, taking in the clutter of files and scattered papers, his eyes narrowing as they flicked from Jonah to me. "I know it's complicated, but this is important," he insisted, his tone urgent, cutting through the awkwardness that lingered between us.

"Important? Or important to you?" Jonah shot back, an edge creeping into his voice that I hadn't heard before. The brotherly rivalry was palpable, crackling in the air like static before a storm.

"Both," Noah replied, taking a step forward. "I wouldn't be here if I had any other choice. There's something you need to know, and it can't wait."

I exchanged glances with Jonah, feeling the undercurrents of tension and concern. "How did you even find me?" he demanded, crossing his arms defensively.

Noah shrugged, his body tense, as if bracing for a confrontation. "I have my ways. The art world is smaller than you think. And trust me, it's getting messier."

"What does that even mean?" I interjected, feeling a mixture of frustration and curiosity. I needed clarity, not cryptic comments that only deepened the mystery.

Noah's gaze darted to me, sizing me up. "You're involved in this too, aren't you? It's about the Rothwell piece, isn't it?"

"The Rothwell piece?" I repeated, my heart racing. "What do you know about it?"

Noah sighed heavily, running a hand through his dark hair. "More than I should. It's linked to something much larger than a simple forgery. There are people who are willing to go to great lengths to protect their interests, and you"—he pointed an accusatory finger at Jonah—"you've already stepped into the deep end."

Jonah shifted, a flicker of worry crossing his face before he masked it with defiance. "And you think running here is going to help? You don't know what you're talking about."

"Actually, I do," Noah replied, the intensity of his gaze unwavering. "I've seen the consequences of this firsthand. You think I just walked away from all of this for fun? You need to listen to me."

Jonah hesitated, the moment stretching taut like a drawn bowstring. "Fine. Then tell me what you know."

"People in our circle are desperate," Noah said, his voice dropping to a conspiratorial whisper. "The Rothwell piece is just the tip of the iceberg. There's a network of forgers, thieves, and worse—connections that reach into galleries and auction houses all over the country."

I felt my stomach twist. "And you're involved with these people?"

"I was," Noah replied, his voice strained. "But I got out before things turned really dark. I thought I could leave it all behind, but I can't let my brother get caught up in this mess."

Jonah stepped closer, his anger simmering beneath the surface. "You think I can't handle myself? I've been dealing with this for weeks."

"No, you don't understand," Noah insisted, desperation creeping into his tone. "I've seen the aftermath of what happens when people dig too deep. If they know you're looking into the Rothwell piece, you could end up—"

"End up what?" Jonah challenged, fists clenched. "Dead? If you're so concerned, then why didn't you warn me sooner? Why did you wait until now?"

The intensity of their exchange was electric, each word a volley in an escalating argument. I felt out of place, caught between the two brothers, the air thick with a mix of brotherly love and bitter rivalry. Yet there was something more—something unaddressed simmering beneath the surface.

"Noah," I said, trying to regain control of the conversation. "If this is as serious as you say, we need to know everything. What do you think they'll do if they find out Jonah's involved?"

Noah's gaze softened slightly as he regarded me. "I don't know. I barely escaped last time, but it wasn't pretty. You don't understand the lengths they'll go to protect their interests. They don't play fair."

Jonah's expression shifted from anger to something more vulnerable, a flicker of fear clouding his eyes. "Then we need to act first. If we know they're watching, we can use it to our advantage."

Noah shook his head vehemently. "That's the problem! You think you can play their game, but they'll always be one step ahead. They have resources we can't even begin to fathom."

"And what do you suggest?" Jonah countered, his voice rising. "We sit back and do nothing? I refuse to let them dictate my life, especially not now that I know there's something bigger at stake."

"Maybe you should consider your life before your pride," Noah replied, an undertone of urgency creeping into his words. "You're not just dealing with art forgers; you're risking everything."

Before Jonah could respond, the doorbell rang, slicing through the tension like a knife. The sound was jarring, and we all froze.

"Who the hell could that be?" I asked, casting a worried glance toward the door.

Jonah's eyes narrowed, the protective instincts flaring again. "Stay behind me." He stepped toward the door, every fiber of his being alert.

I watched, my heart pounding in rhythm with the anxiety swirling in the air. Jonah opened the door cautiously, revealing a tall figure with an unmistakable air of authority.

"Detective Lawrence," the newcomer said, his voice deep and commanding. "I need to speak with you."

The moment stretched, heavy with implications. I could see the recognition in Jonah's eyes, a flicker of fear darting across his face. "What is this about?"

"About your involvement in the Rothwell case," Detective Lawrence replied, stepping into the dim light of the apartment. "And I think you might want to sit down for this."

The detective's presence shifted the atmosphere, the stakes rising higher than I could have imagined. As he surveyed the scene, I felt the weight of our choices closing in, each decision spiraling into a future none of us could foresee. The web of intrigue was tightening, and I realized we were no longer just players in a game; we were entangled in a perilous dance with forces far beyond our control.

The detective's presence was a storm cloud looming over us, dark and foreboding. I stood frozen, my heart racing as he surveyed the room, a mix of authority and something else lurking behind his eyes. His crisp suit seemed to carry the weight of unspoken rules, an armor against the chaos we'd unwittingly stepped into. Jonah's face was a mask of defiance, but I could sense the tension coiling tighter with every passing moment.

"Detective Lawrence," Jonah finally managed, his voice steady despite the turbulence within. "What brings you here?"

"I've been tracking the Rothwell piece for some time now," the detective replied, his tone a blend of professionalism and urgency. "And it seems you've gotten yourself tangled in something much larger than you realized."

The implications hung heavy in the air. I exchanged a worried glance with Noah, whose expression mirrored my own—equal parts concern and confusion. Jonah clenched his jaw, refusing to let fear seep into his voice. "What exactly do you mean by 'tangled'? We're just investigating a forgery."

Detective Lawrence's gaze intensified, locking onto Jonah with an unsettling intensity. "This isn't just about a forgery. There's a criminal network involved, and the Rothwell piece is a key to something bigger—a gateway to the art underworld that's been operating right under our noses."

I felt the walls of my own understanding begin to crumble. "And you think we're involved in this?" I asked, trying to project confidence even as my stomach twisted with unease.

"It's not a matter of 'think,'" he said, his voice firm. "You both are in deep. The connections you've made are raising alarms in places that prefer to stay hidden."

Jonah took a step forward, his resolve unyielding. "We've only been following leads. If someone's pulling strings, we want to know who they are."

The detective studied him, a flicker of something almost resembling respect crossing his features. "That's brave. But the truth is, people don't like to be discovered. Especially those who play in the shadows."

"And I suppose you're here to protect us?" Noah chimed in, skepticism dripping from his words.

"Not exactly," Lawrence admitted, a hint of irony threading through his tone. "I'm here to make sure you don't end up as collateral damage in a game you clearly don't understand."

I felt a wave of anger surge through me. "What does that even mean? You think we're just going to back down because it's dangerous?"

"I think you're both smart enough to know when to walk away," he countered, his eyes narrowing. "You have no idea what you're dealing with. Forgers, smugglers, and people with connections that run far deeper than either of you. This isn't just some little art caper; it's organized crime, and it could get messy."

"Messy?" Jonah's voice raised a notch, his passion igniting a fire I had seen flicker to life before. "You don't think I know that? I'm tired of being in the shadow of my father's legacy, tired of being pushed around by the very people who think they own art and the people who love it."

"Being tired doesn't change the facts, Jonah," Lawrence replied, his tone hardening. "There are stakes here that go beyond ambition. This is about survival. If you keep digging, you'll find yourself in a position where it won't just be your career at risk."

The tension was suffocating, and I could feel my heart pounding in time with the escalating stakes. "What do you suggest we do?" I asked, my voice a mixture of frustration and desperation. "We can't just let this go. There's too much at stake."

Lawrence rubbed the back of his neck, clearly weighing his options. "I suggest you lay low. Disassociate yourself from the Rothwell case. Keep your heads down while we sort this out."

"That's not an option," Jonah said firmly, determination etched into every feature. "We need to know what's happening. If we can expose this network, we can do more than just save ourselves."

The detective's eyes hardened. "You think you can take down a network like this? You have no idea what you're up against."

"Maybe not," I interjected, feeling the flames of defiance spark within me. "But we're not just sitting back and letting it happen. We're already in this, and I refuse to back down. Not when we have a chance to make a difference."

Lawrence's expression softened just a fraction, as if he recognized the fire in my voice. "You're playing a dangerous game. But if you insist on digging deeper, you'd better be prepared for the consequences."

"What consequences?" Jonah snapped. "Are you threatening us? Because if this is about scaring us into submission, it's not going to work."

The detective's gaze flickered between the two of us, assessing. "You think it's just threats? There are people who won't hesitate to silence you if they feel threatened. And they won't leave any trace behind."

An uneasy silence settled over the room, punctuated by the faint sounds of traffic outside, a reminder of the world that continued to spin, blissfully unaware of the turmoil brewing within these four walls.

"Why are you really here, Detective?" Noah asked, cutting through the tension with a sharpness that was almost palpable. "If you know there's danger, why not do something about it? Why not protect us?"

Lawrence hesitated, a flicker of uncertainty crossing his features before he regained his composure. "Because I'm walking a tightrope, and if I tip one way or the other, it could mean trouble not just for you, but for everyone involved. I'm not here to play hero, but I can't just ignore what's happening."

"So, what are we supposed to do?" I asked, the weight of the moment pressing down on me. "We can't pretend this isn't happening. We can't pretend we're safe."

He took a deep breath, a look of resignation crossing his face. "The truth is, you need allies. People who know the territory. But be careful; trust is a luxury you can't afford. And don't assume everyone has your best interests at heart."

As he spoke, I felt the heaviness of his warning seep into my bones. This was no longer just about art or forgery; it was about survival in a world where loyalties were as fleeting as shadows.

"And if we decide to go forward?" Jonah challenged, his gaze unwavering. "What's the worst that could happen?"

The detective met his gaze, his expression serious. "The worst? Let's just say it could get personal."

Before we could process his words, a sudden noise broke through the air—a crash from outside, followed by shouting. The unmistakable sound of chaos erupted just beyond the apartment walls, sending a jolt of adrenaline through me.

"What the hell was that?" I gasped, instinctively stepping closer to Jonah, my pulse racing.

Lawrence's face shifted into a mask of urgency. "Stay here!" he barked, but before he could move, the door burst open again. A figure stumbled in, panting and wild-eyed, and I barely registered the blood on their shirt before the world spun out of control.

"Help! They're coming!" the newcomer gasped, collapsing to the floor, panic etched across their features.

The room plunged into chaos, the gravity of our situation settling over us like a heavy shroud. I looked at Jonah, a thousand unspoken words passing between us. In that moment, the stakes became alarmingly clear. We were no longer mere observers in a dangerous game; we were now players in a perilous dance that could lead to the brink of disaster. The walls were closing in, and I realized with chilling certainty that there was no turning back.

# Chapter 5: A Twist of Fate

The morning sun filtered through the slats of my blinds, casting striped patterns on the wooden floor, but its warmth felt hollow in the wake of last night's revelations. I sat on my couch, clutching a mug of tea as if it could somehow stave off the cold encroaching on my heart. The air was thick with a mix of chamomile and the faint, lingering scent of burnt toast—my morning culinary disaster. I stared into the liquid, willing it to provide clarity, but it swirled back at me like the chaos swirling in my mind.

Jonah had walked through the door last week, his presence shifting the atmosphere in my apartment from mundane to electric. His laughter echoed off the walls, filling the spaces left vacant by solitude. I had reveled in our banter, our playful jabs that danced on the knife-edge of flirtation. But now, as I replayed our conversations, every teasing remark felt laced with potential deception. Could the man who made me laugh so easily really be harboring secrets? The thought twisted in my gut, a knot of suspicion I couldn't easily untangle.

I set the mug down with a gentle clink, the sound sharp against the silence that enveloped me. I tried to think back to the first time we met, his hands animated as he recounted a ridiculous story about getting lost in a corn maze. How could someone so charming become a suspect in my heart's private investigation? I shook my head, pushing away the thoughts like a pesky fly. My phone buzzed beside me, jarring me from my spiraling thoughts. It was Sarah, my ever-optimistic best friend, ready to buoy my spirits with her unwavering belief in love.

"Morning! Just checking in. You okay?" Her text was a lifeline thrown into turbulent waters. I hesitated, my fingers hovering over the screen. Should I unleash my fears onto her? Or should I keep this heartache bottled up, away from her incessant optimism? I opted for honesty, my fingers moving swiftly across the screen.

"Not really. Jonah... there's something off. I think he might be involved with The Raven."

Her response was immediate, a string of exclamation points that could have set off alarms in the quiet of my apartment. "No way! He's too sweet for that. You're overthinking it! Talk to him!"

Talk to him. The very idea made my stomach churn. What could I possibly say? "Hey, Jonah, great to see you! By the way, are you secretly plotting something sinister?" I could already picture the incredulous look on his face, that playful smirk shifting to concern. The thought made my heart clench.

After a moment's hesitation, I hit send, craving the comfort of her reassurance. As I set the phone aside, a shadow flickered across my living room. I turned, heart racing, half-expecting to see The Raven himself lurking in the corner, mocking me with his riddles. Instead, it was just the light playing tricks as the clouds shifted outside, gray and heavy. But my heart didn't settle; it felt more like a sparrow caught in a storm.

The days dragged on like molasses, each one bringing more uncertainty. Jonah had tried to reach me, but I kept my distance. Each text was met with silence; every call went unanswered. I felt like a coward, hiding behind the flimsy walls of my apartment, avoiding confrontation while my mind spun tales of betrayal. I envisioned the look in his eyes as I asked him point-blank about the accusations swirling like autumn leaves outside my window. Was it fear of the truth that held me back, or was it the hope that maybe he was innocent, after all?

By the end of the week, I found myself perched on the edge of my couch, scrolling through social media, and stumbled across a photo that knocked the breath from my lungs. Jonah, standing beside a woman I'd never seen, her arm draped around his shoulders, both of them grinning like they were sharing a private joke. My heart plummeted. There it was, the evidence that pierced through my doubts—Jonah had secrets, and I was the fool for not seeing it sooner.

The image seared itself into my mind, a vivid reminder of the façade I'd mistaken for something real. The room felt smaller as anger surged through me, an insatiable fire that demanded release. I tossed my phone onto the couch as if it were a hot coal, the sudden movement sending my tea sloshing dangerously close to the edge of its mug. With a sudden burst of energy, I marched to the window, flinging the curtain aside. The street below bustled with life, people moving in a choreographed dance I was no longer part of.

The world felt unforgiving, every passerby a reminder of my isolation. Jonah was out there, likely laughing and chatting with that woman, leaving me trapped in this spiral of self-doubt. The sound of my phone chiming broke through my haze, and I snatched it up, my heart racing at the prospect of it being him.

It wasn't. It was Sarah, always the beacon of light, ever-ready with words of encouragement. "You need to confront him. Don't let this eat you alive!"

I tossed the phone onto the couch again, an act of rebellion against her persistent optimism. Confront him? How could I even look him in the eye when all I wanted to do was scream? Instead, I settled back into the cushions, overwhelmed. My mind raced, envisioning all the worst-case scenarios—arguments, accusations, shattered feelings. I felt small and lost, as though the very walls of my apartment were closing in.

That's when I noticed the envelope peeking out from beneath my coffee table, the edge decorated with a familiar flourish. The Raven had struck again, and this time, he was coming for me. My heart thudded, fear and adrenaline coursing through my veins as I reached for the envelope, my fingers trembling as I tore it open. Inside was a single piece of paper, the message inscribed in the same elegant script that had taunted me before.

"Trust is a fragile thing, easily broken. Don't be a fool; choose wisely."

The words reverberated in my mind, igniting the fires of my turmoil. I was caught in a web of uncertainty, torn between the man I had grown to care for and the sinister figure lurking in the shadows. I needed answers, and I needed them fast. The air was thick with tension as I prepared myself for the confrontation I had so desperately been avoiding.

With the Raven's chilling note still fresh in my mind, I knew I couldn't sit in my apartment any longer, drowning in self-doubt and paranoia. The walls that had once felt like a protective cocoon now seemed like a prison, closing in with every passing moment. I needed fresh air, the kind that could cut through the haze of confusion swirling in my thoughts. I slipped on my worn-out sneakers, grabbed my jacket, and made my way out into the bustling streets, where the world moved on blissfully unaware of my turmoil.

As I stepped outside, the crisp autumn air greeted me, its coolness invigorating against my skin. Leaves danced in a chaotic ballet, swirling in the wind like tiny whirlwinds of gold and crimson. I wandered aimlessly, my mind racing. Coffee. I needed coffee. The thought was a beacon, guiding me toward the cozy café down the street, its window frames adorned with ivy and twinkling fairy lights that flickered like a million stars captured in glass.

Pushing open the door, I was enveloped by the rich aroma of freshly brewed coffee mingled with the sweetness of pastries. It was a sanctuary of warmth, filled with the soft chatter of patrons and the clinking of cups. I moved to the counter, scanning the menu with barely a hint of focus. My usual order—a vanilla latte—felt like an anchor in the storm. "One vanilla latte, please," I said, my voice barely above a whisper.

As I waited, I caught sight of a couple seated by the window, their hands intertwined, laughter bubbling up between them like champagne. The scene was so achingly normal, so painfully reminiscent of what I yearned for with Jonah, that I had to look away. My stomach twisted, a familiar ache of longing and betrayal mixing into a cocktail of emotions I wasn't quite ready to drink.

"Your latte," the barista said, interrupting my spiral. I took the steaming cup, its warmth radiating through my fingers, grounding me momentarily. I navigated to a cozy nook in the café, settling into a plush chair, its fabric worn but welcoming. I took a sip, letting the comforting flavors wash over me, the sweetness mixing with the bitterness of my thoughts.

Just then, my phone buzzed on the table, and I glanced down, half-hoping it was Jonah, but the name flashing on the screen was a reminder of the life I had before him. It was my sister, Eliza, calling. I hesitated, but something deep inside urged me to pick up. "Hey, sis!" I forced a smile, knowing she could sense my mood even through the phone.

"Hey! I was just thinking about you. How's the... romantic drama?" Her tone was teasing, but there was genuine concern lurking beneath.

I sighed, running a hand through my hair, the knot of frustration still tight in my chest. "It's a bit complicated. You know the whole Raven situation?"

"Of course. It's like a reality show over there, isn't it?" She laughed, but I could hear the seriousness beneath her words. "What's going on?"

I took another sip of my latte, steeling myself to recount my tangled feelings. "I found this note, and now I think Jonah might be involved somehow. He's... he's been distant, and I saw a picture of him with another woman. I just don't know if I can trust him."

There was a moment of silence on the line, a beat too long for comfort. "Well, did you talk to him about it?"

"Talk to him?" I echoed, a bitter laugh escaping my lips. "And say what? 'Hey, Jonah, so about that photo—care to explain why you're cozying up with someone else?' Sounds like a lovely conversation starter."

"Or you could try asking him directly about his involvement with The Raven. Maybe there's a rational explanation for everything," she suggested, her voice a soothing balm against my agitation.

"Or maybe he'll deny it and I'll look like an idiot," I muttered, glancing around the café, suddenly feeling exposed. I couldn't shake the feeling that everyone could hear my internal struggle.

"Julia, listen to me," Eliza said, her voice firm. "You deserve to know the truth. Even if it hurts, you have to confront it. Don't let fear make the decision for you."

Her words resonated, echoing in the corners of my mind. Maybe it was time to stop running and face the music. I took a deep breath, feeling a flicker of determination igniting within me. "You're right. I need to talk to him."

"Good. And if he is guilty, I'll help you egg his car," she quipped, lightening the mood. "Now, go get your man, Sherlock."

I ended the call, a mix of apprehension and resolve flooding through me. I had to confront Jonah, to pull back the curtain of uncertainty and face whatever lay behind it. I finished my latte, the once warm drink now lukewarm, and stood up, ready to reclaim my narrative.

As I walked back to my apartment, my mind was a tumultuous sea of potential conversations. I pictured the moment I would see him, the charged air thick with unsaid words and unanswered questions. What if I was wrong about him? What if I was right? I had no way of knowing until I faced him.

I reached my apartment door, my heart pounding against my ribcage like a trapped bird, eager to escape. The silence inside felt oppressive, as though the walls themselves were holding their breath, waiting for the outcome of this confrontation. With a steadying breath, I opened the door and stepped inside.

The evening light filtered through the windows, casting a warm glow over the space. But instead of comfort, it felt like a spotlight shining down on my uncertainty. I paced the floor, my mind racing, but there was no escaping the weight of the moment.

I pulled out my phone, staring at Jonah's contact, my thumb hovering over the call button. I knew he would have questions of his own, would want to know why I had been avoiding him, but I had to push through the discomfort. I dialed his number, my heart racing as it rang.

"Hello?" His voice came through the line, warm and inviting, wrapping around me like a familiar blanket.

"Jonah, can we talk?" My voice was steadier than I felt, but I could hear the underlying tremor that hinted at my vulnerability.

"Of course. Where are you?"

"In my apartment."

"I'll be there in ten," he replied, and I could hear the warmth in his tone shift slightly, as if he sensed the weight of my words.

I hung up, setting the phone down as I tried to calm my racing heart. The moments ticked by like a clock counting down to an inevitable explosion. As the sound of his footsteps echoed in the hallway, I took a deep breath, steeling myself for the conversation that could change everything.

The door creaked open, and there he stood, a vision of warmth and confusion. My heart fluttered, but beneath it lay a bedrock of uncertainty. "Julia?" he said, stepping inside, and for a fleeting moment, I allowed myself to bask in the glow of his presence. But the specter of betrayal loomed large, threatening to shatter this fragile moment before it had even begun.

Jonah stepped inside, and the door closed behind him with a soft click that echoed like a gunshot in the tension-laden air. He looked disheveled yet charming, as always, his hair tousled in a way that suggested he had run a hand through it too many times in frustration. The moment our eyes locked, my heart danced between hope and dread, each beat a reminder of what was at stake.

"Julia, what's going on?" he asked, a crease forming between his brows as he stepped closer. The concern in his voice stirred something deep within me—a desire to trust him that was almost palpable. I had rehearsed a thousand scenarios, but now that the moment had arrived, the words stuck like cotton in my throat.

I swallowed hard, forcing my mind to focus. "We need to talk about The Raven. About you." The words slipped out, laden with the gravity of everything I had bottled up.

Jonah's expression shifted, the warmth giving way to caution. "What about me?"

"People are saying you might be involved." The admission hung between us, a fragile thread that threatened to snap at the slightest tug. I could see the color drain from his face, and I braced myself for the denial I expected to come pouring out.

"Who said that?" His voice was steady, but I caught the underlying tremor, the way his hands clenched into fists at his sides.

"I found a note, Jonah. It pointed to you," I pressed, my pulse racing. "And I saw the picture of you with that woman."

The air crackled with unspoken words, the atmosphere heavy with tension. "That was a friend, Julia. Someone I've known for years. We were at a charity event." His tone was defensive, and I could feel the walls of mistrust creeping back in.

"Why didn't you mention her?" I challenged, the familiar sting of betrayal igniting my frustration. "How am I supposed to believe you when you keep these things hidden?"

"I didn't think it was important!" he retorted, and the energy shifted, morphing our conversation into an unexpected confrontation. "You're acting like I'm some sort of criminal, but you don't even know the whole story."

"Then enlighten me!" I shot back, my voice rising. "What's the whole story? Why should I trust you when you're wrapped up in all this?"

His eyes narrowed, a flicker of something—hurt, maybe?—passing through them. "Trust is a two-way street, Julia. You can't just throw accusations at me and expect me to sit here quietly."

I felt the air thicken around us, my heart racing with the truth of his words. "I'm not throwing accusations. I'm trying to understand."

"Understand what? That I'm just as much a victim in this as you are?" His voice had softened, the bite of anger replaced by a desperate sincerity. "I don't want to be part of this mess. I want to be with you."

His admission hung in the air, charged with unspoken implications, and for a brief moment, I felt the swell of longing that had ignited between us before everything spiraled out of control. The gravity of our situation seemed to pulse, drawing me closer to him even as my instincts screamed to retreat.

"But how can I be with you if I can't trust you?" I whispered, feeling vulnerable as the truth settled in my chest like a stone.

Jonah took a step forward, closing the distance between us, his eyes intense. "You have to believe me, Julia. I want to figure this out, but I can't do it alone." His plea tugged at my heart, and despite my doubts, I felt the flicker of connection that had drawn me to him in the first place.

I exhaled sharply, running a hand through my hair. "Then we figure it out together. No more secrets, no more hiding. I need you to be honest with me, Jonah. About everything."

He nodded, his expression earnest. "Okay. Let's start fresh. I'll tell you everything I know about The Raven and how I might be connected. But you have to promise me you'll listen without jumping to conclusions."

"Deal," I said, surprised at how easily the word fell from my lips, a truce offered amidst the battlefield of our emotions.

Jonah shifted slightly, his posture relaxing. "I didn't tell you about the charity event because I thought it was just another night in a long line of them. But something happened there that I didn't expect." He hesitated, as if weighing his words. "There was a woman at the event—a journalist. She was digging into some shady dealings that had happened in the community, and I was trying to help her get the information she needed."

"Why would you do that?" I asked, my curiosity piqued. "What's the connection?"

"She was looking into The Raven's activities," he explained, his brow furrowed. "I thought if I could help her, it would shed light on whatever was happening in our neighborhood. I didn't realize it would put me in the crosshairs."

"So you think that's how you got involved?" I asked, piecing together the puzzle. "Because you were trying to help?"

"Yes," he affirmed, his expression softening. "But it gets more complicated. After the event, I started receiving strange messages—like threats. At first, I thought it was just some prank, but then they became increasingly sinister."

"Threats?" I echoed, my stomach tightening. "What kind of threats?"

"Things like—if I didn't back off, I'd regret it. And the more I tried to help the journalist, the more aggressive the messages became." He raked a hand through his hair, frustration evident. "I didn't want to scare you, so I kept it to myself."

The room was spinning with revelations, the tension ebbing slightly as I processed the weight of his words. "And you think the Raven is behind these threats?"

"I do," he admitted, his voice quiet but steady. "I think he's trying to intimidate me into silence. And if he knows I care about you, that could put you in danger too."

The implications settled heavily between us, the sense of dread creeping back. "We need to go to the police," I said, my heart racing at the thought of involving authorities in our already complicated lives.

"Julia, no," Jonah said quickly, urgency lacing his tone. "If The Raven has connections, it might not be safe for either of us. We need to figure this out quietly first."

My mind whirled with possibilities, anxiety clawing at my insides. "But how? What do we do next?"

"Let me show you something," Jonah said, his eyes flickering with determination. He reached for my hand, and despite my fears, I felt a surge of courage radiate through me. He led me to the small table in the corner, where a pile of documents lay waiting like a damning confession.

"Everything I've gathered about The Raven," he explained, sifting through the papers. "It's not much, but there are patterns here. I think if we can make sense of it all, we might be able to track him down."

As he sorted through the documents, I leaned closer, intrigued despite the nagging sense of danger that lingered in the air. Just as I was about to ask another question, my phone buzzed again, vibrating insistently on the table. I reached for it, only to find a new message that sent a chill through my spine.

It was from an unknown number, but the words sent a jolt of fear straight to my core: "You should have stayed away from him. Next time, it won't just be a warning."

The implication hung heavy, the threat palpable. I looked up at Jonah, my heart racing as the realization washed over us both.

"We're in deeper than we thought," I whispered, dread pooling in my stomach.

Jonah's face had gone pale, the weight of the message settling between us like an avalanche. "Julia, we need to act fast. We might not have much time."

Before I could respond, the sound of hurried footsteps echoed from the hallway outside, each step heavy and urgent. Panic surged through me as I locked eyes with Jonah, a silent agreement passing between us. We weren't just unraveling a mystery; we were now part of a dangerous game.

The footsteps grew closer, and I felt the ground shift beneath me, the walls closing in as I braced myself for whatever—or whoever—was about to enter our lives again.

# Chapter 6: Into the Abyss

I wandered through the shadowed streets of Chicago, the hum of the city swirling around me like a thick fog, obscuring the very air I breathed. Night fell like a curtain, deepening the shades of the alleys where the light dared not tread. Neon signs flickered above me, casting kaleidoscopic colors onto the cracked pavement—a twisted reflection of the vibrant art scene I had once adored. But the allure of beauty had become tainted, as I now found myself ensnared in the sinister web of The Raven's game.

The thrill of the chase pulsed through my veins, each heartbeat a drumroll that echoed in the silence of my solitude. I'd long ago decided that I was done waiting for the authorities to piece together the fragmented puzzle of stolen masterpieces and hidden agendas. With every day that passed, the memory of the latest theft haunted me—an exquisite Van Gogh snatched from the heart of the city, a crime that left ripples of unrest in its wake. I had to know more, and in my relentless pursuit of truth, I had become an amateur detective in a world I once observed from a distance.

My first lead had come from a scruffy man named Felix, who lurked in the dim light of a bar that reeked of stale beer and whispered secrets. He'd looked like a cliché come to life, with a fedora tipped at an angle that suggested both style and desperation. When I approached him, he regarded me with an arched eyebrow, his interest piqued by my audacity. "What's a girl like you doing in a place like this?" he asked, his voice gravelly and teasing.

"Looking for answers," I replied, summoning all the confidence I could muster. I could feel the heat rise to my cheeks, but I pressed on. "I hear you know things. Things about The Raven."

His chuckle was dark, a sound that echoed in the corners of the dimly lit room. "You're chasing shadows, sweetheart. The Raven doesn't play nice with little girls."

"Then what's your price for the truth?" I asked, undeterred.

Felix leaned back, arms crossed, sizing me up like I was a puzzle he hadn't quite solved. "Let's just say, you're not my type. But I might have a tip or two if you're willing to take a stroll down a darker path."

With a sardonic smile, I leaned closer. "I'll take my chances. Just lead the way."

He led me through a maze of alleyways, each step deeper into the unknown. The city had a heartbeat here, a rhythm that thrummed with urgency and danger. I could feel the air thicken with anticipation, a tension that coiled around my senses. Finally, we reached a nondescript door tucked between two larger buildings, barely visible unless you were looking for it. Felix rapped twice in a peculiar sequence, and the door creaked open, revealing a world that felt like stepping into a fever dream.

Inside was an art gallery, though not the kind frequented by the affluent and cultured. The dim lights flickered overhead, illuminating canvases adorned with stolen dreams. Paintings hung haphazardly, their vibrant colors dulled by the shadows that clung to them. The air was thick with the scent of varnish and something acrid, a sharp reminder of the illicit dealings that took place here. I stepped inside, my heart racing, the adrenaline flooding my system as I took in the scene.

A group of men huddled in the corner, their voices low and conspiratorial, eyes darting around the room like wary animals. I could sense the weight of their gazes on me, a mixture of curiosity and suspicion. It was a dangerous game, and I had waded into the deep end. As I approached one of the paintings—a stunning piece reminiscent of a Matisse, bold and colorful—I could feel the prickling sensation of being watched intensify.

"Careful there," a voice purred from behind me, smooth as silk yet laced with an edge. I turned to find a woman standing just a step away, her dark hair cascading over her shoulders like a waterfall of shadows. "You never know what might be hiding behind a pretty façade."

"And you are?" I asked, my tone steady despite the quickening beat of my heart.

"Evelyn. I run this place." She gestured vaguely, encompassing the room with a sweep of her arm. "And you, darling, are far too curious for your own good."

The tension between us crackled like static electricity, and for a moment, the world faded around us. I could feel the energy thrumming in the air, a pulse that seemed to echo my own resolve. "I'm not afraid of a little curiosity," I said, matching her gaze with defiance.

Her smile was enigmatic, as if she appreciated my bravado. "Curiosity can be a double-edged sword. You might just find the answers you seek... but at what cost?"

As we exchanged barbs, the truth of The Raven began to unravel in my mind. It wasn't just about theft; it was a vendetta rooted in a complex web of betrayal, greed, and the insatiable desire for power. Each stolen piece of art was a marker in a twisted game, a calculated move in a much larger scheme. I felt a shiver run down my spine—a warning or an invitation? I couldn't tell.

In that dim gallery, beneath the weight of stolen history, I knew I was dancing on the edge of something vast and treacherous. The thrill was intoxicating, but I couldn't shake the feeling that the shadows were closing in around me, their presence palpable and threatening. Every whisper of the night seemed to hold secrets, and every glance over my shoulder felt like a prelude to danger. I was in too deep, but I had come too far to turn back now. The abyss beckoned, and I had no choice but to answer its call.

The room pulsed with unspoken tension as Evelyn's sharp gaze pinned me in place. She exuded an aura that felt almost magnetic, a mix of danger and allure that made the hairs on my arms stand at attention. I could sense the layers beneath her composed exterior, a web of secrets intertwined with the stolen art surrounding us. As I fought the urge to glance over my shoulder—convinced that someone, or something, lurked just out of sight—Evelyn smiled, the corners of her mouth curling like a cat about to pounce.

"What exactly are you looking for?" she asked, her tone teasing yet laced with a seriousness that silenced the room. The men had gone quiet, their focus shifting to me like moths drawn to a flame. "Or is it more a case of wanting to find trouble?"

"Trouble has a way of finding me," I quipped, leaning into the moment. "But I'm more interested in The Raven. I think he's playing a game, and I intend to win."

A fleeting shadow crossed Evelyn's face, and in that instant, I wondered if I had crossed some invisible line. "Winning can come at a steep price," she warned, her voice dropping to a conspiratorial whisper. "The Raven doesn't take kindly to those who intrude upon his affairs. You may think you're clever, but he'll see you coming. He always does."

Her words echoed in my mind, but the fire of determination flared hotter. "That's precisely why I'm here. I refuse to be scared off by a ghost story."

Evelyn chuckled softly, a sound that was both amused and deeply contemplative. "A ghost, indeed. But even ghosts can cause havoc if you're not careful." She stepped closer, lowering her voice. "If you're really committed to this, you'll need an ally—someone who knows the ins and outs of this world. I could help you, but trust doesn't come easy in these shadows."

"An ally? You're not suggesting I partner with you, are you?" My skepticism dripped from my words, but there was an undeniable spark of intrigue in the idea. A part of me wanted to embrace her world of danger and deception, but the other was anchored by caution. "What's in it for you?"

"Consider it a professional courtesy," she said, her gaze unwavering. "I don't like losing art any more than you do. And The Raven? He's made quite the mess of things."

I considered her proposition, the weight of the decision heavy on my shoulders. I had ventured into this labyrinth of deceit alone, but now, facing the truth of my situation, the thought of an ally was enticing. "So what's the plan?" I asked, a challenge hanging in the air between us.

Evelyn smirked, a spark of mischief lighting her eyes. "We start by visiting a contact of mine—someone who might have insight into The Raven's next move. But be warned, it won't be a tea party." She motioned for me to follow her, the atmosphere crackling with the promise of adventure.

As we navigated through the gallery, the artwork seemed to come alive around us, the painted figures gazing out with knowing eyes. I followed Evelyn into a back room, where the air felt thick with anticipation. She opened another door, revealing a narrow staircase that spiraled down into darkness. "After you," she gestured with a dramatic flourish, a grin playing on her lips.

"Charming," I muttered under my breath, swallowing my trepidation as I descended the stairs. Each step echoed against the walls, the sound amplified in the confined space, heightening my sense of unease. The dim light revealed a small room lined with shelves filled with canvases, crates stacked haphazardly, and a flickering bulb that barely illuminated the corner. The atmosphere felt like a secret kept too long, the kind that whispered of danger lurking just beneath the surface.

"Welcome to my world," Evelyn said, her voice echoing against the walls. "This is a storage space for art that needs a temporary home. And sometimes, it's also a refuge for those who want to escape the spotlight." She moved to the far wall, pulling aside a curtain that revealed a small window overlooking the alley below.

I peered through the glass, my heart racing at the sight of shadows flitting past. "What are we doing here?" I asked, my curiosity piqued.

"Waiting for my contact. He's a slippery fellow, but he knows what's going on in the underbelly of this city." She turned, leaning against the wall with a relaxed demeanor that belied the tension in the air. "Tell me, what do you know about The Raven?"

I hesitated, searching for the right words. "He's a ghost, a myth in the art world—a master thief who targets only the most prestigious pieces. They say he has connections everywhere, like an octopus with arms reaching into every corner of the city."

Evelyn's laughter rang out, bright and clear, cutting through the somber atmosphere. "Very poetic, but there's more to it. The Raven is not just a thief; he's an artist of chaos. He thrives on creating narratives that disrupt the established order. Each heist is a stroke of genius, a statement that art isn't just for the elite—it belongs to everyone."

I could feel the thrill of it all, the way her words wrapped around my imagination, pulling me further into this dark world. "But why does he do it? What's the endgame?"

"Ah, that's the crux of the matter." She glanced toward the window, her expression becoming serious. "It's a vendetta rooted in something personal, something that twists deep within the fabric of his life. I suspect it's tied to betrayal—perhaps even revenge."

Before I could respond, a knock echoed through the small space, sharp and sudden. Evelyn straightened, her eyes narrowing as she approached the door. "This is him. Stay behind me."

The tension thickened as she opened the door to reveal a tall man draped in shadows, a hood pulled low over his face. The air turned electric as he stepped inside, his presence both commanding and unnerving. "You're late," Evelyn said, crossing her arms, but the man merely shrugged, a nonchalance that grated against the gravity of our situation.

"Time is fluid in this line of work," he replied, his voice smooth yet rough around the edges, like gravel coated in honey. He turned his gaze to me, sizing me up with a glance that made me feel exposed. "And who might this be?"

"A friend," Evelyn said curtly, her tone suggesting that any further discussion would be unwise. "We need information about The Raven."

"Ah, the infamous Raven," he mused, his lips curling into a smirk. "And what makes you think you're ready to play his game?"

"I'm not here to play," I interjected, surprising even myself with the confidence in my voice. "I'm here to win."

The man's eyebrows shot up, and for a moment, I thought I saw a flicker of respect in his eyes. "Well, then. Let's see what you're made of."

The man leaned against the wall, his posture relaxed, but his eyes held a glint that spoke of calculated mischief. "So, you're determined to take on The Raven, huh?" he said, his voice dripping with sarcasm. "I admire the bravado, but do you even know what you're up against?"

I squared my shoulders, willing myself to appear unflinching. "I know enough to recognize a man who thrives in the shadows and a woman who thinks she can help me navigate them."

Evelyn shot me a sidelong glance, an expression that combined amusement with disbelief. "That's one way to put it," she replied dryly. "But if you're going to walk this path, you need more than just a good quip. You need information."

"Then give me what I need," I urged, impatience bubbling just beneath the surface. "What do you know about his next move?"

The man smiled, a slow, easy grin that sent a shiver down my spine. "Ah, so eager. But eagerness can be a double-edged sword." He pushed off the wall and took a few steps closer, the flickering light casting shadows across his sharp features. "What if I told you that The Raven is planning something big, something that could change the art world forever?"

"Then I'd say it's time to spill the details," I shot back, crossing my arms defiantly. "Or do you want me to remind you of what happens to those who keep secrets?"

He regarded me for a moment, as if assessing my worth. "You've got guts, I'll give you that," he said, nodding slowly. "Alright, here's the scoop. There's a gala coming up—a high-profile charity event where several priceless pieces will be displayed. Rumor has it that The Raven intends to make an appearance, and not just for the hors d'oeuvres."

"A gala?" I repeated, excitement bubbling in my chest. "Where? When?"

"Next Friday at the Art Institute. It's an open invite, but only the wealthy and influential will be there. And I doubt anyone will notice if a few pieces go missing amid the clinking of champagne glasses and the flurry of well-dressed elites." He paused, letting the weight of his words settle. "You'll want to be there, but I suggest you tread carefully. This isn't just about art—it's about power. The Raven's heists always have a deeper meaning."

Evelyn stepped in, her voice cutting through the tension. "And that deeper meaning could be the very reason why you shouldn't get involved, darling. You're playing with fire."

"Fire? I've always had a knack for dancing with it," I replied, my heart racing with the thrill of the chase. The idea of attending the gala, of mingling with those who wore their wealth like a badge, was intoxicating. I could see it now: the shimmering dresses, the hushed conversations, and the underlying pulse of ambition. "What's life without a little risk?"

The man's laughter filled the small room, dark and rich like a fine wine. "You really are a piece of work, aren't you? Just don't say I didn't warn you when you find yourself in over your head."

"Let's just say I've always preferred a challenge," I said, my resolve firm. "But I'll need your help to make this work. I can't walk into that gala blind."

"Fine. I can give you a few pointers," he replied, his demeanor shifting to one of reluctant respect. "But remember, once you step onto this stage, there's no curtain call. You either play your part, or you'll find yourself exposed—perhaps even removed from the game altogether."

Evelyn's expression darkened, a shadow crossing her features. "And if you get caught, you'll bring more than just yourself into the crosshairs. You'll drag me down with you, and trust me, I'm not ready to dance with the devil."

"I can handle myself," I insisted, though a flicker of doubt crept into my mind. The stakes were higher than I had anticipated, and the thrill that had driven me forward now felt like a tempest raging within. "What's your name, anyway?"

"Jace," he replied, his gaze steady as he studied me. "And I'll help you, but you'd better be ready for anything."

Before I could respond, a loud crash echoed from outside, shaking the walls of our makeshift sanctuary. We exchanged startled glances, and I felt the sudden rush of adrenaline. "What was that?" I asked, my heart thundering in my chest.

"Stay here," Jace instructed, slipping out the door before I could protest. I was left with Evelyn, the silence now heavy with uncertainty. The shadows crept closer, and the flickering light overhead seemed to stutter, as if uncertain of its role in this unfolding drama.

I paced the small room, nerves buzzing in my veins. The world outside felt precarious, like a tightrope stretched above a yawning chasm. I could sense the weight of secrets coiling around me, tightening their grip. Just as I decided to follow Jace, the door swung open, and he stepped back in, his expression grave.

"Someone's here," he said, urgency tinging his voice. "We need to move—now."

"Move? Where?" I asked, panic creeping in.

"Out the back," he replied, pulling a small door I hadn't noticed before. "We'll cut through the alley and circle around. Whatever's going on outside, we can't stick around to find out."

Evelyn cast me a sharp look, her eyes wide. "Do you really think you're ready for this? It's not just art thieves we're dealing with; it's a world filled with merciless players. If you want to survive, you need to keep your head down."

But there was no time for doubt. I had already stepped too far into this abyss. "I'm not backing down now," I declared, steeling myself for the uncertainty ahead. With a nod, I plunged through the door Jace held open, plunging into the darkness of the alley beyond.

The chill of the night air hit me like a slap, and I could hear voices murmuring just beyond the shadows. "What's happening?" I whispered to Jace as we crept along the damp walls.

"Just keep moving. We're close to the exit," he said, his voice barely a breath against the night. But as we rounded a corner, a figure stepped into the dim light ahead, blocking our path. The silhouette was familiar, and my heart sank.

It was Felix, the man I had met in the bar, but he wasn't alone. Behind him stood a group of men, their expressions dark and menacing, eyes glinting with purpose. "You thought you could just disappear?" Felix's voice was laced with a mocking tone. "Looks like the game is just getting started."

A shiver raced down my spine as realization struck. I had unwittingly walked into a trap, and the darkness I had been so eager to explore was now closing in, tightening its grip around me. I glanced at Jace, desperation flickering in his eyes. "What do we do?" I whispered, knowing that the answer could mean the difference between life and death.

Felix grinned, a predator sizing up his prey. "Oh, I think you know exactly what happens next."

# Chapter 7: Beneath the Surface

The gallery buzzes with a frenetic energy, the kind that makes the walls hum and the air shimmer with unspoken tension. I stand amidst the chaos of colors and canvases, my fingers brushing against the cool surface of a metal sculpture, a contorted mass of wires and shapes that somehow mirrors the turmoil inside me. My heart races, the rhythm matching the upbeat tempo of the music pulsing from the hidden speakers. It's supposed to be a night of celebration, but all I can feel is the weight of everything unaddressed pressing down on me like the humid summer air outside.

Then, through the vibrant chaos, I see him—Jonah. He strides in, a beacon of calm amidst the swirling colors, his presence magnetic. The way his dark hair falls effortlessly over his forehead and the sharp angles of his jawline could set off a spark even in the dimmest light. My breath catches, and the anger I had clutched so tightly moments before evaporates, leaving behind a hollow ache that I can't ignore. As he approaches, the world around us fades into a blur. The laughter, the clinking of glasses, the bright flashes of camera bulbs—they all fade, leaving only the tension thrumming between us.

"Hey," he says, his voice low, almost swallowed by the ambient noise. But it pulls me in, wraps around me like a warm blanket on a chilly night. "You okay?"

"Yeah, just admiring the art," I reply, a little too quickly. I force a smile, but the edges of it tremble. How can I stand here, surrounded by art that feels like a lie when everything inside me feels so jagged? My gaze darts away, taking in the vibrant canvases that seem to mock my internal chaos with their perfect strokes. "What about you?"

"I came looking for you." His admission hangs between us, laden with meaning. I feel the heat rise to my cheeks, betraying my attempt to remain composed. "I thought we could talk."

"About?" I ask, my voice barely above a whisper, as if saying it aloud would make it too real. The gallery feels both expansive and constricting, the very walls bearing witness to a conversation that feels monumental.

"About everything," he replies, his eyes searching mine, their depths revealing layers I've yet to unravel. "There's been too much left unsaid."

The sincerity in his voice pierces through the fog of uncertainty that clings to me. I take a step closer, and the space between us shrinks, charged with the electricity of unspoken words and emotions waiting to spill over. "I don't even know where to start."

"Start with what you feel," he suggests, his tone encouraging, gentle yet insistent. "What scares you?"

The question lingers, heavy in the air, and I feel it ripple through my thoughts. My insecurities rise like a tide, each one crashing against the shore of my resolve. "I feel... exposed," I admit, the confession slipping out before I can retract it. "Like I'm standing in front of a canvas with no paint, completely blank. What if I never find the right colors?"

Jonah's expression softens, and I can almost see the gears turning in his mind. "You don't have to have it all figured out," he says, stepping closer. "You're allowed to be uncertain, to be afraid."

I swallow hard, his words threading through my insecurities like a lifeline. "But I feel like I'm drowning in it, Jonah. The Raven is still out there, waiting for me to slip. What if I can't outrun it?"

His eyes darken with understanding, and for a moment, I see a flicker of anger—not directed at me but at the very idea of the threat looming over us. "We face it together. You're not alone in this."

As he speaks, I feel a crack begin to form in the fortress I've built around my heart. I realize I want to believe him, to trust that we can navigate this storm. "You make it sound so easy," I counter, a hint of sarcasm lacing my words. "What if it's not?"

"Then we figure it out as we go," he responds, a small smile breaking through the tension, brightening the corners of his face. "That's the beauty of it, isn't it? Imperfection, uncertainty, and—"

"Chaos?" I interject, a teasing grin finally tugging at my lips. "That's one way to put it."

"Exactly," he replies, his laughter a balm against my fraying nerves. "Life is one big, beautiful mess, and we're just trying to paint within the lines."

The moment lingers, charged with possibility, as I watch Jonah lean closer. The way his gaze flickers from my eyes to my lips feels electric, igniting something deep within me. I feel seen in a way I haven't before, as if he's peering past the layers I've carefully crafted and is unearthing the real me buried underneath. I can't help but wonder if he feels the same pull, the same urgency to bridge the distance that had stretched between us for so long.

Just then, a loud crash reverberates through the gallery, jolting me back to reality. A group of art enthusiasts spills drinks, their laughter cutting through the intimate moment we had forged. Jonah and I pull back slightly, the magic punctured like a balloon. I laugh awkwardly, trying to regain my composure as the raucous energy of the gallery envelops us once more.

"Looks like we're not the only ones creating chaos tonight," he quips, a teasing glint in his eyes that brings back a sense of ease.

"Or maybe it's a sign," I reply, my mind racing. "Maybe it's time to embrace the chaos."

"Then let's dive into it," he says, his voice unwavering and filled with a determination that matches my own. "After all, what's the worst that could happen?"

As the night unfolds around us, the weight of The Raven feels a little lighter, and for the first time, I allow myself to imagine a world where Jonah and I stand shoulder to shoulder against whatever storms lie ahead.

The din of laughter and conversation surrounds us, but within our bubble, there's a clarity that feels almost surreal. Jonah's expression, a blend of determination and warmth, draws me closer as if we're the only two people in the room. I can feel the energy of the gallery vibrating around us, but all I can focus on is the connection that crackles in the air, filling the void of uncertainty with a kind of fragile hope.

"Let's get out of here," he suggests suddenly, his eyes sparkling with mischief. "I know a place where we can actually hear ourselves think."

I raise an eyebrow, half-skeptical and half-intrigued. "Are you about to take me to a secret lair? Should I be worried?"

He grins, a boyish charm lighting up his features. "Only if you're afraid of rooftops and city skylines."

The prospect is tempting, a whisper of adventure tickling at my senses. "Lead the way, then."

We weave through the crowd, Jonah's hand lightly brushing against mine, sending unexpected shivers down my spine. The atmosphere shifts as we step outside into the crisp evening air, a stark contrast to the vibrant chaos we leave behind. The city sparkles under the twilight sky, a tapestry of lights and shadows, each corner holding its own story waiting to unfold.

"Is this where you reveal your true identity as a vigilante?" I ask, trying to match his playful energy.

"Not quite," he replies, his voice a conspiratorial whisper. "But you might discover my terrible taste in music."

"Now I'm genuinely intrigued," I laugh, and the sound feels free, unfettered by the weight of my worries. He leads me through a narrow alley, the distant sounds of traffic fading into a softer hum.

The rooftop is a hidden gem, a secluded space adorned with flickering string lights that twinkle like stars against the night sky. As we emerge into the open air, the view stretches out before us—a breathtaking panorama of the city skyline, illuminated by the glow of countless windows.

"Wow," I breathe, stepping closer to the edge. "This is incredible."

"Right?" Jonah's pride shines through as he watches my reaction. "I come up here whenever I need a break from the noise. The view reminds me that there's more to life than just what's right in front of us."

I nod, feeling a rush of gratitude for this moment, for the sanctuary he's shared with me. "It's perfect. Thank you for bringing me here."

He leans against the railing, his gaze drifting over the horizon. "You've been going through so much. I wanted to give you a little escape, a chance to breathe."

The sincerity of his words settles in my chest, and the barriers I've built around my heart begin to erode. "You have no idea how much I need that," I admit, my voice barely above a whisper. "Sometimes it feels like I'm just... treading water, waiting for the storm to hit."

Jonah turns to face me, his eyes searching mine. "And what if the storm never comes?"

"Then what am I waiting for?" I counter, my heart racing as I lock eyes with him. The question hangs in the air, and the moment stretches out, taut with possibility.

"Maybe it's time to stop waiting," he says softly, stepping closer, our bodies nearly touching. "Start living instead."

His words hang heavy between us, a challenge and a promise all at once. The thrill of uncertainty swirls in my stomach, and for a moment, the rest of the world fades away. It's just Jonah and me, standing on the edge of something transformative.

"What do you suggest we do, then?" I tease, attempting to inject some levity into the heavy moment. "Jump off and embrace the chaos?"

"Only if you're wearing a parachute," he replies, his smile widening. "Or a cape. Capes make everything more dramatic."

"Very true," I agree, a laugh bubbling up as I lean back against the railing, letting the cool metal anchor me to the present. "But I think I'd look better in a nice dress, thank you very much."

"Definitely a dress," he nods seriously. "And maybe a feather boa for flair."

"Now you're talking," I say, enjoying the playful banter that feels so natural with him. "But back to reality. What if I can't let go of the past?"

Jonah sobers slightly, the lightheartedness replaced with something more profound. "Letting go doesn't mean forgetting. It's about recognizing what you've learned from it and using that to move forward. You're stronger than you think."

"Maybe," I concede, my vulnerability creeping back in. "But the fear is always there. What if The Raven comes for me again? I can't shake the feeling that I'm still in danger."

His expression hardens slightly, a flicker of protectiveness sparking in his eyes. "I won't let anything happen to you. We'll face it together."

My heart swells at his promise, the warmth of his words wrapping around me like a comforting embrace. "You make it sound so easy, Jonah. I wish I had your confidence."

"Confidence is overrated," he laughs softly, but there's an undercurrent of sincerity in his tone. "It's more about taking risks, embracing the unknown, even when it scares the hell out of you."

"Are you saying I should jump off this roof?" I challenge playfully, though the deeper meaning isn't lost on me.

"Only if you want to take the plunge," he responds, his gaze steady, unwavering. "But maybe we start with something simpler. Like telling each other our biggest fears."

"Now that's a fun game," I say, biting my lip as I ponder my answer. "Fine, I'll go first. My biggest fear? That I'll never find my place in this world."

Jonah nods, his expression serious as he processes my words. "That's a real fear. But you're on the right path. You're brave, even if you don't see it."

"What about you?" I press, intrigued to peel back another layer of this fascinating man before me.

He hesitates, the lightness in his demeanor dimming momentarily. "I fear losing the people I care about. The thought of it paralyzes me."

His honesty strikes a chord deep within me. "I get that. But you have me, Jonah. I'm not going anywhere."

"Good to know," he replies, his smile returning, a hint of mischief in his eyes. "Because I could really use a partner in crime."

"Partners in crime, huh?" I tease, leaning closer. "What's our first heist? Stealing the moon?"

"Why not?" he chuckles, his eyes glinting with enthusiasm. "Just you and me, up there among the stars."

As the night deepens around us, a sense of peace settles over me. Here, on this rooftop, with Jonah at my side, I feel a flicker of hope igniting within me. The chaos of the world below seems distant, and for a moment, I allow myself to believe in the possibility of something more—something beautiful.

The night air wraps around us like a soft blanket, cool yet inviting, contrasting sharply with the swirling thoughts inside my mind. Jonah leans against the railing, his body relaxed, exuding a calm that draws me closer. The city sprawls beneath us, a living organism with lights flickering like stars fallen to earth, and for the first time in what feels like forever, I start to envision a world without the weight of fear pressing on my chest.

"You know," I say, breaking the comfortable silence, "if I'm ever going to steal the moon, I'm definitely going to need a better plan than just jumping off a rooftop."

Jonah chuckles, the sound rich and warm, dispelling some of the heaviness that lingers in the air. "I could help with that. I'm great at brainstorming bad ideas."

"Is that your secret? A career of terrible plans?" I retort playfully, nudging him gently with my shoulder.

He feigns offense, placing a hand over his heart. "You wound me. I prefer to think of it as creative problem-solving."

"Creative, huh? Sounds much more impressive," I quip, unable to suppress my grin. There's something refreshing about our banter, like a breath of fresh air slicing through a thick fog. "So what's your next 'creative' project?"

"I was thinking about painting an enormous mural of us stealing the moon," he replies, his eyes sparkling with mischief. "I'll need your help for inspiration, of course."

"Of course! I'm practically an art guru now," I say, striking a mock pose as if I'm an expert in some grand gallery. "What would I wear? A glamorous cape, or perhaps a stylish jumpsuit?"

"Definitely the cape," he insists, laughing. "But it has to be sequined. You can't steal the moon without a little sparkle."

"Then I shall demand a proper budget for this caper," I declare dramatically, spinning around to survey the skyline. The moon hangs low, full and luminous, casting a silvery glow over the city. "Look! There's the target! But I'll need a distraction. Any ideas?"

"Maybe I could set off some fireworks?" he suggests, his tone playful yet earnest.

"Fireworks? You might attract attention from more than just the moon," I say, my voice dropping an octave as I pretend to look serious. "What if the police show up? I don't want to spend my nights in jail for moon theft."

"Fine, I'll scratch that idea," he replies, holding up his hands in mock surrender. "What if we just tell them we're artists at work?"

"Brilliant! And when they ask for our permits?" I shoot back, a smirk spreading across my face.

Jonah rolls his eyes. "You really know how to kill the mood, don't you?"

"Oh, come on! You love it," I tease, nudging him again. But beneath the lighthearted banter, an unsettling thought creeps in: what if this moment is fleeting? What if the looming shadow of The Raven crashes down at any second, breaking this bubble of peace we've found?

"Tell me something real," Jonah says suddenly, his voice dipping into seriousness, grounding me. "What's one thing you want that you think you'll never have?"

I hesitate, the question hanging in the air like a fragile bubble, waiting to pop. "I want... I want to feel safe," I admit finally, my voice barely above a whisper. "Not just from The Raven, but in every aspect of my life. I want to wake up without that pit in my stomach."

Jonah's expression softens, the playful glint in his eyes replaced by something deeper. "You deserve that. We all do," he replies, his tone firm yet compassionate. "But safety can be an illusion. It's about finding the right people to share the journey with."

My heart swells at his words, but a shadow lingers at the edges of my mind. "What if I can't find those people? What if I'm always looking over my shoulder?"

"You're not alone anymore," he assures me, his voice steady. "I'll be there. We'll face whatever comes together."

His promise sends a shiver through me, igniting a spark of hope, but it also stirs a whirlpool of conflicting emotions. "What if it's not enough?" I ask, vulnerability creeping back into my voice.

"Then we'll find another way," he replies, unwavering. "We'll keep looking until we figure it out."

I want to believe him, to trust in this connection that feels so genuine, but the fear gnaws at me, an insistent reminder of the danger that lurks beyond the comfort of this rooftop.

"Let's make a pact," I say suddenly, my tone shifting to a more playful one to mask the fear bubbling beneath the surface. "If we're caught by the moon police, we blame each other. Sound good?"

"Deal," he agrees, grinning widely. "You can take the blame for the sequined cape."

We share a laugh, the sound echoing in the night, but beneath it, an undercurrent of tension lingers. Just as I'm about to suggest we retreat from the edge, my phone buzzes violently in my pocket, slicing through the moment like a knife. I pull it out, my heart racing as I read the message.

It's a group chat, the name flashing ominously: The Hunt. My stomach drops. The last time this group reached out, it was to warn me of The Raven's presence.

Jonah leans closer, curiosity flickering in his eyes as I frown at the screen. "What is it?"

I shake my head, the words caught in my throat. "It's... it's nothing." But my heart races, a relentless drumbeat that drowns out the laughter.

"Liar," he counters, his voice low and insistent. "Show me."

I hesitate, the gravity of the situation weighing heavily on me. I glance at the glowing message again, my hands trembling as I finally relent and turn the screen toward him. His brows furrow in concern as he reads the words, his expression darkening.

"We know where you are. The Raven is coming for you."

The laughter dies in my throat, replaced by a cold dread that washes over me. Jonah's eyes widen, his playful demeanor shifting into something more serious, more protective.

"What does this mean?" he demands, the energy between us snapping taut like a wire about to break.

I can only stare at the screen, the implications swirling in my mind, panic clawing at the edges of my reason. "I— I don't know," I manage to stammer, my voice barely above a whisper. "But we need to go. Now."

Before I can react, a sharp noise erupts from below—a loud crash, followed by shouting. My heart pounds in my chest as I look at Jonah, the reality of the situation settling like a stone in my stomach. The night that felt so full of promise has twisted into a nightmare, the vibrant city now a dangerous landscape.

"Stay close," Jonah orders, his tone commanding as he grabs my hand. Together, we dart toward the edge of the rooftop, adrenaline coursing through our veins. Just as we reach the ladder leading down, a shadow flickers in the periphery of my vision, a figure emerging from the darkness, tall and menacing.

My breath catches, dread pooling at the base of my throat. "Jonah, we have to—"

But the words die on my lips as the figure steps into the light, and the world tilts beneath me.

# Chapter 8: Shadows of the Past

The storm had rolled in with all the subtlety of a freight train, black clouds roiling overhead like angry spirits, while the first drops of rain splattered against the pavement, a harbinger of the chaos that was about to unfold. I watched from my perch on the dilapidated porch of the old Whitmore estate, the wood creaking beneath me as if protesting my presence. The house loomed large and menacing, its once grand facade now a patchwork of peeling paint and creeping ivy, a reflection of the tangled secrets it held within. This place was a relic of Jonah's past, and it felt like an uninvited guest at our already tumultuous gathering of emotions.

Jonah stood a few paces away, his silhouette stark against the darkening sky, the tension in his shoulders betraying a man fighting against invisible chains. I could see the storm in his eyes, a tempest of regret and fear flickering just beneath the surface, battling against the determination that had driven him this far. Every instinct within me screamed to reach out, to bridge the chasm that had suddenly opened between us, but the weight of his secrets hung heavy in the air, thick as the oncoming rain.

"Why didn't you tell me?" I finally asked, my voice barely cutting through the thrum of the storm. I hated how it trembled, betraying the hurt lodged deep in my chest. I felt the distance between us, not just physically but in the very essence of who we were. The air was charged, and I couldn't tell if it was the impending rain or the unresolved tension crackling like static electricity.

Jonah turned to face me, his expression caught between anguish and defiance. "Because it's complicated, Maddie," he replied, his voice gravelly as if he had been chewing on his words for too long. "The Raven... it's not just a name, it's a part of me. A part I thought I could outrun."

"The Raven," I echoed, the name tasting bitter on my tongue. It was the dark figure that had shadowed our every move, the specter that had threatened to unravel the delicate thread of trust we'd built. "You're connected to them, Jonah. How could you not tell me?"

"I didn't want you to see me that way," he admitted, stepping closer, his dark hair dampening under the drizzle that began to fall in earnest. "I wanted you to see me as I am now, not as I was then."

I studied him, trying to peel back the layers that concealed his truth. In the dull light, I could see the soft contours of his face illuminated with raindrops like tiny diamonds, and my heart ached with a fierce longing to understand him. "But I can't be in this with you if I don't know all of you. It feels like... it feels like you're hiding behind shadows."

Jonah's brow furrowed, the rain mingling with the sweat of his earlier exertions as he reached for me, his fingers brushing against my arm. The contact sent a jolt through me, igniting a warmth that fought against the chill of the storm. "You think I want this? You think I chose this life?" His voice trembled with an intensity that both scared and excited me. "Every day is a battle, Maddie. The Raven was not just an organization; it was a family. A sick, twisted family that twisted everything into a nightmare."

"Then let me help you," I urged, my own determination rising in tandem with the swell of the rain. "You don't have to face this alone. I won't let you."

A flicker of something—hope, perhaps—crossed his features, but it was gone as quickly as it came, replaced by the shadows that seemed to follow him like a loyal hound. "You don't understand. This isn't just about me anymore. The deeper we dig, the more danger we invite. They'll come for you, too."

I squared my shoulders, the rain soaking through my shirt, chilling me to the bone but igniting a fire within. "If they come for me, then they'll have to deal with both of us. We'll face it together.

I'd rather fight beside you than stand back and let you go through this alone."

The silence stretched between us, thick and heavy, as thunder rumbled in the distance, but something shifted in his gaze. I could see the walls he had built around himself begin to tremble, cracks appearing in his carefully constructed facade. "You're brave, Maddie. Braver than I've ever been," he said, his voice low and reverent, as if I were a delicate thing he was afraid to touch too hard. "But bravery doesn't always win against shadows."

"Maybe not," I replied, my heart pounding with a mix of fear and exhilaration. "But love does. It has to."

The rain fell harder now, washing away the dirt and grime of the past, a baptism of sorts, and in that moment, surrounded by the ghosts of Jonah's history, I made a silent vow. I would not let his past define him—or us. I stepped closer, a reckless abandon flooding my senses as I reached up to cup his face, my thumb tracing the line of his jaw.

He leaned into my touch, and for a moment, the chaos outside faded into the background, leaving only the quiet storm brewing between us. The tension thickened, coiling tightly around us as I felt the warmth of his breath mingle with the cool droplets that clung to our skin.

Then, in that heart-stopping second, everything shifted. A crack of thunder split the sky, and with it came a chilling realization—Jonah's past was not just a shadow; it was a living, breathing entity that had claws and teeth. If we were to move forward, we had to confront it head-on, embracing the storm that was bound to come.

As I pulled back slightly, searching his eyes, a spark ignited within me. The fight wasn't over. It was just beginning.

As the storm unleashed its fury, the world around us transformed into a swirling mosaic of gray and silver. Rain hammered against the ground, creating puddles that reflected the tumult of our emotions, each drop echoing like a heartbeat in the chaos. I could feel the weight of Jonah's past pressing down on us, a dense fog that threatened to suffocate any remaining glimmers of hope. Yet, in the middle of this tempest, a spark flickered—something undeniable that whispered that we could forge a path through the darkness together.

"Let's go inside," Jonah finally suggested, his voice low and urgent, as if he feared that the storm might overhear our plans. He took my hand, and I felt the warmth of his skin, grounding me amid the onslaught of fears and uncertainties swirling around us. We stepped into the house, the door creaking ominously as it swung open, revealing an interior steeped in shadows and memories. Dust motes danced in the scant light that filtered through the grimy windows, and the scent of old wood and dampness enveloped us like a forgotten embrace.

Inside, the walls felt like they were closing in, thick with unspoken histories. The floorboards groaned underfoot, a symphony of creaks and whispers as we made our way through the dimly lit corridor. I could see photographs lining the walls—smiling faces trapped in time, oblivious to the storm brewing outside. Each picture told a story, and I felt a pang of envy for their carefree moments. I wished I could peel back the layers of Jonah's history like the wallpaper peeling away from the corners, revealing the raw truths beneath.

"Do you ever think about what it would be like to erase everything?" he asked suddenly, stopping in front of a particularly faded photograph of a young boy with bright eyes and a toothy grin. "To start fresh, without any ghosts hanging around?"

I considered his words carefully, realizing how deeply they resonated with my own desires. "It sounds tempting," I replied, leaning closer to inspect the picture. "But those ghosts are part of us, aren't they? They shape who we become."

Jonah was quiet for a moment, his gaze distant, as if he were wandering through the echoes of his own memories. "You don't understand what it means to be haunted," he said finally, a trace of bitterness creeping into his tone. "Every decision I made, every path I chose, was shadowed by The Raven. They don't just let you go."

"Then let's make our own decisions," I countered, my heart racing with the challenge. "Let's write a new chapter together, one that doesn't include them."

He turned to me, the storm raging outside mirroring the tempest in his eyes. "It's not that simple, Maddie. I wish it were. But their claws are deep, and the moment we dig too far, they'll come for us both."

I stepped closer, determined to bridge the gap between us. "Then let's dig smart. Let's outmaneuver them." The words tumbled out, fueled by a mix of adrenaline and an unwavering belief that we could forge a path through the shadows.

"Outmaneuver them?" Jonah scoffed, a hint of a smile breaking through the storm clouds of his expression. "You make it sound so easy. What do you suggest? A game of chess with a bunch of mobsters?"

"Why not?" I shot back, grinning. "I happen to be excellent at chess. Besides, I like my odds better when I'm playing against the house."

He chuckled softly, the sound a welcome respite from the weight of our situation. "You're something else, you know that?"

"Yeah, but you still haven't answered my question. Are you ready to stop letting them dictate your life?" I pressed, holding his gaze steady.

Jonah's breath hitched, and I could see the flicker of hope battling against the shadows within him. "I don't want to lose you," he admitted, his voice almost a whisper. "If I dive back into that world, it could pull you in with me."

"Then I'm diving in with you," I said fiercely, feeling the conviction settle in my bones. "We can't live in fear of what might happen. We have to confront it together. I won't let you face this alone, no matter how deep the darkness goes."

He studied me, his eyes searching for something, perhaps a flaw in my resolve, but all he found was a steadfast determination that mirrored his own. The weight of our shared burdens hung between us, yet amidst it all, a fragile thread of connection began to weave itself tighter.

A sudden crash of thunder shook the house, rattling the windows as the storm reached its zenith outside. We both jumped, a reminder of the chaos that awaited us, both within and without. But instead of pulling apart, we stood rooted, our fingers entwined, drawing strength from one another.

"Alright," Jonah said, the resolve returning to his voice. "Let's figure this out. But we have to be careful. We'll need a plan, a way to gather intel without drawing attention."

I nodded, the excitement of action replacing the earlier weight of uncertainty. "We can start by researching The Raven's connections. They have to have some kind of network—contacts, records. If we can find a way to access their information..."

He interrupted, a grin creeping across his face. "You think you can crack a safe or something?"

"Pfft, please. I'm more of a digital-age sleuth," I replied, smirking. "But I do know a thing or two about security systems."

Jonah's expression shifted, a glimmer of admiration sparking in his eyes. "You're brilliant, you know that? I've always admired how you think on your feet."

"Flattery will get you nowhere, Mr. Ex-Underworld," I quipped, unable to suppress a laugh. "But it's nice to hear. And honestly, it's easy to admire someone who's a walking, talking mystery."

With a newfound sense of purpose, we began brainstorming ideas, sharing plans and possibilities that felt almost exhilarating against the backdrop of the storm. It was like we were plotting our escape from a life we didn't want, our laughter echoing off the walls as we pieced together a strategy that felt both audacious and thrilling.

As the rain beat relentlessly against the roof, I felt the dark clouds of Jonah's past begin to part, revealing the possibility of something brighter—a future that, against all odds, might just include both of us. We would face the storm together, and maybe, just maybe, we could weather whatever came next.

The air crackled with excitement as Jonah and I mapped out our plans, the storm outside a mere backdrop to the whirlwind of thoughts racing through our minds. The flickering light from the old chandelier overhead cast playful shadows on the walls, reminding me of the very ghosts we were trying to escape. It was as if the house itself was holding its breath, waiting for us to make our move.

"Okay, so we've got your insider information about The Raven. What's next?" I asked, tapping my fingers against the coffee-stained table that looked like it had seen its fair share of secrets. I glanced up at Jonah, who had leaned back, his expression both thoughtful and a bit apprehensive.

"The next step is to find out where they operate. They have safe houses around the city—places where they can regroup and plan without fear of being watched. If we can figure out where those locations are, we can get ahead of them," he said, his voice steady yet edged with tension.

"Sounds like a plan," I replied, enthusiasm bubbling up within me. "And you have connections, right? Old friends in the 'business' who could help us?"

He hesitated, the flicker of doubt clouding his eyes. "It's risky. I haven't spoken to anyone from that life in years. I'm not sure they'll be willing to help me, especially since I'm not exactly a part of their world anymore."

I leaned closer, my heart racing at the thought of him reaching out to his past. "But that's the beauty of it, Jonah. You're not just some pawn in their game anymore. You're a player on the board, and you've got me on your side. Besides, what's life without a little risk?"

His gaze softened, and I felt the weight of unspoken gratitude between us, mingled with the tension of what was to come. "You make it sound so easy," he mused, a hint of a smile playing on his lips.

"Maybe I'm just too stubborn to see the impossible," I replied with a wink, trying to lighten the mood. "Besides, if anyone can navigate a web of deceit, it's us. We're practically professionals now."

As we plotted our next steps, a sudden crash of thunder rattled the windows, and the lights flickered ominously. A shadow crossed my mind—was it truly just the weather, or was it a harbinger of something more sinister lurking just beyond the periphery? Shaking off the feeling, I focused on Jonah's determination, which ignited a spark of hope in my chest.

Hours melted away as we dove deeper into our plans, poring over maps and old contact lists that Jonah had unearthed from the dark recesses of his past. Each name sent chills down my spine, a reminder of the labyrinthine connections that could either lead us to safety or drag us into the abyss.

"There's someone I can reach out to," Jonah said suddenly, a resolute gleam lighting up his eyes. "A guy named Marco. He's always been a straight shooter, even when things got dicey. If anyone knows the whereabouts of the safe houses, it's him."

"Marco?" I replied, arching an eyebrow. "Sounds like a real stand-up guy. What's his deal? Is he trustworthy?"

"Trustworthy is a strong word. He's opportunistic but has a code. If I can convince him that helping us serves his interests, he might just come through." Jonah's expression turned serious, and I could sense the weight of his past creeping back in, ready to pull him under. "But I need you to promise me something."

"Anything," I said, my pulse quickening at the intensity of his gaze.

"If things go south—if he doesn't want to help or if it gets too dangerous—I need you to walk away. I can't lose you to this world."

I felt a swell of warmth at his concern, but it was quickly overshadowed by the reality of the situation. "You're not getting rid of me that easily," I replied, my voice firm. "We're in this together. I won't let you face this alone."

Jonah held my gaze for a long moment, his expression a mixture of admiration and apprehension. Just then, the lights flickered again and plunged us into darkness, the sudden quiet punctuated only by the distant roar of the storm. My heart raced, caught between excitement and fear, as I fumbled for my phone, its glow illuminating Jonah's face, casting him in an otherworldly light.

"Guess the storm's really trying to set the mood," I joked, trying to cut through the tension that had seeped into the air.

"Or maybe it's a warning," he replied, his voice low and serious.

Before I could respond, a loud knock reverberated through the house, echoing off the walls like an ominous drumbeat. I froze, the laughter dying on my lips as adrenaline shot through my veins. Jonah's expression shifted from playful to grave in an instant, and I could see the muscles in his jaw tense as he glanced toward the door.

"Did you invite anyone?" he asked, his voice barely above a whisper.

"No, I—" I started, but another knock followed, this one louder, more insistent. It sounded as if it were demanding entrance, the sort of knock that screamed trouble.

Jonah moved closer to me, the light from my phone casting sharp shadows across his face. "Stay behind me," he instructed, taking a step toward the door, his body a barrier between me and the unknown.

My heart thudded in my chest as I obeyed, the air thick with anticipation. The second knock came again, and this time I could hear a voice, low and gravelly, murmuring something I couldn't quite make out.

"Jonah," I breathed, my instincts screaming that we were no longer alone. "What do we do?"

He hesitated, then grabbed my hand, squeezing it tightly. "We don't open that door," he said, his voice firm. "Not until we know who it is."

As the voice grew clearer, my stomach dropped. "Jonah! I know you're in there! Open up, it's Marco!"

A chill ran down my spine as I processed the name, the very person Jonah had just mentioned. But something about the urgency in Marco's voice felt wrong, a primal instinct warning me that this was not the casual reunion we had hoped for.

Jonah's eyes locked onto mine, and I could see the wheels turning in his mind, weighing the risks of trusting the man on the other side of the door. "What if it's a trap?" he murmured, just loud enough for me to hear.

The storm raged on outside, and in that moment, I realized that the shadows weren't just memories of Jonah's past—they were creeping closer, closing in on us like a thick fog. "What if we don't open the door?" I whispered back, panic threading through my words.

Marco's voice rose, urgent and desperate. "Please! I don't have much time! They're coming for you, Jonah!"

The weight of his words hung in the air, an impending sense of doom crashing over us like the thunder outside. I squeezed Jonah's hand, and the tension coiled tighter, the world around us spiraling into uncertainty.

"Jonah," I urged, my heart racing as the realization dawned—this was more than a simple knock at the door. The storm outside was a prelude to the tempest that was about to break in our lives.

Before he could answer, the sound of shuffling feet echoed from the other side, and my breath caught in my throat. "Open the door, Jonah! We need to go—now!"

In that heartbeat of hesitation, I understood the choice before us: open the door and step into the unknown, or remain cloistered in the shadows, hoping to outlast the storm. With each passing second, the weight of our decision pressed down like the rain outside—dark, heavy, and relentless.

"Do we trust him?" Jonah asked, his voice strained as he grappled with the reality of our situation.

The sound of footsteps grew louder, a reminder that time was slipping away. "We have to make a choice," I replied, my voice steadying against the rising tide of fear.

Jonah took a deep breath, his eyes searching mine for the courage we both needed. And just as he opened his mouth to speak, a loud crash from outside silenced us both, followed by the unmistakable sound of shattering glass.

In that moment, I realized that the shadows of the past weren't the only threat closing in on us. The storm was only beginning, and we stood on the precipice of something far darker than we could have ever imagined.

# Chapter 9: Threads of Deceit

The sun dipped low in the sky, casting a golden hue over the bustling streets of downtown. People hurried along the sidewalk, their footsteps a rhythmic percussion against the pavement, but I felt detached from the world around me. My thoughts spun like a tornado, whirling around the shocking revelations I had unearthed about Jonah's family and their murky ties to The Raven's web of crime. The air was thick with the scent of roasted coffee and fresh pastries from the nearby café, but all I could taste was the bitterness of betrayal.

Jonah and I had spent so many evenings in that very café, our laughter mingling with the rich aroma of espresso. We had crafted a cocoon of warmth amid the city's chaos, two souls seeking solace in each other. But now, as I walked toward him, each step felt heavier than the last, a lead weight dragging me down into an abyss of uncertainty. Would he understand? Could he bear the truth?

"Hey," I said, my voice barely above a whisper as I approached him. He was seated at our usual table, his fingers absently tracing the rim of his coffee cup, lost in thought. The shadows beneath his eyes betrayed his restless nights, and I wished I could ease his burden, even for a moment.

He looked up, and for a heartbeat, everything else faded away. His warm brown eyes sparkled with the remnants of our shared laughter, but as I took a seat across from him, the light dimmed. "What's on your mind?" he asked, concern creasing his brow. I admired that about him, how he always put my feelings first, even when his own heart was heavy with secrets.

"Jonah, we need to talk," I said, my stomach tightening in knots. I could feel the intensity of the moment crackling between us, like the charged air before a storm. He nodded, his expression shifting from warmth to wariness.

"What is it?" His voice was steady, but I could sense the tremor beneath it, the unspoken fear of what might come next.

I took a deep breath, the weight of my discovery pressing down on me like an anchor. "I ran into Mia today," I began, choosing my words carefully. "She told me about the connections between your family and The Raven." Each syllable felt like a dagger, the truth slicing through the delicate fabric of our relationship.

For a moment, silence enveloped us, thick and suffocating. Jonah's eyes widened, the warmth draining from his face, leaving behind a mask of shock. "What do you mean?" he asked, his voice a low rumble, as if he were struggling to contain a tempest of emotions.

"Mia has evidence," I pressed on, unable to hold back the torrent of thoughts racing through my mind. "She said there are financial records linking your family to The Raven's operations. It's all tied to that warehouse fire from last year, the one that nearly took your brother's life."

His fingers clenched around the cup, knuckles white against the ceramic. "You don't understand," he said, his voice trembling with a mix of anger and confusion. "My family... they're not involved in that. They've worked hard to distance themselves from that world."

"But what if they haven't?" I shot back, the desperation creeping into my tone. "What if they've been lying to you all along? I don't want to believe it, Jonah, but the pieces fit too well. The connections are there."

He leaned back in his chair, the space between us suddenly vast and unfathomable. "You think I haven't asked myself those questions? You think I haven't searched for answers?" His voice was strained, the hurt evident in his gaze. "I grew up in that environment. I know the darkness that lurks in the corners of my family's past."

My heart ached at the pain in his eyes. "Then let's confront it together. You deserve to know the truth, Jonah. We both do." I reached across the table, my fingers brushing against his, a lifeline in the chaos. But he pulled away, his expression hardening.

"I need time to think," he said, rising from his seat. The air between us crackled with unresolved tension, the space once filled with warmth now suffocated by the shadows of uncertainty.

"Jonah, wait!" I called after him, but he was already slipping away, swallowed by the throngs of people milling about. The café that had once felt like our sanctuary now stood as a monument to our fractured bond.

I sat alone, staring at the half-empty cup of coffee, its steam curling upward like a ghost. The room buzzed around me, but I was ensnared in a web of my own making, caught between love and betrayal. The world outside continued its dance, but my heart felt like a lead balloon, heavy and grounded.

Mia's words echoed in my mind, her warning a constant reminder of the danger lurking in the shadows. I couldn't shake the feeling that the truth would lead us to a crossroads—a place where we would have to choose between our love and the loyalty to our families. What lay ahead felt like a minefield, each step fraught with the possibility of explosion.

Determined not to let fear paralyze me, I pulled out my phone, fingers shaking as I typed a message to Mia. "We need to meet. I have more questions." The click of the send button felt like a promise, a vow that I wouldn't back down. No matter how deep the rabbit hole went, I would uncover the truth for Jonah, even if it meant exposing secrets that could tear us apart.

As the evening sun dipped below the horizon, painting the sky in hues of orange and purple, I took a deep breath. The weight of the day pressed down on me, but beneath it all was a flicker of hope. We would face this together, no matter how many threads of deceit we had to unravel.

The following day unfolded with the weight of unspoken words hanging between Jonah and me like a thick fog. I tried to shake the feeling off, but it clung to me, heavy and inescapable. The city buzzed around me, alive with laughter and chatter, but I felt like a ghost drifting through a party I wasn't invited to. I pushed through the streets, my mind racing with the implications of what I'd discovered.

As I entered the office, the fluorescent lights flickered overhead, casting a sterile glow that made everything seem unreal. The usual hum of conversations faded into background noise as I settled into my desk, thoughts swirling. I glanced over my shoulder, half-hoping to see Jonah stride through the door with that casual confidence of his, but he didn't appear.

"Hey, you look like you've seen a ghost," Lisa, my ever-cheerful coworker, quipped from across the room. Her bright blue blouse stood out against the drab office decor, a beacon of positivity. I managed a weak smile, trying to mask the turmoil beneath my skin.

"Just trying to solve a mystery," I replied, feigning nonchalance as I flipped through my notes.

Lisa leaned in closer, her curiosity piqued. "Ooh, a mystery? Spill it. I'm all ears!"

I hesitated, the temptation to share my burdens fighting against the need to protect Jonah. "It's... complicated," I finally said, casting my gaze toward the window where clouds gathered, mirroring my mood.

"Complicated is my middle name," she shot back, her eyes glinting with mischief. "Come on, what's going on? You can't leave me hanging here!"

I sighed, torn between the desire for comfort and the instinct to guard my heart. "It's about a friend... and some troubling family secrets."

Lisa nodded, her expression softening. "Family can be messy. Believe me, I know."

Just then, the door swung open, and in walked Mia, her presence a whirlwind of energy that instantly filled the room. Her dark curls bounced as she walked, and she wore an expression that suggested she'd just come from a breaking news story. "Sorry, I'm late! You won't believe the gossip I just heard!"

"Perfect timing, Mia!" I called, waving her over. My heart leapt at the thought of getting the answers I needed, but there was a nagging feeling of dread as well.

"Tell me everything," she said, sliding into the seat next to me, her eyes sparkling with intrigue. "I have some juicy intel on The Raven."

"About that..." I began, hesitating as I caught Lisa's interested gaze. I shot her a warning look, and she held her hands up in mock surrender, mouthing, "I'm out."

Once we were alone, I leaned closer, lowering my voice. "You mentioned something about Jonah's family being connected to The Raven."

Mia's expression shifted, a mixture of concern and determination washing over her features. "Yes. I dug deeper, and it's worse than I thought. His family has been funding some of The Raven's operations, probably without Jonah's knowledge."

A wave of nausea crashed over me. "But why would they do that?"

"Money. Power. The usual motivations. There's a lot at stake, and they're playing a dangerous game." Her voice dropped to a whisper. "Jonah's brother has been implicated in several suspicious transactions. If this gets out, it could ruin them."

"What do I do?" I felt the panic rising within me, my chest constricting. The thought of Jonah being caught in this web made me feel sick. "He deserves to know, but..."

"But it might tear him apart," Mia finished, her eyes dark with understanding. "You have to be careful how you handle this."

My phone buzzed on the desk, pulling my attention away from the conversation. It was a message from Jonah: Can we talk? My heart fluttered at the thought of seeing him again, but a sharp pang of anxiety followed quickly. What if he already knew? What if he was angry?

"I need to go," I said, pushing back from the desk.

"Wait," Mia said, her voice steady. "Whatever happens, you've got to stand by him. Love is messy, but it's also powerful."

I nodded, but doubt lingered like smoke in the air. With a swift goodbye, I made my way to the park where we had often met. The grass swayed gently in the breeze, but the bright colors of the flowers around me felt muted, overshadowed by my impending confrontation.

I spotted Jonah sitting on a bench, his silhouette stark against the backdrop of the vibrant autumn foliage. The way he held himself—shoulders hunched, hands clasped tightly—told me all I needed to know about the turmoil brewing inside him.

"Hey," I said softly, taking a seat beside him.

"Hey," he replied, his voice a low murmur. The silence stretched between us, thick and uncomfortable, as we both struggled to find the right words.

"I got your message," I ventured, my heart racing. "I want to help."

He turned to me, the hurt in his eyes cutting deeper than I anticipated. "You think you can help me? You think you can fix this?"

"I'm not trying to fix anything, Jonah. I just want us to be honest with each other."

"I don't even know what honesty looks like anymore," he snapped, frustration bubbling to the surface. "My family is a tangled mess of lies, and I'm right in the middle of it. What am I supposed to do with that?"

I reached for his hand, desperate to bridge the gap between us. "You don't have to face it alone. I'm here."

He looked down at our hands, and for a moment, the tension eased. "I wish I could believe that," he whispered.

Before I could respond, his phone buzzed, breaking the moment. He glanced at the screen, his expression shifting from vulnerability to something guarded. "I need to take this," he said, pulling away.

As he answered, I felt an icy chill seep into the space between us. What could be so urgent that it pulled him away from me at such a critical moment? I watched as he spoke, the lines of worry etching deeper into his face. Whatever was said seemed to confirm the chaos swirling around us, and my heart sank.

As he hung up, I steeled myself for what was to come. "What was that?"

His eyes were clouded, frustration simmering just below the surface. "My brother. He's in trouble—again. I have to go."

"Wait, Jonah—"

But he was already standing, urgency propelling him away. "I'll call you later," he tossed over his shoulder as he hurried down the path, leaving me standing alone, the warm afternoon sun suddenly feeling cold and distant.

The weight of the world pressed down on me, and I stood there, the vibrant colors of the park around me fading into the background as I tried to process the chaos that had overtaken my life. Jonah was slipping away, and the truth felt like a boulder sitting on my chest. What lay ahead was uncertain, a storm brewing in the distance that could either tear us apart or bind us closer together. I had to find a way to navigate this labyrinth of deceit before it swallowed us whole.

The wind rustled through the trees, the leaves swirling in a dance that echoed the turmoil within me. I stood in the park, my mind racing as I processed the abrupt end of my conversation with Jonah. The vibrant hues of autumn around me seemed to dim, casting everything in a gray wash of anxiety. I felt like a lone tree, stripped bare, waiting for the storm to pass, not knowing if I'd survive its wrath.

With Jonah gone, a disquieting silence settled over the space where warmth and laughter used to thrive. I had to find a way to reconnect with him, to bridge the chasm that was rapidly widening between us. But how? The urgency of the situation pressed heavily on my chest. His brother was in trouble, and whatever that meant could have disastrous consequences for both of them—and for us.

I pulled my phone from my pocket, fingers hovering over the screen. Texting him felt inadequate, like sending a message in a bottle into an unforgiving ocean. Instead, I resolved to find Mia again; her tenacity had been a guiding light, and I needed her insights more than ever.

The little café where we had met earlier was a short walk away, its familiar aroma of coffee and pastries beckoning me like a siren song. I stepped inside, greeted by the comforting hum of conversation and the clinking of cups. Finding Mia was easy—she was seated in the corner, her laptop open and papers strewn across the table like the aftermath of a battle.

"Mia!" I called out, weaving through the crowded space to reach her. Her head snapped up, and a grin broke across her face.

"Good timing! I have some new information that might interest you." She closed her laptop and gestured for me to sit.

"Let's hear it," I said, a mix of eagerness and dread coiling in my stomach.

"Okay, so I dug into the financial records a bit deeper, and it turns out that the transactions between Jonah's family and The Raven weren't just isolated incidents. They've been funding multiple operations under the radar for years. It's all very hush-hush, but the implications are huge."

I felt a chill creep up my spine. "Huge how?"

Mia leaned in, her voice dropping to a conspiratorial whisper. "There's a pattern to the timing of these transactions—correlating with several crimes that have been pinned on The Raven. It seems they were setting up Jonah's family to take the fall if anything went wrong."

I couldn't believe what I was hearing. "So they're being used as a cover?"

"Exactly. It's as if The Raven is playing chess while everyone else is stuck on checkers. They have their eyes on something big, and Jonah's family is part of the game."

My heart raced as the pieces started to align. "Then Jonah's brother might not just be in trouble; he could be the target."

"Precisely," Mia confirmed, her eyes bright with the thrill of the chase. "And if they're really deep in this, Jonah could be in danger too. We have to figure out a way to protect him."

I took a deep breath, my mind whirling. "What do we do?"

"We gather evidence. We need to get proof of what's really happening. If we can expose The Raven, it might just sever their hold on Jonah's family."

Mia's determination resonated within me, sparking a flicker of hope. "Let's do it," I said, my voice firm. "I'll do whatever it takes to keep Jonah safe."

The plan took shape quickly. We would dig through records, find out everything we could about Jonah's family's finances and their links to The Raven. As we worked, a sense of urgency enveloped me, mingling with the fear that lurked just beneath the surface. This was bigger than us, bigger than our love; it felt like we were diving headfirst into a dark abyss.

As the sun began to set, the café dimmed, shadows stretching like dark fingers across the table. With each passing moment, I felt a mixture of excitement and dread. What if we stumbled upon something we weren't meant to find? Or worse, what if we put ourselves in the crosshairs of those who thrived in the shadows?

"Do you think Jonah will be okay?" I asked, the question slipping from my lips before I could stop it.

Mia's expression softened, and she reached across the table to squeeze my hand. "He's stronger than he knows. And you are too. Remember, you're not in this alone."

"Thanks, Mia," I said, her words a balm to my fraying nerves.

As the evening wore on, we pored over papers, the two of us like detectives piecing together a complex puzzle. The hours slipped away, marked by the click of keys and the rustle of paper. My heart thudded in my chest, not just from the caffeine but from the enormity of what we were uncovering.

Just as I was starting to feel overwhelmed, my phone buzzed again. It was a message from Jonah: We need to talk. Meet me at the old warehouse.

A chill raced down my spine. The warehouse was a place of bad memories, a remnant of his family's tangled past. "Mia, I need to go. Jonah wants to meet."

"What? Now?" she asked, concern knitting her brow.

"Yes, now. I have to find out what's going on. If his brother is in trouble, he might need me."

"Be careful," she cautioned, her voice low and serious. "You don't know what you're walking into."

"I'll be careful," I promised, though the weight of uncertainty pressed down hard.

As I rushed out of the café and into the night, the city felt different, shrouded in an air of foreboding. The streetlights flickered overhead, casting long shadows that danced ominously along the pavement. I took a deep breath, willing myself to remain calm, to focus on the steps ahead.

When I arrived at the warehouse, the imposing structure loomed before me, its metal façade reflecting the dim light of the moon. I hesitated at the entrance, the foreboding aura wrapping around me like a shroud. Every instinct screamed at me to turn back, but I pushed the door open and stepped inside.

The air was stale, heavy with the scent of rust and dust. Shadows lurked in the corners, making the space feel alive, as if it held its breath in anticipation of what was to come. I called out softly, "Jonah?"

Silence answered, and a knot of anxiety twisted in my stomach. As I ventured deeper, the beams of my flashlight sliced through the darkness, illuminating old crates and remnants of past lives. My heart raced as I scanned the shadows, my pulse echoing in my ears.

"Jonah!" I called again, more urgently this time.

Suddenly, I heard a noise—a soft scuffle followed by a low murmur. I turned, my heart pounding in my chest. Was that him? I moved toward the sound, every instinct heightened.

Just as I rounded a corner, I froze. Jonah stood there, his back turned to me, and beside him, a figure cloaked in darkness loomed. The glint of a blade caught the light, and my breath hitched in my throat.

"Jonah, no!" I screamed, fear igniting in my veins.

He turned, his expression shifting from surprise to alarm, just as the shadowy figure lunged. Time seemed to slow, the world around me fading away as adrenaline surged through my body. This was it—the moment where everything would change.

"Get down!" Jonah shouted, and I dove for cover as chaos erupted, the sound of metal clashing against metal reverberating through the cavernous space.

The stakes had never been higher, and I realized in that split second just how far I was willing to go to protect him—and ourselves. In the swirling shadows of the warehouse, with danger closing in, we were about to discover just how deep the threads of deceit ran, and whether love could withstand the unraveling.

# Chapter 10: Allies and Enemies

The mansion loomed like a ghostly giant against the indigo sky, its ornate turrets jutting into the night like fingers grasping at secrets. As I stepped from the sleek black car, a shiver danced down my spine, but it wasn't from the cool autumn air; it was the sense that the evening was steeped in danger, a feeling that had become my constant companion since our investigation began. Jonah adjusted his cufflinks, the glint of diamond catching the light as he glanced at me, an unspoken question lingering in his sharp gaze. Tonight, we were supposed to be nothing more than players in a game of high stakes, but beneath our tailored suits and bright smiles, the weight of our shared mission pressed heavily.

Inside, the atmosphere crackled with a blend of laughter and clinking glasses, the kind of refined revelry that seemed to mock the shadows we'd been chasing. I tucked a loose strand of hair behind my ear, taking a moment to absorb the scene. Golden chandeliers dripped with crystals that caught the light like stars fallen from the sky, illuminating faces that wore masks of polite intrigue. The scent of expensive perfume mingled with the crispness of white wine, wrapping around me like a silken shroud. Yet, despite the glamour, an undercurrent of tension thrummed through the crowd, a whisper of secrets waiting to be unveiled.

"Stay close," Jonah murmured, his voice low and firm, cutting through the din of conversation. His eyes scanned the room, alert and focused, while I tried to mirror his poise despite the butterflies dancing in my stomach. We were here to find out more about The Raven, a shadowy figure whose machinations had left chaos in their wake. Rumors swirled like the smoke from the elegant cigars being puffed in the corners, hinting at a stolen artifact that would be on display tonight—an ancient pendant rumored to have the power to sway fortunes. It was exactly the kind of bait The Raven would relish.

As we navigated through clusters of elite chatter, I caught sight of a figure standing alone, leaning against a marble column. The man exuded a magnetic charisma, his dark hair tousled just enough to be effortlessly stylish, his tailored suit hugging his frame in all the right places. He held a glass of champagne with an ease that suggested he was no stranger to this world. The moment our eyes met, a playful smirk danced across his lips, and I felt my heart skip—a sensation I wasn't sure I could afford tonight.

"Care to indulge in a moment of distraction?" he said, his voice smooth like the finest silk. It was the kind of charm that could sweep anyone off their feet. "I promise I'm more entertaining than the gilded conversations surrounding us."

"Depends on what kind of entertainment you're offering," I replied, my tone light yet edged with caution. Jonah stood beside me, his tension palpable, radiating protectiveness like a shield.

"Ah, a woman who knows her worth," the stranger chuckled, his dark eyes glinting with mischief. "I'm Theo, by the way. Just a humble connoisseur of fine art and the occasional intriguing conversation."

Before I could respond, Jonah interjected, his voice laced with barely concealed annoyance. "We're actually here on business, Theo. So if you'll excuse us..."

Theo raised an eyebrow, clearly unfazed by Jonah's bristling demeanor. "Ah, but isn't business often the most riveting form of entertainment? Surely, your 'business' might benefit from a bit of insight." He leaned in closer, lowering his voice as if sharing a secret. "I happen to know a thing or two about The Raven's plans for tonight."

Jonah stiffened, and I felt a mixture of intrigue and unease coil within me. "And why would you want to share that with us?" I asked, cautious yet unable to hide my curiosity.

"Because," Theo replied with a sly smile, "I enjoy watching the game unfold. And I'm not fond of our mysterious friend ruining the night for everyone."

The tension in the air thickened, and Jonah's jaw clenched. "We don't need your help," he said, his tone brusque.

I could see the flicker of jealousy in Jonah's eyes as he glared at Theo, but the stranger merely shrugged, unbothered by the hostility. "Suit yourselves. Just remember, when the lights dim and the auction begins, shadows will linger. And those who are unprepared will find themselves on the wrong side of the game."

As he turned to leave, I felt a strange pull, a desire to know more. "Wait!" I called, taking a step forward. "What do you know?"

Theo paused, glancing over his shoulder. "Meet me in the garden after the auction. There are things you'll want to hear—things that could change the course of your evening."

With that, he vanished into the crowd, leaving me with a swirling mix of excitement and apprehension. I turned to Jonah, who was still radiating a mix of annoyance and protectiveness. "We should follow him," I suggested, the thrill of potential information coursing through me.

Jonah sighed, his brows furrowed in frustration. "And what? Trust a charming stranger who could be leading us into a trap? I don't like this, not one bit."

"Neither do I," I admitted, my heart racing. "But what if he's telling the truth? We need every advantage we can get against The Raven. If Theo knows something, we can't let jealousy dictate our decisions."

His gaze softened for a fleeting moment, but the tension didn't dissipate. "Fine," he relented, albeit grudgingly. "But I'll be watching him. No more distractions, understand?"

"Understood," I replied, feeling a rush of adrenaline. The night was still young, and the stakes were higher than ever. As the crowd buzzed around us, I took a deep breath, ready to dive into the mystery that awaited in the shadows.

The garden was a maze of fragrant blooms and shadowy alcoves, illuminated by the soft glow of lanterns swinging gently in the night breeze. I lingered at the entrance, my heart thumping like a drum as I scanned the foliage for any sign of Theo. The scents of blooming jasmine and damp earth mingled in the air, intoxicating and heavy with unspoken promises. It was a stark contrast to the glittering chaos of the auction inside, where wealth and ambition collided in a dizzying display.

"Why do I let you drag me into these situations?" Jonah muttered beside me, arms crossed over his chest like a fortress wall. He stood vigilant, an ever-watchful guardian, but there was a trace of curiosity in his tone. I could see the internal struggle flickering behind his eyes—his protective instincts wrestling with the undeniable intrigue this evening had sparked.

"Because I have a knack for adventure, and you like to keep me out of trouble," I replied with a teasing smile, trying to lighten the mood. "Besides, this could be our best lead yet. Theo seemed to know more than he let on."

"I don't like that guy," he grumbled, shifting his weight as he surveyed the garden. "He's too charming. It's a red flag, and I'm not about to ignore it."

"Charm is just a surface, Jonah. What matters is what lies beneath," I said, glancing over my shoulder to ensure no one was lurking nearby. "And right now, we need to uncover as much as we can about The Raven's plans. The longer we wait, the closer they get to executing whatever scheme they have in mind."

Just as Jonah opened his mouth to argue further, Theo emerged from the shadows, his presence both electrifying and unsettling. "You're both far too serious for such a delightful evening," he said, his voice smooth like the finest whiskey. "I was beginning to think you'd stood me up."

"Not quite," I said, my heart racing as his gaze locked onto mine. "But your timing could use some work."

Theo grinned, an easy, disarming smile that made it hard to remember that we were supposed to be cautious. "Touché. But let's get down to business, shall we? There's a storm brewing, and it's not just the kind that brings rain."

Jonah's posture tightened as he stepped slightly closer to me, an instinctive move of protection that sent a rush of warmth through my chest. "What do you know about The Raven's plans?" he asked, his voice clipped and authoritative, a clear indication of his discomfort with Theo.

"Ah, direct to the point. I like that," Theo said, his eyes sparkling with mischief. "I overheard some interesting conversations tonight. You see, The Raven is planning something big—an acquisition, if you will. The pendant on display is merely a distraction, a beautiful bauble designed to lure in the unsuspecting."

I exchanged a quick glance with Jonah. "A distraction for what?" I pressed, leaning in, eager for details.

"A more valuable item, hidden away in the mansion," Theo explained, his voice lowering conspiratorially. "Rumor has it, an ancient manuscript containing secrets that could topple empires. The kind of thing that attracts not only thieves but powerful players from all walks of life. If The Raven succeeds, it will change everything."

"Why should we trust you?" Jonah asked, skepticism etched across his features. "You could be leading us into a trap."

"I could be," Theo conceded, a smirk playing at the corners of his mouth. "But I assure you, I have no love for The Raven. My interests lie in art and truth, not in shadowy dealings. We're in a position to help each other."

"Right," Jonah replied, his voice laden with doubt. "Help or manipulate? I'm not sure which is your forte."

Theo laughed, the sound bright and charming. "You have a sharp tongue, Jonah. It's refreshing. But let's focus on what matters. The auction will begin shortly, and you'll want to keep an eye on that pendant. The moment it's displayed, all eyes will be on it, creating the perfect opportunity for a distraction."

"And you think we can just walk in and take it?" I asked, trying to suppress my excitement at the prospect.

"With a little finesse, yes," he said, his eyes glinting with mischief. "You'll need to play the game, act like you belong. Once the auction starts, the security will be lax, distracted by the show. That's your moment."

Jonah's jaw tightened, but I could see the gears turning in his mind. "And what do you get out of this?" he asked, skepticism still evident.

"A seat at the table," Theo replied smoothly. "An opportunity to shift the balance of power. But enough about me. Are you in or out?"

I felt a rush of adrenaline, the thrill of the unknown mingling with the anxiety that had been building since we entered the mansion. This was a risk—a big one—but it could be our only chance to thwart The Raven. I turned to Jonah, searching his eyes for a flicker of agreement.

"Jonah," I began softly, "we can't pass this up. We need to act. We can't let fear dictate our moves."

He hesitated, his protective instincts clashing with the urgency of our mission. Finally, he let out a long breath, the weight of resignation settling in. "Fine," he said, his voice low. "But I'm watching you, Theo. One wrong move, and I'll drag her out of here myself."

Theo raised his glass, a grin spreading across his face. "Cheers to a new alliance then. Let's shake things up a little."

As we moved deeper into the garden, the air thick with anticipation, I couldn't shake the feeling that we were standing on the precipice of something much larger than ourselves. The evening had transformed from a mere gala into a battlefield, with secrets lurking behind every bush and shadows stalking our every move. The thrill of the chase surged through me, invigorating yet unnerving, and I couldn't help but wonder if this alliance with Theo would lead us to victory or betrayal.

In that moment, the line between ally and enemy blurred, and I knew we were about to step into a game that would test not only our skills but our trust in one another. With hearts racing and uncertainty lingering, we ventured further into the darkness, the promise of danger and adventure swirling around us like the intoxicating fragrance of the flowers blooming in the moonlight.

The dim light of the garden lanterns flickered, casting playful shadows that danced around us as we trailed after Theo. He moved with an effortless grace, weaving through the hedges like a thread through fabric. My heart thrummed with a mix of anxiety and exhilaration; this was the kind of adventure I had only ever read about, yet it felt all too real, as tangible as the crisp night air. Jonah walked beside me, his shoulders tense and his expression locked in a careful blend of wariness and curiosity.

"So, what's the plan, Mr. Charisma?" Jonah challenged, his voice low but edged with skepticism as we stepped further into the labyrinth of greenery. "You're the one with all the ideas. How do we get our hands on this manuscript?"

Theo glanced back, a mischievous glint in his eye. "Ah, the eager pup is worried about the game plan. Relax; I've got this down to an art. All we need is a little finesse, a sprinkle of charm, and a dash of distraction."

I raised an eyebrow, unsure whether to be impressed or concerned by his casual demeanor. "And if things go south? You can't charm your way out of every situation, Theo."

"True, but I can certainly try," he replied, his voice dripping with playful confidence. "Now, listen closely. The auctioneer will be a showman, all flair and drama. The moment he lifts that pendant, the attention of the entire room will pivot to him. That's when we make our move."

Jonah shot me a glance that clearly said, This better work, but I nodded. "And what's our cover? How do we blend in without attracting unwanted attention?"

"Leave that to me," Theo said with a wink, moving closer as he lowered his voice conspiratorially. "You'll both play the role of wealthy bidders—high-stakes players in this extravagant game. I'll be your smooth-talking friend who knows the ins and outs. Just follow my lead, and remember, confidence is key."

"Confidence, right," Jonah muttered under his breath, his skepticism palpable. "I just hope confidence doesn't get us arrested."

"Now you're getting it!" Theo laughed lightly, his demeanor infectious. "If you believe you belong, no one will question it. Besides, it's the thrill of the chase that keeps things interesting, isn't it?"

As we approached the back entrance of the mansion, the atmosphere shifted; the air felt charged with anticipation, thick with the scent of opportunity and risk. The chatter of the auction-goers inside pulsed like a heartbeat, underscoring the urgency of our mission.

We slipped through the grand doors, re-entering the ballroom, where the clinking of glasses and bursts of laughter enveloped us like a cozy blanket. The sight was almost surreal: glittering chandeliers illuminated a sea of designer gowns and tailored suits, each face a mask of confidence. It was a world where wealth reigned supreme, and the stakes were as high as the ceilings above us.

"Right, here we go," Theo said, straightening his jacket as he stepped forward, his demeanor shifting into that of an insider. "Remember, we're here to observe, to learn, and maybe to play a little. Just smile and nod, and let me do the talking."

With a shared look of determination, Jonah and I followed Theo into the thrumming heart of the event. I kept my focus ahead, but the atmosphere thrummed with an energy that was almost palpable. I caught glimpses of familiar faces—art dealers, socialites, and a few notorious figures I'd only seen in tabloids. Each one was more extravagant than the last, a parade of wealth that made my heart race.

As the auctioneer took the stage, a hush fell over the room. A spotlight flickered on, illuminating him like a celebrity. "Ladies and gentlemen, welcome to the Auction of the Century!" His voice boomed with theatrical flair, and I could feel the energy shift in the room, the collective breath held in anticipation.

Theo leaned in, whispering, "Now's our time. Watch for the pendant, and stay sharp."

As the auctioneer began, the first few items flew off the block, but my heart raced with impatience, waiting for the pendant to make its debut. Finally, he gestured grandly toward a covered display. "And now, the pièce de résistance—a stunning pendant, believed to be from the ancient royal family of Elysia, adorned with sapphires and diamonds!"

He pulled the cloth away, and the pendant sparkled under the lights, drawing gasps from the crowd. A hush settled over the room, every eye trained on the exquisite piece. "Who will start the bidding at a modest ten thousand dollars?"

The moment was electric. My pulse quickened as I caught Jonah's gaze; the urgency between us was unmistakable. "We need to act," I said softly, feeling the weight of the moment.

"On it," Theo replied, his voice a low murmur as he moved toward the front, seamlessly blending into the crowd of wealthy bidders. I followed closely, my heart pounding with adrenaline.

"Ten thousand!" A voice rang out, and I turned just in time to see an elderly gentleman raise his paddle, the first bid initiated. The auctioneer nodded, urging for higher stakes, and as the numbers climbed, I felt the tension rising with them.

With every increase, Theo navigated the crowd with uncanny ease, drawing closer to the auctioneer while maintaining the façade of an eager bidder. I watched him, admiring his confidence but also wishing I could shake off the flutter of unease that wrapped around my chest like a vice.

Then, just as I was about to join the fray, a chilling sensation crept up my spine. I turned, and my blood ran cold. A figure lurked at the entrance—a man in a dark suit, his expression shadowed beneath the brim of a hat, his posture radiating menace.

I couldn't shake the feeling that he was watching us, specifically me. The atmosphere shifted, a wave of tension washing over the room, and my heart raced. Jonah noticed my sudden change in demeanor and turned to see what I was staring at.

"Who is that?" he whispered, his voice taut with concern.

Before I could respond, the lights flickered. The auctioneer's voice faltered for a moment, but he quickly regained his composure. "A hundred thousand! Do I hear one hundred and twenty?"

The man moved stealthily, inching closer as if stalking prey. I felt my breath quicken, panic bubbling just beneath the surface. "We need to go," I hissed to Jonah, but before we could make a move, the lights dimmed entirely, plunging the room into darkness.

Gasps erupted around us as chaos ensued. My heart thundered in my chest as I grabbed Jonah's arm, feeling the tension in his muscles. "This isn't good," I muttered, searching for a way out amidst the confusion.

Suddenly, a piercing scream sliced through the air, and in that split second, I knew we were no longer just players in a game—we were pawns caught in a deadly chess match, and the stakes had just been raised to life or death.

Before I could grasp the enormity of what was happening, a sharp laugh echoed through the darkness, followed by the unmistakable sound of shuffling footsteps. It was a promise of chaos, and we were right in the thick of it, unprepared for the onslaught that was about to unfold.

# Chapter 11: In the Lion's Den

The auction hall buzzed like a hive of restless bees, the atmosphere thick with the sweet scent of polished wood and the subtle musk of expensive perfumes. Flickering chandeliers cast a golden glow over the throngs of elegantly dressed patrons, their laughter and chatter mingling with the clinking of crystal glasses. I clutched Jonah's arm, my pulse racing with a mix of thrill and trepidation, as the evening unfurled like a velvet curtain, revealing secrets that lay hidden just beneath the surface.

"Are you sure about this?" I whispered, the words escaping my lips before I could catch them. My eyes darted across the room, lingering on the shadows that seemed to linger too long, the smiles that felt just a bit too wide. Jonah's presence beside me grounded me, yet the air around us crackled with tension.

"Trust me," he replied, his voice a low rumble, a promise and a warning wrapped in one. "Stick close. The Raven's not the only one interested in what's up for bid tonight."

He guided me deeper into the crowd, our movements fluid as we weaved through clusters of art collectors and thrill-seekers. Each step took us closer to the main display, where an opulent canvas hung, its colors vibrant and tumultuous, echoing the storm brewing within me. The painting was a chaotic dance of blues and reds, a tempest that seemed to pulse with life, but the true allure lay not in its strokes but in the symbol etched discreetly in one corner—a raven, its wings poised for flight.

"Look," I murmured, pointing subtly to the emblem. It felt like fate itself had drawn me to this moment, the whispers of the past colliding with the present. "It's the same mark I saw on the note."

"Keep your voice down." Jonah's sharp gaze swept the room, his protective instincts flaring. "We can't let anyone know we're onto them."

As the auctioneer began to speak, I felt the pulse of excitement surge through the crowd. Bidders raised their paddles like warriors ready for battle, eyes glinting with greed. The anticipation was palpable, the thrill of competition electrifying. But just as I began to lose myself in the moment, the lights flickered ominously, plunging us into fleeting darkness. Gasps rippled through the room, and the mood shifted like a tide—an undercurrent of unease began to pull at my heart.

"Stay close," Jonah said, his hand tightening around mine. I nodded, though my mind raced with thoughts of the emblem, the potential secrets hidden within that painting. It felt like a key, one that could unlock doors I didn't even know existed. But with that thought came a sinking dread; the raven was a symbol of danger, a warning shrouded in intrigue.

The lights burst back to life, and a cacophony erupted from the far side of the room. I turned just in time to see a figure shove another against a wall, voices raised in angry confrontation. The laughter and excitement morphed into chaos, a whirlwind of panic as people began to scatter in all directions. My heart raced as I instinctively looked to Jonah, who was already pulling me away from the fray.

"Run!" he shouted, and I didn't need to be told twice. We dashed through the crowd, the world around us a blur of color and sound. My breath came in short gasps, a mix of fear and exhilaration propelling me forward as we navigated the chaos. Jonah's grip on my hand was firm, his presence a steadying force against the rising tide of uncertainty.

As we stumbled into the night, the cool air hit me like a refreshing wave, grounding me amidst the storm of emotions. The moon hung high above, casting silvery shadows that danced along the pavement, and for a fleeting moment, I felt a rush of freedom. But just as quickly, that exhilaration was snuffed out when I caught sight of a familiar figure stumbling through the dark—a flash of long dark hair, a silhouette too vivid to be a mirage.

"Mia!" I shouted, breaking free from Jonah's hold and rushing toward her. Her face twisted in fear, wide eyes searching the night as if looking for a way out. The moment felt surreal, as if time had slowed to capture this shocking reunion amidst the turmoil.

"Lia, you have to go!" she cried, urgency lacing her voice. "They're coming! The Raven's men—"

Before she could finish, a heavy thud echoed through the air, and shadows loomed at the edges of the alley. My heart plummeted. Jonah joined me, his body rigid beside mine, as we both faced the encroaching threat. The men emerging from the shadows wore dark suits, their expressions cold and calculating, as if they thrived on the fear they instilled.

"Mia, get behind us!" Jonah commanded, a fierce protector in a moment of impending danger.

I could feel the tension thickening, wrapping around us like a noose. "What do they want?" I gasped, torn between the urge to flee and the instinct to stand my ground.

Mia swallowed hard, her voice trembling. "They want the painting... and anyone who knows about it." Her eyes flickered between us, fear and something else—something deeper—sparking in their depths.

I stepped forward, adrenaline surging through my veins. "Then we can't let them have it." A determined fire ignited within me, stronger than the fear gnawing at the edges of my mind. I looked to Jonah, whose fierce expression mirrored my resolve. Together, we were more than just two frightened souls; we were a force poised against the unknown, ready to defy the shadows that sought to consume us.

As the darkness of the alley enveloped us, the night felt alive with tension, each shadow a potential threat lurking just out of sight.

Jonah stood protectively in front of me, his stance unwavering as the men approached, their intentions as inscrutable as the flickering streetlights overhead. I felt my heart hammering in my chest, a frantic drumbeat urging me to act, to do something—anything—other than simply stand there and wait for the inevitable.

"Mia," I breathed, desperation curling around my words. "What do we do? They're right there!"

"I don't know!" she exclaimed, her voice rising with panic. "We need to find a way out of here. Fast."

The men were closer now, their features sharpened by the harsh glow of a nearby lamppost. The leader, tall and imposing, wore a smirk that twisted his features in a way that made my stomach churn. "Well, well, what do we have here?" he drawled, taking a step forward. "Little birds caught out in the night, far from their nest."

"Just leave us alone," Jonah snapped, stepping forward with a bravado that belied the tension radiating off him. "We don't want any trouble."

"Oh, but trouble has a way of finding those who seek it," the man taunted, his eyes glinting with malicious delight. He motioned to his companions, and they fanned out, blocking any potential escape routes.

My mind raced, a thousand thoughts colliding in a chaotic whirlpool. The painting—the emblem—the secrets hidden within those strokes. What did these men know? More importantly, what were they willing to do to get it? I stepped forward, my pulse quickening with a mix of fear and determination. "You don't have to do this. We can just walk away."

"Walk away?" the leader laughed, a sound devoid of humor. "And leave without what we came for? Not a chance."

"Then what do you want?" I challenged, my voice stronger than I felt. "If you're after the painting, then you'll have to go through us."

Jonah shot me a glance, a mix of admiration and concern swirling in his eyes. The leader's expression shifted, a flicker of surprise crossing his face before it was replaced with a mocking grin. "Ah, I see. We have ourselves a little fighter, don't we?"

Before I could respond, the men moved, their intentions clear. One lunged toward Jonah, and instinct kicked in. I grabbed Mia's arm, dragging her backward while Jonah sidestepped the attack, using the momentum to land a swift kick that sent the man stumbling.

"Run!" Jonah shouted, and we needed no further encouragement. We darted down the alley, the sound of footsteps pounding behind us like a sinister drumbeat. The air was thick with adrenaline, each breath a desperate gasp as we rounded a corner, seeking refuge in the labyrinthine streets.

"Where do we go?" I panted, glancing back to see the dark figures chasing us. Jonah's grip tightened around my hand, his presence a fierce anchor amidst the chaos.

"There's a café nearby," he said, breathless but focused. "If we can make it there, we can call for help."

"Then let's move!" I urged, pushing forward, my heart racing not just from fear but from an exhilarating sense of agency. For the first time, I felt a surge of defiance bubbling within me, a refusal to let fear dictate my actions.

As we sprinted, the café's neon sign glowed like a beacon, illuminating the cobbled streets with a warm, inviting light. It felt surreal, a juxtaposition to the danger that loomed just behind us. We burst through the door, the scent of rich coffee and sweet pastries enveloping us in a comforting embrace, but there was no time to linger.

"Back entrance!" Jonah barked, leading us through a narrow corridor that led to the kitchen. The clatter of dishes and the chatter of staff provided a stark contrast to the chaos outside, and I clung to that normalcy as we pushed through the heavy door at the back.

We stepped out into an alley that was quieter, the sounds of the café fading behind us. "We need to call the police," Mia said, her voice trembling. "They can't keep coming after us like this."

Jonah nodded, his expression grave. "I'll make the call. You two keep an eye out."

I leaned against the wall, the cool brick grounding me as I watched Jonah dial. He was calm under pressure, a reassuring force amidst the swirling uncertainty. But my thoughts were a tempest, a chaotic mix of dread and the nagging question of why this was happening. Why were they after the painting? And what did it have to do with us?

A moment later, Jonah hung up and turned to us, his brows furrowed. "Help is on the way, but we need to keep moving. They could catch up."

"Where to now?" I asked, scanning the alley for any sign of danger.

"We should head to my apartment. It's closer, and we can figure out our next move there," he replied, determination lining his features.

As we navigated through the dimly lit streets, my mind raced with possibilities. The raven emblem kept resurfacing in my thoughts, a dark omen that seemed to weave through the fabric of this night. What was hidden within the painting that made it so valuable? Why did it matter to The Raven?

"Lia," Mia broke into my reverie, her voice steady despite the situation. "What do you think they want with the painting? It can't just be about money."

"Maybe it's more than that," I replied, piecing together the fragments of information. "What if it's tied to something bigger? Something dangerous?"

Jonah glanced back at us, his eyes sharp. "You're onto something. The Raven is more than just a group of criminals; they have their fingers in a lot of shady dealings. If they're after this painting, it's likely connected to their operations in ways we can't even begin to imagine."

As we approached Jonah's apartment building, the weight of uncertainty settled heavily on my shoulders. The night was far from over, and the shadows were closing in. But with Jonah and Mia by my side, I felt a flicker of hope amidst the storm. We would unravel the secrets of the raven, even if it meant facing the darkness head-on. Together, we were not just pawns in someone else's game; we were players, and it was time to turn the tide.

The walls of Jonah's apartment felt like a fortress, yet I could hardly shake the feeling that they were merely a thin veneer against the chaos that had erupted just outside. We slipped through the door, and he quickly locked it behind us, the reassuring click a small comfort amidst the storm of emotions swirling in my chest. The faint glow of the streetlights filtered through the blinds, casting stripes of light and shadow across the cluttered living space. Art supplies lay strewn about, half-finished canvases leaning against the walls like lost souls yearning for completion.

"I thought you said you were an artist, not a hoarder," I quipped, trying to lighten the mood, though my heart raced as if it were trying to escape my ribcage.

Jonah shot me a half-smile, the tension in his features easing slightly. "It's called 'creative chaos,'" he replied, moving to the window to peek outside. "And I'm a firm believer that a little mess is a sign of brilliance."

Mia settled onto the couch, her expression still tense but tinged with curiosity as she surveyed the room. "Brilliance or just procrastination?" she teased, attempting to break the ice.

"Probably both," he admitted, shaking his head. "But let's focus on the current crisis instead of my questionable organizational skills."

I pressed my palms together, the weight of the night's events crashing down like a wave. "Do you think they followed us?"

"I don't know," Jonah murmured, drawing the curtains tighter as if the fabric could shield us from the dangers lurking just beyond the glass. "But we need to be careful. If they're as connected as I think, we might have stirred up a hornet's nest."

Mia's brow furrowed, her voice low and serious. "Do you think they'll come here? They could know where you live."

"Let's hope not. This is a low-profile kind of place," Jonah replied, glancing around as if the clutter could provide some semblance of security. "But we can't just sit here waiting for the other shoe to drop."

I nodded, the reality of our situation crashing down on me like a thunderclap. We had stumbled into something far more dangerous than I had anticipated. "So what's our plan? We can't just let them get away with whatever they're after."

Jonah paused, his eyes narrowing in thought. "We need to find out what's so important about that painting. If we can figure that out, maybe we can leverage it against them or get someone who can help us."

"Like who?" I asked, feeling the weight of the uncertainty in my chest. "Who can we trust?"

"I have a few contacts," Jonah said, rubbing his chin thoughtfully. "But the fewer people who know about this, the better. We don't want to raise any more alarms than necessary."

"Great," Mia said with a hint of sarcasm, running a hand through her hair. "So we're flying blind, then?"

"It's not ideal," Jonah admitted, the corners of his mouth twitching in a wry smile. "But what's life without a little risk?"

I couldn't help but chuckle despite the circumstances. "Well, I'm not a fan of high-risk living. I prefer my thrills in the form of bad rom-coms and cupcakes."

"Cupcakes could definitely come in handy right now," Mia agreed, a spark of humor breaking through her worry.

Jonah moved to the small kitchenette, his brows furrowing in concentration as he rummaged through the cluttered shelves. "I can whip up something. It might not be gourmet, but I can at least provide caffeine to fuel our brainstorming session."

"Instant coffee? Great. Just what I need for my nerves," I replied, settling onto the couch beside Mia, who was tapping her fingers on her knee in a nervous rhythm.

As Jonah busied himself with the coffee maker, I couldn't shake the feeling that we were on borrowed time. The air in the apartment felt heavy, as if it were saturated with secrets and unsaid words. "What if we don't have time to wait?" I said, my voice edged with urgency. "What if they come here before we can figure things out?"

Jonah turned, mug in hand, his expression thoughtful. "Then we need to be ready for whatever comes next. We can't let fear control us."

"Right. Fear is overrated," I said, trying to muster a sense of bravado. "Besides, I'm just a girl who came to an auction for some art. I didn't sign up for a high-stakes heist."

"Welcome to the club," Jonah said, a glimmer of mischief in his eyes. "You've officially been inducted into the 'Winging It' Society."

Before I could respond, a loud bang echoed through the building, sending a jolt of adrenaline coursing through me. The sound was followed by muffled voices and heavy footsteps that resonated like thunder through the hall.

"Did you hear that?" Mia whispered, her eyes wide with fear.

Jonah's expression shifted, a seriousness settling in. "Yeah. It sounds like trouble." He moved to the window, peering out cautiously. "We need to—"

The front door burst open, and a shadow loomed in the entrance. The figure was tall, dark, and imposing, with a demeanor that exuded authority and menace.

"Where are they?" the voice boomed, cold and demanding, causing my breath to catch in my throat.

Jonah stiffened beside me, his hand tightening around a makeshift weapon—a heavy glass vase from the coffee table. "Stay behind me," he urged, positioning himself between me and the intruder.

"Get out!" I shouted, panic rising within me like a tidal wave. "Whoever you are, you're not welcome here!"

The intruder stepped forward, revealing a face partially obscured by shadows but unmistakably fierce and intent. "You're in way over your head, little girl. Hand over the painting, and this can all end peacefully."

Mia gasped, her eyes darting between Jonah and the looming figure. "We don't have it!"

A sinister smile spread across the intruder's face, revealing a glint of something dangerous in his eyes. "Oh, I think you do. And if you don't hand it over willingly, I assure you, I have ways to make you talk."

In that moment, the weight of my choices bore down on me. I glanced at Jonah, the fear mirrored in his eyes mingled with fierce resolve. This wasn't just a fight for survival anymore; it was a battle for our lives and the secrets that had entwined us in this web of darkness.

The air crackled with tension as the intruder stepped closer, and with a sudden surge of courage, I made a choice. "You want the painting?" I said, my voice steadier than I felt. "You'll have to get through me first."

The smirk faded from his lips, replaced with an unsettling glimmer of intrigue. "So you do have spirit. I'll enjoy breaking it."

As the darkness closed in, I braced myself for what lay ahead, determined to confront whatever threat stood between us and the truth. The clock was ticking, and the danger was only just beginning.

# Chapter 12: Chasing Shadows

The air in my apartment felt charged, thick with the remnants of the evening's chaos. Jonah stood by the window, silhouetted against the soft glow of the streetlights, his profile sharp and defined, yet etched with an unmistakable tension. I could feel my heart racing, not just from the adrenaline of the auction but from the weight of the words we had exchanged, words that hung in the air like storm clouds threatening to unleash a downpour.

"Mia, what do you mean he's after revenge?" I asked, the tremor in my voice betraying the calm façade I desperately tried to maintain. The room felt smaller somehow, as if the walls themselves were closing in, absorbing the heavy secrets we were uncovering. I could sense Jonah's gaze on me, a mixture of concern and something darker—an acknowledgment of a threat that loomed larger than both of us.

Mia, sitting cross-legged on my worn-out couch, leaned forward, her hair falling over her eyes like a curtain shielding her from the truth. "It's not just about the art, Claire," she said, her voice steady yet tinged with urgency. "The Raven is a ghost from Jonah's past—a haunting that won't rest until it settles the score." The way she spoke made the air quiver, as if we were discussing a curse rather than a person.

"Settle the score?" I echoed, feeling the words twist in my gut like a serpent ready to strike. I glanced at Jonah, searching for reassurance, but his eyes held a flicker of fear that sent a chill down my spine. I had thought I knew the man beside me—the charming wit, the easy laughter—but this revelation shattered my illusions, revealing a jagged truth hidden beneath the surface.

"Mia, you need to tell us everything," Jonah urged, his voice a low rumble, one that echoed the gravity of the situation. The shadows danced across his features, amplifying the sharp angles of his jaw and the haunted look in his eyes. I could feel the air crackle with unspoken words, the tension between us palpable and electric.

She nodded slowly, her expression serious. "Years ago, Jonah's family was embroiled in a scandal. There was betrayal, secrets exchanged for power, and The Raven—he's a part of that history." Each word hung in the air, thickening the atmosphere, wrapping around us like an ancient spell we were powerless to break.

As she spoke, images flickered through my mind: opulent ballrooms filled with laughter that turned to whispers, glances exchanged over crystal goblets, secrets woven into the very fabric of society. It was a world I had only glimpsed through the lens of art and elegance, a world that now felt suffocatingly close. "What did they do?" I pressed, unable to keep the tremor from my voice. The need to understand pushed me forward, even as the answer felt like a blade poised to cut deep.

"Jonah's family took something that didn't belong to them. A piece of art, yes, but also a life—a man who crossed them, who knew too much." Mia's words fell like stones, each one heavy and sharp, creating ripples of unease. "The Raven is that man's son. He wants vengeance, Claire, and he's not going to stop until he gets it."

The revelation landed with a dull thud in my chest, reverberating through my thoughts like an echo of dread. "So he's coming after Jonah?" I asked, my voice barely above a whisper. The thought curled around my mind, a tight knot of fear and confusion. I could feel the heat of Jonah's presence beside me, a flicker of warmth amid the chill of our circumstances, but it was overshadowed by the looming threat of revenge.

Jonah turned to face me fully, his expression fierce yet vulnerable. "I won't let him hurt you, Claire. I'll do whatever it takes." There was a fire in his voice that ignited something deep within me, a spark that flared into defiance. But beneath the bravado,

I could sense the cracks forming in his armor, the weight of history pressing down on him like an anchor.

"And what exactly do you plan to do?" I asked, challenging the resolve in his tone. "You can't fight shadows with bravado, Jonah."

"I have to protect you," he replied, determination lacing his words. "You don't understand the lengths he'll go to, the lengths I've already gone to in order to stay ahead of this. It's not just art anymore; it's a game of survival."

In that moment, I understood. This wasn't just about me or Jonah; it was about a reckoning that was long overdue, a confrontation with the past that threatened to engulf us both. "You're not alone in this," I said, my voice steadier than I felt. "We'll face it together, whatever it is."

Mia watched us, her eyes flickering with a hint of admiration mixed with concern. "It's not just a game, Claire. The Raven will stop at nothing. You need to be prepared for the worst."

The words sank deep, igniting a fire within me. I could feel the adrenaline pumping through my veins again, a rush that sharpened my senses. "I'm not afraid of the shadows," I declared, each word punctuated by a surge of conviction. "If we're going to do this, we do it together. No more running, no more hiding."

Jonah's gaze softened, a mixture of pride and worry washing over him. "You're incredible, you know that?" he said, his voice barely above a whisper. But beneath the praise, I sensed a warning—a reminder that the path ahead was fraught with danger.

As the weight of our decision settled around us, the shadows in the room seemed to deepen, wrapping us in a shroud of uncertainty. Yet amid the darkness, a flicker of light emerged—our resolve, our shared determination to confront the ghosts of the past. We stood at the precipice, ready to leap into the unknown, our fates entwined in a web of secrets and revenge. The Raven was coming, but we were no longer just pawns in his game. Together, we would reclaim our story, rewriting the narrative of betrayal and vengeance that had bound us for far too long.

The rain began to patter against the windows, a soft percussion that both soothed and unsettled. Each drop echoed like a reminder of the storm brewing within us. I stood in the kitchen, brewing coffee with a sense of urgency, as if the simple act of preparing the drink might somehow ward off the brewing chaos outside. Jonah leaned against the doorframe, arms crossed, watching me with an intensity that made my skin prickle.

"Do you always make coffee like it's an Olympic sport?" he quipped, a hint of a smile creeping onto his lips, but his eyes held the shadow of the conversation we had just shared.

"I'm just trying to keep us alert. We might need to outrun a ravenous ghost, after all," I replied, turning to flash him a teasing grin. But the reality settled like a weight on my chest. I needed to stay sharp.

"Right," he said, pushing off the doorframe and crossing the room to stand beside me. He peered out the window, watching the droplets race each other down the glass. "Do you think Mia's right? That he really wants revenge?"

"Who knows what he wants? The Raven sounds like a character from one of those melodramatic novels," I mused, pouring the steaming coffee into two mismatched mugs—one bright yellow, the other a deep forest green. "But if he's connected to your family's past, it's likely he means business."

Jonah took the mug I offered him, our fingers brushing for a brief moment that felt like a spark igniting a flame. "It's just a lot to process," he said, his voice low. "I can't believe this is happening. I thought my family's past was buried, forgotten."

"Buried, yes, but never forgotten," I replied, feeling a shiver run down my spine. "Secrets have a way of clawing their way back to the surface, especially when they involve betrayal."

A silence settled over us, thick and heavy. I could almost hear the wheels turning in Jonah's mind, the gears of his thoughts clicking into place as he tried to navigate the terrain of his family's history. It was strange, standing together in this intimate space, yet feeling like we were both walking on the edge of a precipice, teetering between uncertainty and the depth of what lay ahead.

"Do you ever feel like you're in a movie?" Jonah said, suddenly breaking the tension with an unexpected chuckle. "You know, the kind where the hero uncovers a family secret, and suddenly everyone's in danger?"

I laughed, the sound breaking through the heaviness in the air. "Right, and I'd be the quirky sidekick who gives terrible advice."

"Hey, you've got the coffee part down. That's a solid start."

Just as I was about to reply, a loud crash echoed from the hallway, jolting us both into a state of alertness. I exchanged a worried glance with Jonah, my heart racing. "What was that?" I asked, setting my mug down as I moved toward the door.

"Stay here," he instructed, the protective glint in his eyes surfacing again. I bristled at the command but held my ground, my curiosity piquing.

Jonah edged toward the door, his movements deliberate, as if every step could trigger a trap. "Maybe it's just the wind," I suggested, though I didn't quite believe it myself.

"Right, because the wind sounds like a party crashing through the front door."

With a determined nod, he opened the door, and the sight that greeted us froze my heart in my chest. There, sprawled on the floor, was Mia, tangled in a heap of coats and her own limbs, a look of sheer panic etched across her features.

"I didn't mean to scare you!" she exclaimed, scrambling to her feet. "I just—I thought I saw someone lurking outside. I was trying to sneak in and warn you."

Jonah frowned, concern flickering across his face. "Lurking? Did you see who it was?"

Mia shook her head, her wild hair bouncing around her shoulders. "No, but it felt wrong. I swear, there was a figure, and then they disappeared before I could get a good look."

Jonah's jaw clenched, and I could almost see the protective instincts surging within him. "We need to check it out," he said, a new edge to his voice.

"Are you crazy? You can't just go out there," I protested, the idea of stepping into the stormy night, chasing after shadows, sent adrenaline coursing through me.

"We can't hide forever," he replied, and for a brief moment, I saw the boy I had met at the gallery, confident and daring, standing before me. "We need to know what we're up against."

Mia nodded, her expression a mix of fear and determination. "I'll go with you. I'm not about to sit here while you two play hide-and-seek with a ghost."

"Great, then it's settled," Jonah declared, his voice carrying a firmness that left little room for dissent.

"Settled? No one actually asked me," I muttered, but a surge of excitement and dread rippled through me. I had never been one to shy away from danger; the idea of facing whatever lurked outside felt exhilarating, almost intoxicating.

As Jonah grabbed his jacket and slipped it on, I followed suit, my heart pounding like a drum in my chest. We stood at the threshold, the world outside beckoning, cloaked in shadows and uncertainty. I felt a strange mixture of fear and exhilaration, as if we were stepping into an adventure that could either end in disaster or reveal the truth we desperately sought.

"Remember," Jonah said, turning to me, "we stick together. No matter what."

"Got it. Together," I echoed, even as the weight of the night pressed down on us. We stepped into the hallway, the echoes of our footsteps bouncing off the walls, each step drawing us closer to the unknown.

The atmosphere outside was electric, the air thick with the promise of rain and the lingering scent of damp earth. As we stepped into the street, the shadows danced around us, teasing and taunting. A flash of movement caught my eye, and I felt the thrill of fear clawing at my throat.

"Did you see that?" I whispered, leaning closer to Jonah.

"Yeah," he replied, his gaze narrowing. "Stay alert."

As we ventured further into the night, the adrenaline surged through my veins, drowning out the fear. We were no longer just three individuals caught in a web of secrets; we were hunters now, chasing down the shadows of our past, ready to confront whatever—or whoever—was waiting for us.

The street was eerily quiet as we stepped outside, the damp air clinging to our skin like an unwelcome cloak. The distant sound of thunder rumbled, a reminder of the tempest both outside and within our hearts. As I walked beside Jonah and Mia, I felt an electric current of fear and exhilaration swirling in the atmosphere. The city, usually vibrant and alive, felt like a labyrinth of secrets, every corner harboring hidden dangers.

"What's our game plan here?" I asked, trying to keep my voice steady despite the fluttering in my stomach. "Do we just wander around and hope we bump into a ghost?"

Jonah shot me a sideways glance, half-smirking, half-serious. "If we can lure it out with our charm, maybe it'll just show up and have tea with us."

"Tea? Really? Because I'd prefer something stronger right about now," Mia chimed in, her voice playful yet laced with anxiety. The banter, however light, seemed to infuse us with a sense of unity, a reminder that we were in this together.

I let out a nervous laugh. "Right, because ghosts are known for their refined taste in beverages."

We moved down the narrow street, illuminated only by the flickering streetlights that cast ominous shadows across the pavement. The wind picked up, rustling the leaves in the trees, a sound that felt almost conspiratorial. The rhythm of my heartbeat seemed to synchronize with the rustle, each thud echoing my unease.

Mia stopped suddenly, her eyes scanning the area. "Wait, did you hear that?"

I strained my ears, catching a faint sound—a soft whisper carried on the wind. "What did it say?" I joked, trying to cut through the tension, but my voice trembled slightly.

"It sounded like—" Jonah began, but he halted mid-sentence, his expression shifting to one of focus. "There it is again."

We paused, every nerve ending on high alert. The sound grew clearer, a low murmur that seemed to swirl around us like a ghostly fog. "This isn't funny," I muttered, glancing over my shoulder as if expecting to see something—or someone—materialize from the shadows.

"It's not funny at all," Jonah replied, his tone serious. "We need to find out where it's coming from."

Following the sound, we stepped deeper into the heart of the city, weaving through alleyways lined with graffiti and crumbling bricks, the urban decay reflecting our own inner turmoil. Each step felt laden with the weight of what was at stake—betrayal, revenge, and the possibility of losing everything.

Just as I was starting to feel the chill of the night seep into my bones, we stumbled upon a dimly lit courtyard. The bricks were slick from the earlier rain, and a single, feeble light flickered from above, casting an ethereal glow over the scene. In the center stood an old stone fountain, the water trickling slowly, each drop echoing like a heartbeat in the silence.

"This place feels...wrong," Mia said, her eyes wide. "Like it's hiding something."

"Yeah, like a ghostly speakeasy for lost souls," I added, attempting to lighten the mood, but my voice lacked its usual confidence.

Jonah stepped closer to the fountain, peering into the shallow water. "What do you think we're supposed to find here?"

Suddenly, a figure darted from the shadows, moving with a speed that sent my heart racing. "Did you see that?" I gasped, instinctively grabbing Jonah's arm.

"I did," he said, his expression turning grave. "Stay close."

The figure disappeared into the darkness of the courtyard's far corner, and before I could voice my objections, Jonah took off after it, with Mia and me trailing behind. My breath came in quick bursts, panic rising in my throat. What were we doing? Chasing shadows?

We rounded the corner and skidded to a stop, hearts pounding in unison. The figure stood silhouetted against the wall, a cloak billowing around them, masking their features. "You shouldn't have come here," a voice said, smooth and low, sending a shiver down my spine.

"Who are you?" Jonah demanded, stepping forward with a bravado I hoped masked his unease.

The figure chuckled, a sound rich with menace. "I am the one you seek—the Raven."

"What do you want?" I blurted, the question escaping my lips before I could stop it.

"To finish what was started," the Raven replied, stepping closer. The dim light revealed a mask covering their face, ornate and shimmering, glinting in the faint light like the scales of a serpent. "You've dug up secrets better left buried."

"Secrets? We're not digging up anything," Jonah shot back, his voice steady despite the growing dread in my stomach. "You're the one hiding in the shadows."

The Raven tilted their head, the mask reflecting a twisted smirk. "Hiding? Hardly. I've been waiting for you to uncover the truth. But be warned, the truth can be a deadly companion."

The wind howled, and a chill swept through the courtyard, causing the fountain to ripple, the water shimmering as if alive. I glanced at Jonah and Mia, my heart pounding, the reality of the situation crashing down like a tidal wave.

"And what if we don't want to play your little game?" I challenged, my voice stronger than I felt.

"Then you will face the consequences of your ignorance," the Raven said, their tone dripping with disdain. "You've tangled yourselves in a web far more complex than you realize. But don't worry; I'll make sure you enjoy the show."

Before we could react, the figure darted away, disappearing into the shadows like smoke in the wind. The air felt thick with tension, the weight of their words hanging heavily over us.

"Did that just happen?" Mia whispered, her voice barely audible over the pounding in my ears.

"We need to regroup," Jonah said, urgency fueling his voice. "We have to figure out what they know and how they're connected to your family."

But just as we turned to leave the courtyard, a piercing scream shattered the night, echoing off the walls, slicing through the tension like a knife. I froze, dread creeping up my spine.

"Claire!" Jonah shouted, panic lacing his voice.

The scream faded into the distance, swallowed by the night, leaving us standing on the precipice of fear and uncertainty. A decision loomed before us—follow the sound and plunge deeper into the mystery, or retreat and hope to salvage what was left of our fragile safety.

As the rain began to fall, heavy and relentless, I caught Jonah's eye, and in that moment, we both understood: there was no turning back. We were already entangled in a web of shadows, and now, the only choice left was to chase them down, even if it led us straight into the heart of darkness.

# Chapter 13: A Dangerous Game

The faint flicker of candlelight danced against the aged stone walls of the cellar, casting shadows that swayed like restless spirits. I stood at the table, a battered wooden surface strewn with sketches of elaborate paintings and notes scribbled in frantic scrawl. Jonah leaned closer, his breath warm against my ear as he pointed out the intricacies of our plan, but I couldn't focus on the words. The urgency of our situation clawed at my mind, and I was painfully aware of his presence, an intoxicating mix of strength and vulnerability.

"Are you sure about this?" My voice was barely above a whisper, heavy with the weight of what we were contemplating. The air felt charged, thick with the promise of something dangerous. The thought of baiting The Raven, a criminal mastermind whose gaze could slice through the darkness like a knife, sent chills down my spine. The man was elusive, a specter woven into the fabric of the city's underground, and here we were, poised to lure him in with a painting that was as fake as the false bravado we wore like armor.

Jonah's fingers brushed against mine as he adjusted the blueprints, a seemingly innocent gesture that sent a jolt through me, igniting a fire that burned hotter than the flickering candles. His eyes, usually so calm, danced with a storm of emotions—fear, determination, and something else that made my heart race. "We have to do this. It's the only way to stop him," he insisted, his voice steady but laced with an urgency that betrayed the confidence he tried to project.

I nodded, though doubt gnawed at the edges of my resolve. The idea of drawing The Raven out was reckless, and we both knew it. Every instinct screamed at me to step back, to seek safety in the shadows where I could remain untouched by the chaos of the world we were entangling ourselves in. Yet, here we were, unwilling participants in a deadly game.

As we worked, the tension between us crackled like static in the air. Every time our fingers brushed, an electric thrill surged through me, leaving a trail of heat that lingered long after he moved away. I caught myself stealing glances at him, studying the way the light caught in the tousled strands of his dark hair and how his jawline tightened in concentration. He was a contradiction, a man who fought against the darkness while drawing me into it.

"We can't let him think we're afraid," Jonah continued, his gaze locking onto mine with an intensity that made the air feel thick and heavy. "Fear is what keeps him in power."

There it was, the underlying current of our situation—the fear that held us in its grip, squeezing tighter with every passing moment. I swallowed hard, aware that the very essence of our lives had become entwined with this audacious plan. The weight of our choices hung over us like a storm cloud, threatening to burst at any moment.

"Right. No fear," I murmured, trying to infuse my words with confidence I didn't feel. "Just a fake painting and a dangerous criminal."

Jonah chuckled, the sound low and rich, breaking through the tension. "Just another day at the office, right?" His smile was infectious, a fleeting reminder of the man beneath the layers of peril we were navigating.

But beneath that humor lay an unspoken truth—our lives were no longer defined by the mundane. The stakes had shifted dramatically, and I was painfully aware that with each step forward, we were walking a tightrope stretched over an abyss. One miscalculation, one moment of hesitation, and we could plummet into the depths of despair.

"I can't shake the feeling that we're being watched," I confessed, my voice barely above a whisper, the shadows around us suddenly feeling suffocating. "What if we're walking into a trap?"

Jonah's expression hardened, a flicker of concern flashing across his face. "Then we adapt. We're not alone in this." The conviction in his words wrapped around me like a protective shroud, urging me to believe in our ability to navigate the dark waters ahead.

"Right." I took a deep breath, trying to gather the fragments of my shattered confidence. "We can do this."

We moved back to our preparations, piecing together our façade with care. Each brushstroke I painted felt like a promise—an oath to myself that I would not let fear dictate my actions. We were stepping into the lion's den, ready to confront the beast that had haunted our steps for far too long.

And yet, as the candlelight flickered, casting playful shadows across the room, an undercurrent of longing surged between us, more potent than the fear that threatened to overwhelm. My heart raced as Jonah drew closer, the air between us thickening with unspoken words.

"Before we step into the abyss, there's something I need to tell you," he said, his voice low and serious.

My heart quickened, a wild flutter that sent my thoughts spiraling. Had he felt it too? The spark that ignited in those fleeting moments, the magnetic pull that drew us together? The world around us faded, and it was just the two of us, suspended in time, on the precipice of something extraordinary.

But before I could respond, before I could voice the truth that hung in the air like an unfinished sentence, a noise echoed from the shadows, snapping me back to reality. The sound—soft, yet distinctly unsettling—filled the space around us. I froze, every instinct screaming that we were no longer alone.

"Did you hear that?" I whispered, my pulse racing.

Jonah's expression shifted, alert and fierce. "Stay close," he ordered, his voice barely above a breath.

The tension surged between us, the danger we faced morphing from a distant threat into an immediate reality. We had walked willingly into the lion's den, and now, it seemed, the lions were stirring.

The tension in the cellar coiled tighter, almost palpable, as the shadows deepened around us. My heart thudded in my chest, each beat a reminder of the stakes we faced. I leaned against the cool stone wall, feeling the chill seep through my clothes, contrasting sharply with the warmth radiating from Jonah. The flickering candles cast a soft glow on his face, highlighting the determination etched in the lines of his jaw and the intensity in his eyes.

"Do you think he's out there?" I asked, my voice a whisper as I searched the dim corners of the room, half-expecting The Raven to materialize from the gloom.

Jonah shook his head, a hint of a smile playing at the corners of his lips. "If he is, I'm sure he's busy polishing his villain cape." The levity in his tone was a welcome balm, a momentary reprieve from the heavy atmosphere pressing down on us.

"You know, if we survive this, I might have to write a bestselling thriller about our escapades," I shot back, a teasing smile creeping onto my face. "I can picture the cover now—two ridiculously attractive protagonists caught in a web of intrigue."

Jonah raised an eyebrow, his smirk widening. "I'd prefer 'daring duo outsmarting a dangerous criminal' rather than 'ridiculously attractive,' but I'll let it slide if it means I get a spot on the cover."

Our laughter echoed through the cellar, cutting through the tension like a knife. It was a fleeting moment, a reminder that even in the most perilous situations, joy could seep in through the cracks. Yet, as quickly as it came, the weight of reality pressed down on us again.

"Okay, enough of the banter," I said, shaking off the giddy warmth of our moment. "What's the next step?"

Jonah gestured to the makeshift table littered with paint tubes and brushes, the crude replica of the painting we were set to use as bait. "We need to finalize the details. The Raven is cunning, and if there's even a hint that this isn't the real deal, we're toast."

My stomach twisted at the thought. The last thing I wanted was to face the wrath of a man whose reputation was built on fear and brutality. "Right. Let's make it flawless."

We fell into a rhythm, our movements synchronized as we worked together to perfect our ruse. As I dabbed paint onto the canvas, I caught glimpses of Jonah's concentration—the way his brow furrowed and how he occasionally licked his lips when he was deep in thought. Each flick of my brush against the canvas became a metaphor for the pulse of our unspoken connection, both thrilling and terrifying.

"Just think of it," Jonah mused as he mixed colors, the vibrant hues swirling together like the chaos of our lives. "This could be the turning point. Once we pull The Raven into the open, we can expose him. End this nightmare once and for all."

"Or we could become his next victims," I interjected, my voice wavering. "There's a fine line between bravery and stupidity."

He turned to face me, his gaze piercing. "It's a risk we have to take. For too long, we've been running scared. I refuse to let him dictate our lives any longer."

In that moment, I felt the gravity of his words settle over me, heavy yet invigorating. The fire ignited within me was not just desire; it was a hunger for liberation, for the chance to reclaim our lives from the clutches of fear.

As we worked, our shoulders brushed, a gentle reminder of our proximity. The heat between us simmered, an undercurrent that made each brushstroke feel charged with an electric energy. The world outside faded into a distant murmur, replaced by the intimacy of our shared mission.

"Just one more touch," I murmured, focusing intently on the canvas as I added delicate strokes to the corner. "Then we can lay our trap."

"Lay our trap and maybe lay our cards on the table," he said, a playful smirk dancing across his lips.

My heart raced at the implication behind his words, and I met his gaze, the intensity between us thickening. "You mean our feelings? Or are we talking about the kind of cards that might get us killed?"

"Both," he replied, his tone serious yet playful, grounding us in the gravity of our situation while igniting a playful spark. "I'd prefer to be straightforward rather than play poker with a guy who holds all the aces."

"Good point," I said, laughter bubbling up despite the impending danger. "But if we're being honest, I'm not sure I'm ready to reveal my hand."

"Neither am I," he admitted, the warmth in his gaze deepening. "But maybe we'll surprise ourselves."

As I finished the final details on the painting, my thoughts drifted to what lay ahead. The game we were playing was one of life and death, but beneath that danger was something raw and unfiltered. The fear that gripped us was real, but so was the connection we had forged in the flames of adversity.

"We need to decide how we'll get the painting to him," I said, stepping back to admire our work, the canvas a beautiful deception.

Jonah nodded, his expression shifting to one of determination. "I'll arrange a meeting. He trusts certain channels to deliver messages, and I have a contact who can help."

"Are you sure that's wise?" I asked, unease creeping back in. "What if he sees through it?"

"Then we adapt. Just like we've been doing all along," he said, confidence coloring his words.

I drew in a shaky breath, letting the moment stretch between us. There was an undeniable allure in the way he carried himself, a calm amidst the chaos that anchored me. "And what about us? What happens after this?"

The question hung in the air, weighted and electric, and for a moment, I feared that the danger outside would seep into the sanctity of our shared space.

"I want to find out," he replied, his voice steady, each word laden with intention. "But first, we need to survive tonight."

"Right. Survive first, kiss later," I quipped, trying to lighten the gravity of the moment.

"Hey, if we pull this off, there's going to be a very public celebration. Just you wait."

As he spoke, a sudden sound pierced through the cellar's stillness, a faint echo of footsteps approaching from outside. My heart lurched, adrenaline flooding my veins.

"Jonah," I whispered, panic creeping in.

He stiffened, instinctively moving closer, a protective barrier formed between me and the unknown. "Stay behind me."

The shadows seemed to deepen, and as the footsteps grew louder, the weight of impending danger descended upon us. The moment of reckoning had arrived, and I could feel the world shifting, the fragile balance we had fought to maintain teetering on the edge. We were no longer merely players in a game; we were the pieces on a board, and the stakes had never been higher.

The sound of footsteps grew louder, reverberating off the stone walls and creeping into my bones like a chill wind. Jonah tensed beside me, the playful banter that had filled the room moments ago evaporating into an urgent silence. I felt my heart leap into my throat, the warmth we had shared now overshadowed by an icy dread that pooled in my stomach.

"Get down," he whispered, urgency slicing through his tone. Without hesitation, he pushed me behind a stack of crates, their rough wood scraping against my skin. We crouched in the shadows, barely breathing as the footsteps neared, their rhythm steady and unyielding.

In the dim light, I caught a glimpse of Jonah's face, shadowed and serious. The flicker of the candle cast a glow that danced across his features, highlighting the determination etched there. I wanted to reach out, to assure him that we could face this together, but the danger was palpable, a suffocating blanket pressing down on us.

The door creaked open, the hinges protesting as a figure stepped into the cellar, draped in a long coat that billowed like a cape. My breath caught in my throat as the silhouette moved further into the room, revealing a man whose face was obscured by the shadows.

"Raven's men," Jonah whispered, a mixture of fear and anger coloring his voice.

"Do you think they know we're here?" I asked, my voice barely a breath.

"Not yet, but we need to move. If they catch us..."

Before he could finish, the figure paused, glancing around with a predatory grace. "You know the Raven doesn't like to be kept waiting," he called out, his voice smooth like velvet but laced with an underlying menace.

Jonah's grip tightened around my wrist, a silent command to remain silent and still. I nodded, forcing myself to breathe steadily, though every instinct screamed at me to flee. I could feel the tension crackling between us, a mix of fear and something else—a shared resolve that pulsed like electricity in the air.

The man began to search the room, moving closer to our hiding spot. I could see the glint of a knife sheathed at his side, its blade sharp enough to cut through the shadows, and my stomach twisted at the thought of what would happen if we were discovered.

"What's the plan?" I whispered, panic creeping into my voice as he moved within a few feet of us.

"Wait for my signal," Jonah murmured, his eyes narrowing as he gauged the situation. "If he comes too close, we'll make a break for it."

My heart raced, a relentless drumbeat echoing the urgency of our predicament. Every instinct screamed for me to act, to take control of the situation, but I stayed still, focusing on Jonah, drawing strength from his presence.

"Any idea how long we'll be waiting?" I quipped, desperate to keep the tension at bay with humor, even as it fluttered dangerously close to despair.

"Long enough for me to rethink our entire life choices," he replied dryly, a hint of a smile teasing his lips despite the gravity of our situation.

The man turned, his attention drawn away for a moment, and I seized the opportunity to study him. He had the sharp features of a predator, eyes dark and calculating as they roamed the room, seeking any sign of us.

"Where are they?" he muttered under his breath, frustration evident in his tone. "They wouldn't dare—"

Before he could finish, Jonah shifted slightly, and a loose crate shifted ominously, the wood groaning in protest. The man's head snapped in our direction, eyes narrowing as he zeroed in on our hiding spot.

"Found you," he sneered, lunging forward with a predatory grace that sent adrenaline coursing through my veins.

"Go!" Jonah shouted, his voice fierce as he pushed me out from behind the crates. I stumbled forward, heart pounding as I darted toward the far side of the cellar.

I barely glanced back, but I could hear Jonah's voice, low and commanding, as he confronted the man. "You don't want to do this."

"Tell me something I don't know," the man hissed, a cruel edge in his voice. The clash of bodies echoed, the sound of a scuffle igniting a primal fear deep within me.

I reached the wall, my mind racing as I searched for an escape route. The cellar was a labyrinth of shadows and crates, and I needed to find a way out before the situation escalated beyond our control.

"Jonah!" I called, panic lacing my voice as I pressed against the cold stone, the rough surface digging into my palms. "We have to move!"

He was still fighting, the sound of flesh meeting flesh ringing out as I turned to look back at him. I could see the man's knife glinting in the dim light, and a surge of terror gripped me.

"Hold on!" Jonah's voice sliced through the chaos, fierce and unwavering.

I could see he was gaining the upper hand, but the man was relentless, and my heart dropped as I heard a heavy thud echo in the confined space. Jonah staggered back, and for a moment, time seemed to freeze.

"Go!" he shouted again, his eyes locking onto mine, filled with fierce determination. "I'll handle this!"

"No!" The word burst from my lips, a desperate plea against the impending darkness that threatened to engulf us both.

But before I could make sense of what was happening, the cellar door burst open with a loud crash, a flood of light spilling into the dim space. Figures swarmed in—more men, their faces hidden beneath hoods, eyes glinting with malice.

"What the hell is going on here?" one of them shouted, their voice booming, slicing through the chaos.

The sudden influx of intruders shifted the tides, and I felt the world tilt dangerously on its axis. Jonah's fierce determination turned to a new kind of resolve as he realized the odds had shifted.

"Get out!" he yelled again, urgency in his tone as he struggled against the man still grappling with him. "I'll find you!"

But before I could react, a pair of strong hands grabbed me from behind, yanking me back into the shadows. I kicked and struggled, panic rising as I fought against the grip that held me captive.

"Let her go!" Jonah's voice cut through the chaos, but the struggle was no longer just between us and The Raven's men—it was a full-on assault, a whirlwind of violence that surged around us.

"Take her!" the man from before spat, his voice filled with contempt. "She's the bait we've been waiting for."

Everything shifted in an instant, the walls closing in as I realized the precariousness of our situation. I was being pulled away, away from Jonah, from the only person who understood the depths of this twisted game we had found ourselves in.

"No!" I screamed, my voice raw with desperation as I strained against my captor. "Jonah!"

In that moment, I caught a glimpse of him—determined, fierce, fighting with everything he had. But the shadows loomed larger, and I could feel the weight of fate pressing down upon us as my world began to spiral out of control.

Then, just as suddenly as it began, the chaos erupted into a crescendo, and I felt myself being yanked backward, the world fading away, leaving only the echo of Jonah's voice ringing in my ears as the darkness closed in around me.

# Chapter 14: Into the Darkness

The moon hung low, a sliver of silver peeking through the jagged remnants of the city's skyline, casting ghostly shadows on the cracked pavement. I pressed my back against the cold, unyielding wall of the warehouse, the rough texture scraping against my skin like the memories I couldn't shake. The air was thick with the smell of rust and decay, a fitting tribute to the secrets the building had long kept buried. Each heartbeat echoed in my ears, a reminder that I was very much alive in this moment, and oh, how I wished I weren't.

I glanced sideways at Jonah, whose brow was furrowed with a mix of determination and something else I couldn't quite place—fear, perhaps. He always wore his emotions like armor, but tonight, they felt like a weight pulling him down. The shadows danced around us, and the eerie stillness of the night was punctuated only by the distant sound of traffic, a reminder that life was normal just beyond the confines of our chaotic reality. But we weren't normal. Not anymore.

"Do you think he'll come?" I asked, trying to keep my voice steady, though the tremor gave me away. The thought of The Raven loomed like a specter, haunting my dreams and taunting my waking hours.

Jonah shifted, casting a sideways glance at the old wooden crates that lined the warehouse, their surfaces mottled with age. "He has to," he replied, his voice low and gravelly. "This is the moment we've been waiting for."

I nodded, but the knot in my stomach tightened. Our plan was both reckless and brilliant, a delicate dance on the razor's edge of danger. The fake painting we'd hidden among the crates was a lure, bait for a predator who thrived in darkness. We wanted to draw him out, to confront him on our terms. But the deeper I delved into the scheme, the more I realized how quickly the tables could turn.

Moments stretched like taffy in the silence. I could feel the humidity clinging to my skin, mixing with the adrenaline coursing through my veins. Every creak of the warehouse sent a jolt through me, igniting memories of my past—of fear and betrayal, of moments where trust was a fragile thread about to snap. I closed my eyes, willing myself to focus on the here and now, on Jonah beside me, the only thing tethering me to reality.

Then, a sound pierced the night, a soft footfall barely disturbing the quiet. My heart raced, and I straightened instinctively. The darkness shifted, and there he was. The Raven stepped out from the shadows, clad in black, a wraith-like figure that sent shivers up my spine. His presence was magnetic yet repulsive, like a black hole that threatened to consume everything in its path. The stark white of his mask glowed in the dim light, a reminder that behind the façade lay a monster.

"Ah, the heroes of the hour," he said, his voice smooth like silk but laced with a sinister edge. "I must admit, I'm surprised you managed to summon the courage to face me."

Jonah stepped forward, his body tense and ready, a coiled spring about to unleash its energy. "This isn't a game, Raven. We know what you've done, and it's time you pay the price."

The Raven chuckled, a low, menacing sound that echoed in the cavernous space. "You think you can intimidate me? How quaint." He took a step closer, and the air seemed to thicken with his arrogance. "Do you even know what you're up against?"

I shivered, the instinct to flee bubbling just beneath the surface. But the thought of retreating, of letting this man slip through our fingers, ignited a fire within me. "You think we're afraid?" I shot back, surprising even myself with the steadiness of my voice. "You don't know us at all."

"On the contrary," he replied, a gleam in his eye that made my stomach drop. "I know you better than you think. Your fears, your desires, your every weakness laid bare." He smiled, and it felt like a dagger poised at my heart. "I could break you with a whisper."

I forced myself to hold his gaze, to remain anchored in the moment. Jonah's shoulder brushed against mine, an unspoken promise of solidarity. "We're not here to play your twisted games. We're here to end this."

"End this?" The Raven laughed, a chilling sound that echoed off the walls. "You are but two moths fluttering around a flame, and I am the one holding the match."

The weight of his words hung heavy in the air, and I felt the tension ratchet up, a taut line ready to snap. The realization crashed over me like a wave—this was more than a confrontation; it was a battle for our very survival. The pulse of danger throbbed in my ears, drowning out rational thought.

In that instant, everything shifted. Jonah stepped forward, fists clenched, but before he could make a move, The Raven lunged, and the world turned chaotic. I barely registered the shift in the air, the flash of movement, as I instinctively ducked to the side. My heart thundered as I tried to process what was happening—this was a fight, a desperate dance on the edge of chaos.

"Get down!" Jonah shouted, and the command jolted me back into reality. My instincts kicked in, and I dove behind a stack of crates, my breath ragged as I scrambled for cover. I could hear the scuffle of feet, the sound of something heavy crashing against the ground.

My pulse quickened as I peeked around the corner, my heart sinking at the sight before me. Jonah was locked in a fierce struggle with The Raven, the two figures grappling in a deadly embrace. Every punch thrown and kick landed was a testament to the stakes we faced. This was not just about a painting; it was about everything we had fought to protect.

"Think you can take me?" The Raven taunted, a twisted smile on his lips as he shoved Jonah backward, sending him sprawling against a crate.

"Just watch me," Jonah spat, determination blazing in his eyes as he charged again, fueled by a fury that was palpable.

The fight erupted into a whirlwind of movement, and I was paralyzed for a moment, caught between fear and the desperate need to help. But what could I do? My mind raced, searching for something—anything—that could tip the scales in our favor. The warehouse loomed around us, dark and forbidding, but I was not about to let it swallow us whole.

Then I spotted it: a rusty metal pipe, half-hidden beneath a layer of dust. I grabbed it, feeling the weight settle comfortably in my grip. The sound of flesh hitting flesh rang in my ears as I prepared myself. This was no longer a battle for a painting; it was a fight for our lives, and I would not stand by and watch.

The clang of metal against metal shattered the tense silence as I lunged from my hiding place, pipe gripped tightly in my hand. Jonah was on the ground, grappling with The Raven, who had him pinned, an insidious grin curling his lips as he relished the control. It was time for me to intervene. I swung the pipe with every ounce of adrenaline pumping through my veins, aiming for The Raven's shoulder.

"Hey, batman!" I yelled, channeling every ounce of bravado I could muster. "Didn't your mother teach you not to play with your food?"

The Raven turned his head, surprise flickering across his features, just long enough for Jonah to capitalize on the moment. He shoved The Raven off him, creating a gap that felt like a lifeline. I swung again, catching The Raven off balance, and we both stumbled back.

"Nice shot!" Jonah exclaimed, scrambling to his feet, breathing heavily.

"Yeah, well, I've always preferred my art with a side of danger." I shrugged, the wry grin on my face betraying the tumult inside. "And I definitely don't do well with being anyone's appetizer."

The Raven growled, straightening himself with a fluidity that belied the aggression simmering beneath the surface. "You think you can take me on with a pipe and some clever quips?" He laughed, the sound slicing through the air, taunting us. "I've dealt with far worse than you two."

"Yeah, well, we're not done yet," Jonah said, stepping beside me, his stance unwavering. "This is our turf now."

"I'd love to see you try," The Raven sneered, shifting his weight, preparing for the next round.

Our eyes locked for a fleeting moment, and I saw the fire in Jonah's gaze. We were more than allies now; we were a united front, forged in desperation and defiance. I could feel the electricity crackling between us, a shared understanding that we were fighting not just for ourselves but for everything we held dear.

The Raven lunged forward, but this time I was ready. I dodged, the pipe sweeping through the air like a dancer's arm, and I landed a strike against his knee. He hissed, the pain snapping his focus back to me.

"Is that all you've got?" he taunted, though I could see the flicker of uncertainty in his eyes.

"It's enough to keep you on your toes, isn't it?" I shot back, heart racing as I prepared for his next move.

As we exchanged blows, the warehouse felt like a boxing ring, with shadows for spectators and the echoes of our struggle bouncing off the walls. Jonah managed to deliver a solid punch to The Raven's jaw, but he was quickly met with a counter that sent him staggering back.

"Get up!" I urged, my voice slicing through the chaos. "You can't let him win!"

Jonah gritted his teeth and sprang back into action, his determination shining brighter than the dim overhead lights. "I'm not going down that easily," he grunted, pushing forward again.

In a sudden burst of rage, The Raven shoved Jonah hard against a stack of crates, the sound of wood splintering ringing out like a death knell. I gasped, but I couldn't afford to panic. I rushed forward, brandishing the pipe like a sword, my heart pounding with a mix of fear and fury.

"Get away from him!" I yelled, swinging at The Raven's head, the pipe connecting with a satisfying thud. He staggered back, momentarily stunned, and I seized the opportunity to grab Jonah and pull him to safety.

"What were you thinking?" he panted, rubbing the back of his head as we ducked behind a crate.

"I was thinking that you'd better not get yourself killed," I shot back, trying to keep my voice light despite the gravity of the situation. "You know how much I hate paperwork."

"Is that really what you're worried about right now?" he chuckled, even as adrenaline coursed through him.

"Hey, a girl has to prioritize!" I shot back, a grin breaking through the fear. The moment felt surreal, a strange dance of laughter amidst the chaos.

The Raven recovered, his eyes narrowing in fury as he stalked toward us. "You think this is a game? You're nothing but pawns in a much larger scheme. You have no idea what you're dealing with."

I straightened, feeling the weight of my resolve solidify. "Then enlighten us. Because from where I stand, you look like a man cornered by his own arrogance."

The tension crackled in the air like a live wire, and for a heartbeat, The Raven hesitated, the certainty in his expression wavering. "Arrogance? Hardly. You don't know the power I wield."

"Power?" Jonah scoffed, regaining his footing beside me. "The only thing you wield is fear. And we're not afraid of you anymore."

"Oh, how naive." The Raven smirked, but it didn't reach his eyes. "You'll regret this decision. I'm not just a shadow; I'm the darkness that consumes everything."

I could see Jonah's jaw tighten, determination flooding his features. "Then we'll fight the darkness together."

With a surge of confidence, I swung the pipe again, aiming for The Raven's legs, but he sidestepped, letting out a low growl. In that split second, I felt a rush of realization. We had momentum, a spark of unity igniting our spirits, and we couldn't let it go to waste.

"Now!" Jonah shouted, charging forward, forcing The Raven into a corner. I followed, closing in from the side, adrenaline electrifying my every movement.

The fight raged on, a chaotic ballet of fists and resolve. I ducked under The Raven's flailing arm, swinging the pipe wildly, the metal singing through the air. I could feel the tide shifting, the balance tilting in our favor as Jonah landed a series of solid punches.

The Raven, now visibly rattled, started to retreat, his bravado cracking like glass. "You think you can win? This isn't over!"

"It's not over until you're out of our lives for good," Jonah replied, and I could see the fierce resolve in his eyes.

With one last desperate lunge, The Raven turned to flee, his shadow disappearing into the depths of the warehouse. The tension hung in the air, and for a moment, we stood still, breathless, the thrill of the fight leaving us dizzy.

"Did we just win?" I gasped, my heart racing.

"I think we did," Jonah said, his voice shaky yet triumphant. "But I don't think he's gone for good."

The thought sent a chill down my spine, but I met his gaze with fierce determination. "Then we'll be ready for him. Together."

And just like that, the darkness seemed a little less daunting, the night a little less oppressive, as we stood side by side, resolute against whatever storm was still to come.

The air hung heavy with the scent of dust and the remnants of something long forgotten. As Jonah and I shared a glance, an unspoken vow lingered between us—a promise to hold the line against the encroaching darkness. The Raven's retreat had thrown us into a whirlwind of questions. What did he mean by saying this wasn't over? The thought gnawed at me as we stepped out of the shadows, adrenaline still thrumming in my veins.

"Where do we even begin to piece this together?" I muttered, brushing off my clothes, the grime sticking to my palms like unwelcome memories.

Jonah leaned against the nearest crate, his brow furrowed in thought. "We need to find out who he really is and what he's after. This isn't just a personal vendetta; there's something bigger at play here."

"Great, more mysteries. Just what I wanted," I replied, sarcasm tinging my voice. "How about a nice beach vacation instead? A little sun and sand would do wonders for our sanity."

He chuckled softly, the tension easing momentarily. "Yeah, well, the beach can wait. We have a war to wage."

I peered around the warehouse, its skeletal structure looming like a graveyard of forgotten dreams. "So what's next? We turn this place upside down and hope for clues?"

"Something like that," he said, pushing off the crate. "Let's see what we can find. Maybe The Raven left us a calling card."

As we moved deeper into the shadows of the warehouse, each creak of the floorboards beneath us echoed in the vast emptiness, amplifying our uncertainty. I swiped a hand across the dusty surface of a nearby crate, revealing a smattering of symbols painted in a dark, unyielding color.

"Jonah, look at this," I said, kneeling to inspect it closer. "Do you see these marks? They look... ritualistic."

He crouched beside me, his eyes narrowing as he examined the symbols. "This isn't just a hideout. It looks like it was used for something sinister."

A chill crept up my spine, and I fought the urge to shiver. "So, we're dealing with a dark arts enthusiast on top of everything else? Just fantastic."

"I'd say it's a good bet that whatever he's involved with is more than just art theft," Jonah replied, his voice low and steady. "We need to tread carefully. This could go from bad to worse in a heartbeat."

With a deep breath, I stood, my resolve hardening. "Well, then, let's get to it. We didn't come here to play detective for nothing."

We moved through the labyrinth of crates and debris, the air thickening with tension as shadows danced across the walls. I could feel the weight of history in the building, a haunting echo of past deeds that loomed over us like a specter. Each corner we turned felt like an invitation to face more secrets, each sound a reminder that we weren't alone in this desolation.

As we reached the far end of the warehouse, I stumbled upon a dusty, half-open door. It creaked ominously as I pushed it wider, revealing a dimly lit room that sent a thrill of apprehension racing down my spine. The flickering light inside illuminated shelves lined with faded documents and peculiar artifacts, each one seemingly drenched in darkness.

"Jonah, come look at this," I called, stepping tentatively into the room.

He joined me, his expression shifting from curiosity to concern. "This looks like some sort of archive," he observed, scanning the shelves laden with dusty tomes and jars filled with strange substances. "We might find something useful here."

I picked up a leather-bound book, the spine cracked and weathered, and opened it to reveal pages filled with illegible scrawl and diagrams that made my head spin. "This is like something out of a horror novel. What are we even looking at?"

Jonah leaned in closer, his brow furrowed. "It's hard to tell, but some of these symbols... they match those on the crates outside. We might be onto something big here."

Suddenly, a soft sound caught my attention—a faint rustling from behind one of the shelves. My heart raced, and I exchanged a worried glance with Jonah.

"Did you hear that?" I whispered, tension coiling in my stomach like a tightly wound spring.

"Yeah," he replied, his voice barely above a whisper. "Stay alert."

As we both turned our attention to the source of the noise, the air seemed to thicken around us, anticipation hanging like a fog. I inched closer, the floorboards creaking underfoot, my heart pounding against my ribcage.

"Show yourself!" I called out, trying to keep my voice steady despite the fear coiling in my chest.

To my shock, a figure stepped out from behind the shelves, cloaked in shadows. My breath caught in my throat as I recognized the familiar silhouette—the last person I expected to see.

"Sam?" I breathed, disbelief washing over me. "What are you doing here?"

He stepped closer, his face partially illuminated by the dim light. "I came to warn you," he said, urgency etched into his features. "You need to get out of here, now."

"What do you mean? We're close to uncovering something big," Jonah interjected, stepping protectively in front of me.

"No, you don't understand," Sam insisted, his voice laced with panic. "The Raven is not just a thief. He's part of something much darker. They're coming for you."

A cold wave of realization crashed over me, and the implications of his words sent a chill down my spine. "Who's coming?"

Before Sam could respond, the lights flickered violently, plunging us into an oppressive darkness. The echo of heavy footsteps reverberated through the warehouse, sending a jolt of fear through my veins.

"Hide!" Jonah urged, shoving me behind a stack of crates as he positioned himself between us and the approaching danger.

I pressed my back against the rough wood, my heart thundering in my chest as the footsteps grew louder, reverberating like a drum of impending doom. Sam's presence felt like an anchor in the swirling chaos, but I couldn't shake the sense of dread that settled over me.

"Jonah," I whispered, fear gripping my throat. "What if this is it? What if we're not ready for whatever's coming?"

He turned slightly, his expression fierce yet tender. "We've come this far. We can't back down now."

The footsteps halted abruptly, and an eerie silence enveloped the room. I held my breath, the tension palpable, as I strained to hear any sound over the pounding of my heart.

Then came the voice, smooth and chilling, cutting through the darkness like a blade. "Ah, I see we've gathered a little party. How quaint."

The Raven stepped into the light, flanked by a group of shadowy figures whose faces were obscured. My pulse raced, panic clawing at my insides.

"I was hoping to have a more intimate reunion," he continued, his tone mocking. "But it seems I'll have to settle for a grander audience."

As he stepped forward, the shadows around him shifted, and my breath caught as I realized the true nature of his accomplices. They were unlike anything I had ever seen—eyes glinting like shards of glass in the dim light, a predatory grace to their movements that sent a chill racing down my spine.

In that instant, the weight of our situation crashed down on me like a wave, and a single thought crystallized in my mind: We were outmatched, and this wasn't just a fight for our lives; it was a battle against a force far more powerful than we could have imagined.

"Get ready," Jonah murmured, and I could see the resolve in his eyes as we braced ourselves for the storm that was about to break over us.

But as The Raven stepped closer, a sinister smile spreading across his face, I realized with a sinking feeling that this was only the beginning of something much darker—and I feared we might not survive to see the end.

# Chapter 15: Betrayal in the Night

The moon hung high, a sliver of silver slicing through the night's velvet embrace, illuminating the chaos that had erupted in the narrow alley behind the crumbling facade of the old theater. Shadows twisted and danced around me, the dim glow creating a theatre of horror where I was unwillingly cast as the lead. Jonah stood beside me, his frame tense and resolute, yet I could see the weariness etched into the lines of his face, each one a testament to the trials we had faced together. It was a face I had come to cherish, each line telling a story I wanted to hear over and over again.

The air crackled with tension, and the smell of rain-soaked asphalt mingled with something darker—an undercurrent of dread that prickled at my skin. I knew, deep in my bones, that tonight was unlike any other. The Raven, our adversary cloaked in shadows and whispers, was here. The very thought sent a shiver down my spine. It was one thing to fight against the rumors, to confront the tales spun in the dim corners of our town; it was entirely another to face the embodiment of those fears, lurking just beyond the reach of light.

"Stay close," Jonah murmured, his voice steady, yet there was an urgency beneath it that made my heart race. I nodded, though my breath hitched in my throat. I could see his determination, but I also felt the weight of the night pressing down on us like a heavy blanket, stifling and oppressive.

The first blow came without warning, a sharp crack that shattered the stillness of the night. Jonah instinctively moved in front of me, his body a shield against the unseen threat. I felt a rush of panic, the kind that grips you like a vice, and then I saw him falter. A glint of metal flashed through the dark—a blade, wicked and sharp—before I registered the chaos unfolding around us.

"Jonah!" I screamed, my voice cutting through the darkness as I rushed to his side. Blood marred the fabric of his shirt, a vivid scarlet against the pale cotton, and a surge of panic rose in my throat like bile. His gaze locked onto mine, fierce and protective, even as he grimaced in pain.

"I'm fine," he gritted out, though the pallor of his face told a different story. The Raven's laughter echoed through the alley, a cold sound that twisted my insides. It was a sound I'd come to associate with malice and cunning, a prelude to something terrible.

"You think you can protect her?" The Raven's voice dripped with disdain, slithering around us like a serpent ready to strike. "You're a fool, Jonah. She's nothing but a pawn in a game you cannot win."

In that moment, the world around us narrowed to just Jonah and me. The chaos faded into a distant roar, and I could feel the weight of our situation pressing down on me. A part of me wanted to fight, to rise against the fear that clawed at my insides, but I knew I was helpless. My heart raced, a frantic drumbeat echoing the turmoil within.

"Listen to me," Jonah said, his grip tightening on my wrist as he leaned closer. "You have to get out of here. Find a way to—"

"Not without you!" The words tore from me, desperation coating each syllable. I couldn't bear the thought of leaving him behind, of walking away while he faced whatever darkness The Raven had in store for us.

Before he could respond, the shadows shifted, and suddenly, The Raven was upon us, a figure draped in darkness, eyes glinting with an unsettling glee. My breath caught in my throat as he raised his knife, the cold steel catching the moonlight, reflecting a world of nightmares.

I could feel my heart pounding in my chest, fear coiling tightly around my ribs, but I refused to cower. "Let him go!" I shouted, my voice trembling but resolute.

The Raven's laughter was a sharp, cruel sound that sliced through the air. "Oh, sweet girl. You're far too late. You think you can save him? Look around. You're already trapped."

In that moment, time seemed to freeze. Jonah's eyes searched mine, pleading for me to understand, to see the truth buried beneath our circumstances. "You don't have to do this," he said, his voice a whisper, a soft plea beneath the thunderous chaos.

But The Raven had other plans. With a swift motion, he twisted my arm, the sharp bite of pain jolting me back to reality. "Now, let's see how far your love will take you," he hissed, the knife pressing dangerously close to my throat. I could feel its cold kiss against my skin, and my heart raced, a wild thing desperate to escape.

As fear threatened to consume me, memories of Jonah flooded my mind—moments stolen between the shadows of our lives, laughter shared in quiet corners, the warmth of his hand in mine. Each memory wrapped around my heart like a lifeline, and I clung to them fiercely, drawing strength from the love that had blossomed amidst the chaos.

"Jonah!" I cried, the name spilling from my lips like a prayer.

"Don't let him win!" he shouted, his voice fierce, igniting a spark of defiance within me. I looked into his eyes, and for a moment, the world faded away, leaving just us—two souls intertwined, fighting against the darkness that threatened to tear us apart.

In that instant, I realized I would do anything to save him, to protect the fragile threads of our shared existence. The Raven's dark presence loomed, but I could feel a fire igniting within me, a fierce determination that rose above the encroaching fear. I wouldn't let this end without a fight.

The air crackled with tension, the kind that makes your skin prickle and your heart race. As The Raven's laughter echoed through the dimly lit alley, the world around us seemed to blur, a chaotic swirl of shadows and threats. Jonah lay sprawled on the ground, his breath shallow and pained, the crimson stain on his shirt growing more prominent with each passing second. I could see the glimmer of defiance in his eyes, but it was dulled by the fear creeping in. "Stay back," he gasped, his voice strained. But there was something primal in his gaze, a fierce determination that made my heart swell even amidst the turmoil.

"Look at you," The Raven mocked, circling us like a predator, the knife in his hand glinting ominously under the flickering streetlight. "So noble, yet so foolish. You think you can save him? This ends tonight." He stepped closer, and I instinctively moved to shield Jonah, my body acting on impulse as I placed myself between him and our adversary. My heart thundered against my ribs, a wild drumbeat urging me to find a way out, to protect what was mine. "You won't lay a finger on him," I shot back, my voice trembling with a mix of bravado and terror.

The Raven paused, his eyes narrowing. "Is that so? And what will you do? Your bravery is commendable, but utterly useless." He lunged forward, knife poised, and in that split second, adrenaline surged through me. I had to act. I had to fight. The world faded into a blur of instinct and desperation. Grabbing a discarded piece of metal from the ground, I swung it toward him with all my might. The blade clattered to the pavement, and in the chaos, I caught a glimpse of Jonah, his face a mask of anguish.

"Run!" he shouted, the desperation in his voice cutting through the fog of my fear. But how could I abandon him? The thought twisted in my gut like a serrated knife. I couldn't leave him behind, not now. "No, I won't leave you!" I screamed back, my voice rising over the cacophony of the night. The Raven recoiled, surprised by my sudden burst of defiance. "Ah, but you see, darling, that's where you're mistaken. You've already lost," he sneered, advancing once more.

In the dance of shadows and light, I felt an unusual calm wash over me as I drew a deep breath, channeling every ounce of strength I possessed. "You underestimate us," I said, forcing confidence into my words, though my insides twisted with dread. "Jonah and I are stronger together."

Jonah shifted, trying to push himself upright, his face pale but his spirit unyielding. "We can do this, trust me," he murmured, though I could see the pain etched in every line of his features. The Raven's eyes glinted with malice, but there was also a flicker of something else—curiosity, perhaps? "How quaint. A love story in the face of death. But love won't save you from me," he taunted, lunging forward once again.

With a surge of adrenaline, I moved to Jonah's side, ready to tackle our foe. "Maybe not, but it gives us strength." With a swift motion, I threw the metal shard toward The Raven, hoping to distract him long enough for Jonah to regain his footing. It missed its target but caught him off guard, causing him to stumble. "Now!" I yelled, pulling Jonah up with me.

He winced as he stood, but there was a fierce spark in his eyes. Together, we backed away, seeking the safety of the shadows while our enemy recovered. "We need to get out of here," I urged, glancing over my shoulder. Jonah nodded, though his breath came in ragged gasps. "Right behind you," he assured, and I could see the resolve building within him. But just as we turned to flee, a piercing shriek split the night air, and a figure burst from the shadows—a woman, wild-eyed and desperate.

"Help! Please!" she cried, rushing toward us, her hands outstretched. The Raven's expression twisted into rage. "You meddling fool!" he shouted, lunging toward her, but Jonah reacted faster. He grabbed my arm, and together we pulled the stranger into our circle. "Stay close!" he commanded, and the three of us huddled together, forming a fragile barricade against the encroaching darkness.

"Who are you?" I demanded, eyeing the newcomer. She looked disheveled, her clothes torn and dirty, a smudge of dirt streaked across her cheek. "I'm... I'm just trying to escape him," she stammered, fear etched in her features. "I saw what he did to my brother. Please, we can't let him take anyone else."

Jonah's grip on my arm tightened as The Raven laughed mockingly from the shadows. "You think this is a game? You think I'm going to let you walk away?" he spat, the menace dripping from his words. The atmosphere shifted; an electric current of danger hung in the air, the tension palpable as we stood, caught in a web of fear and uncertainty.

"Stay back!" I shouted, steeling myself for whatever came next. In the flickering light, The Raven's eyes gleamed with malicious intent. But there was something unsettling in the depths of his gaze, a hint of vulnerability perhaps, beneath the facade of menace. What had made him like this?

Suddenly, the ground trembled beneath us, and the world seemed to lurch as if reality itself was fraying at the edges. Jonah steadied himself, but I could see the fear creeping back into his expression. "We have to go now!" he urged, but I felt rooted to the spot, a storm of questions swirling in my mind.

Just as we were about to turn and run, the shadows around us twisted, and a bright flash illuminated the alley, blinding me momentarily. I stumbled, trying to shield my eyes, and when I looked again, The Raven was gone, leaving only a lingering echo of his laughter, mocking and hollow.

"Where did he go?" I whispered, my voice trembling as I scanned the alley for any sign of our tormentor. The woman clutched at my arm, her eyes wide with panic. "He's toying with us," she said, her voice barely a whisper. "He knows we're scared."

Jonah stepped forward, a frown creasing his brow. "This isn't over. He'll come back," he warned, determination lacing his tone. But in that moment, uncertainty seeped into my heart like a chilling breeze. We were not safe yet, and the game was far from finished. As I glanced down the darkened alley, the shadows loomed ominously, and I knew we were walking a tightrope between survival and despair.

# Chapter 16: Rescue and Reckoning

The warehouse loomed before us, a hulking mass of steel and shadow, its walls heavy with the secrets of those who had dared to trespass its threshold. I felt the chill of the early morning air biting through my thin jacket, a stark contrast to the heat radiating from my pounding heart. Each breath came with the metallic tang of fear, yet in that moment of palpable danger, a strange clarity settled over me. Jonah stood beside me, a steadfast presence, his jaw set and eyes ablaze with determination. I could feel the weight of his gaze, a silent promise that we would not succumb to this darkness without a fight.

As we edged closer to the entrance, the remnants of last night's storm clung to the ground, slicking the pavement and glistening like tiny diamonds. I had always found beauty in the aftermath of a storm—the way nature seemed to breathe anew, but here, surrounded by decay and neglect, the beauty felt like a cruel joke. I could almost hear the echoes of despair whispering from the peeling paint, urging us to turn back. But retreat was not an option. Not now, not after all we had faced.

We stepped into the dimly lit cavern of the warehouse, the air thick with the scent of rust and something more sinister, something that twisted in my stomach like a coiled snake. Shadows danced along the walls, stretching and retracting like the lingering remnants of nightmares, and my instincts screamed at me to flee. Jonah's hand found mine, grounding me. He squeezed gently, a lifeline in the storm of uncertainty. "We're in this together," he murmured, his voice a steady anchor amidst the chaos.

The stillness was deceptive, broken only by the distant drip of water echoing through the empty space. My senses heightened, I felt the prickling awareness of danger lurking just beyond our sight. Jonah's breath was warm against my ear as he leaned closer. "Stay close. We need to find a way to outsmart The Raven." I nodded, determination washing over me like a wave, though the fear coiled tighter around my heart.

We navigated the labyrinth of rusting machinery and broken crates, moving like shadows ourselves, quiet and deliberate. Each creak of the floorboards underfoot echoed like thunder, a reminder of the fragile line we walked between life and death. As we turned a corner, a flicker of movement caught my eye—a figure, cloaked in darkness, stalking through the wreckage. My breath caught, and I instinctively pulled Jonah back, our bodies pressing together in a protective cocoon.

"Jonah," I whispered, my voice trembling with the weight of unspoken fears. "What if he finds us?" The thought hung heavy in the air, a question laced with desperation.

"Then we fight," he replied, his voice a low growl of defiance. I admired his resolve, even as my heart raced with dread. I had seen the depths of his bravery before, but now I wondered if we were in over our heads.

Before I could respond, a sudden crash echoed through the warehouse, startling us both. The sound reverberated through the empty halls like the tolling of a bell, signaling our imminent confrontation. A surge of adrenaline propelled me forward as I slipped through the shadows, my instincts screaming for action. Jonah was right behind me, our synergy forged through the fires of hardship.

The figure emerged from the darkness, a familiar silhouette cloaked in menace—The Raven. His eyes glinted with malice as he stepped into the dim light, a predator reveling in the moment before the kill. "I've been expecting you," he sneered, his voice like gravel scraping against glass. "You thought you could escape your fate?"

I felt the heat of anger swell within me, igniting a fire I didn't know I possessed. "You don't know what we're capable of," I shot back, my words fierce and unyielding. Jonah stepped forward, standing shoulder to shoulder with me, our unity palpable. Together, we were stronger than the shadows that threatened to engulf us.

The Raven's laughter echoed, a sound devoid of joy, twisted and dark. "Ah, but I do know. You're nothing but a flickering flame, ready to be snuffed out." He lunged forward, and instinct took over. I ducked low, adrenaline coursing through my veins as I grabbed a nearby metal pipe, swinging it with all my might.

The clang of metal meeting flesh rang out, a sickening sound that reverberated through my bones. The Raven stumbled back, a look of shock etched across his face. In that instant, everything slowed—the world narrowed to the space between us, the palpable tension thickening the air. Jonah's presence bolstered my resolve as he charged forward, tackling The Raven to the ground. The struggle was fierce, a whirlwind of fists and fury as we fought for our lives, our dreams, our future.

I could hear Jonah's grunts of effort, the sounds of our struggle blending into a chaotic symphony. The warehouse, once an echoing void, transformed into a battleground where hope and despair clashed violently. My breath quickened, but I didn't waver. Every swing, every kick, was fueled by the love I felt for Jonah and the life we had envisioned together—a life that would not be extinguished by this malevolent force.

With a final push, we managed to pin The Raven to the cold, unforgiving floor. He thrashed against us, but our determination was unyielding. Jonah's eyes met mine, a shared understanding passing between us. In that moment, I knew that we would emerge from this darkness together, hand in hand, stronger than before.

As dawn began to break outside, the first rays of light spilling through the shattered windows, a sense of liberation washed over me. We had faced the monster, and against all odds, we had triumphed. The warehouse that had felt like a tomb now opened before us like the dawn of a new day, and I felt a flicker of hope ignite within my chest. But as we stood over our defeated captor, a haunting realization crept into my mind: the battle might have been won, but the war was far from over. What lay ahead, in the light of day, was a reckoning that would test the very fabric of our love and the strength we had yet to discover within ourselves.

The light of dawn seeped into the warehouse, illuminating the chaos we had just endured. Dust motes danced in the golden rays, casting a surreal glow over our bruised bodies and disheveled clothing. Jonah stood beside me, panting, his chest heaving as if he were trying to exhale the very fear we had just fought against. I could still feel the adrenaline coursing through my veins, a wild, exhilarating rush that made every small sound seem amplified, like a symphony of survival playing around us.

As we made our way toward the exit, the weight of what we had just experienced pressed down on my shoulders. I glanced back at The Raven, sprawled on the ground, his face contorted in anger and disbelief. A rush of triumph surged within me, but it was quickly chased by a flicker of concern. Had we truly defeated him, or was this merely a temporary reprieve? Jonah must have sensed my hesitation because he placed a reassuring hand on my back, guiding me forward as we stepped out into the crisp morning air.

The world outside felt like a different realm, untouched by the horror we had just left behind. The sky stretched above us in brilliant hues of orange and pink, the promise of a new day washing over the remnants of our struggle. "Do you think it's really over?" I asked, my voice quieter than I intended, as if speaking too loudly might shatter the fragile peace we had regained.

Jonah paused, his brow furrowed as he contemplated my question. "I want to believe it is," he said, his tone thoughtful, "but we can't let our guard down. The Raven won't just walk away from this. He's not the type to give up easily." His words struck a chord deep within me. I had witnessed his resilience and resourcefulness, yet the gravity of our situation made my heart sink.

A sudden rustling sound nearby made us both jump, adrenaline sparking anew. We turned, only to see a group of workers arriving to begin their shifts. They looked at us with a mix of curiosity and concern, the remnants of last night's storm still hanging in the air. "Are you two okay?" one of them called, concern etched on her face.

"We're fine," I managed to say, forcing a smile that felt more like a grimace. "Just... taking a moment to breathe." Jonah nodded, standing a bit taller, a silent shield at my side. The worker's eyes darted to the entrance we had just exited, but thankfully, she didn't press further. Instead, she went back to her duties, casting one last wary glance our way.

As we stepped away from the warehouse, the familiar sights of our neighborhood began to emerge. Sunlight kissed the sidewalks, glimmering against the dew-soaked grass, and the scent of fresh coffee wafted from a nearby café, tugging at my senses. A part of me craved that comforting normalcy—the simple joy of a warm cup in hand, the mundane chatter of morning commuters. Yet, another part felt tainted, as if the shadows of the past few hours had etched themselves into the very fabric of my being.

"Let's grab a coffee," Jonah suggested, his voice steady, a hint of the familiar warmth creeping back. "We could use a moment of normalcy after all that."

"Normalcy?" I raised an eyebrow, the corners of my mouth twitching upward. "What, you mean like discussing our new superhero status? 'Survivors of the Warehouse Wars'?"

He chuckled, the sound melting some of the tension still knotted in my chest. "Exactly. We should get capes. That would really enhance our credibility."

As we walked toward the café, I felt a soft swell of hope rising within me. Perhaps this was what we needed—a break, a reprieve before facing whatever storm still lingered on the horizon. Jonah's hand slipped into mine, a simple gesture that grounded me. The contact was electric, a reminder of our bond forged in fire and fear.

Inside the café, the aroma of coffee wrapped around us like a warm blanket, and the soft hum of conversation created a comforting backdrop. We found a small table near the window, sunlight streaming through, casting playful shadows on our faces. I could see the concern etched in Jonah's features as he surveyed the crowd. "You sure you're okay?" he asked, his voice low and careful.

"I will be," I replied, hoping to believe my own words. "Just a little shaken. But I'm here. We're together."

Jonah nodded, his eyes searching mine as if trying to read the depths of my soul. "Together," he echoed softly, a promise that lingered between us like an unbreakable thread.

After ordering our coffees, we settled into an easy conversation about everything and nothing—the kind of banter that felt both light and necessary, a balm for our bruised spirits. But underneath the surface, an undercurrent of tension remained, a silent acknowledgment of what we had escaped and the uncertainty that lay ahead.

"Do you ever think about what comes next?" I asked suddenly, the question slipping out before I could catch it. "Now that we've faced The Raven, what if there's more to uncover? More darkness lurking in the shadows?"

Jonah's expression shifted, the warmth fading slightly as he considered my words. "I think about it a lot," he admitted, his voice grave. "We've made it this far, but we need to stay vigilant. It's what we do now that matters. We can't let fear dictate our lives."

"I know." I took a sip of my coffee, the warmth spreading through me, a small comfort amidst the storm. "But I also want to live, you know? I want us to find joy in the little things, not just survive."

His eyes lit up at my words, a spark igniting something deep within him. "Then let's do it," he said, the challenge clear in his tone. "Let's find joy in the madness. Starting now."

With that, he leaned across the table, a playful grin spreading across his face. "I challenge you to find the most ridiculous thing on the menu. Loser buys dinner tonight."

I laughed, feeling lighter as we slipped back into our familiar rhythm. "You're on. But don't blame me when you end up eating something outrageous."

The playful banter continued, a sweet distraction as we let the weight of our worries drift away, at least for the moment. Yet, even in our laughter, the specter of uncertainty loomed large. The dawn had broken, but shadows still lurked just out of sight, waiting for the right moment to pounce. We were determined to embrace our freedom, but somewhere deep within, a question remained: How long could we hold on to this fragile peace before the storm returned?

With the warmth of coffee still lingering on my tongue, I leaned back in my chair, momentarily lost in the cozy buzz of the café. Outside, life buzzed with the ordinary—the soft whirr of bicycles passing, laughter from children darting down the street, and the occasional bark of a dog breaking through the hum of morning conversations. It felt surreal to be in the heart of normalcy after the storm we had just weathered. Yet, even in this sanctuary, I sensed a storm brewing beneath the surface, a whisper of unease that wouldn't quite leave me.

"What if we started a new project?" Jonah suggested, tilting his head slightly as he sipped his coffee. The steam curled around his face, creating an almost ethereal glow that softened his features. "Something that would give us a focus, a way to channel all this energy we've got buzzing around us."

I raised an eyebrow, intrigued yet cautious. "Like what? A secret club for survivors of warehouse confrontations?" The idea danced playfully on my lips, a small rebellion against the heaviness that still clung to us.

He chuckled, his eyes sparkling. "Actually, I was thinking something more like a community garden. We could grow our own vegetables, make our own salsa, you know, like a fresh start with a twist of irony."

"A community garden?" I mused, the thought tickling my imagination. "You mean turning our collective trauma into tomatoes? That's surprisingly optimistic of you."

"Why not? It'd be a safe space, something that grows over time. Besides, tomatoes are very forgiving." He leaned in closer, lowering his voice conspiratorially. "And we can always sneak in some hot peppers. Can't have it all be bland."

I laughed, picturing us, shovels in hand, defiantly cultivating life amidst the remnants of our fears. "You might be onto something," I said, warming to the idea. "It could be our way of reclaiming what we've lost—something tangible we can nurture."

As the idea took root between us, the café door swung open with a sharp jingle, the bell announcing a new arrival. A figure stepped inside, shaking off rain that had begun to drizzle again, their silhouette shrouded in a dark trench coat. The atmosphere shifted, tension rising as the stranger scanned the room with an intensity that made my skin prickle.

I caught Jonah's gaze, and the lightness of our conversation faded in an instant. "Do you know them?" he whispered, eyes narrowed, every muscle in his body tightening.

"No idea," I replied, my pulse quickening. The stranger took a few steps deeper into the café, and I couldn't help but notice the familiar outline of a face hidden beneath the shadow of the brim of their hat. It felt like a scene from a thriller, where the protagonist is suddenly thrust back into a world they thought they had escaped.

The stranger walked purposefully toward us, and my breath caught in my throat. "Is that...?" I began, but Jonah squeezed my hand, a silent warning to keep my voice low.

The figure stopped at our table, the light catching the edge of their features just enough for recognition to crash over me like a wave. It was Ava, a former friend from our shared past, someone I hadn't seen since the fallout of our tangled lives. Her once vibrant smile was now a ghost of what it used to be, replaced by a look of grave determination.

"Hey, I'm not interrupting, am I?" she said, her voice steady but laced with an edge of urgency. "We need to talk."

"What's going on?" I asked, trying to process the rush of emotions battling within me. A flicker of hope mingled with the anxiety tightening my chest. Was she here to help, or had she brought more trouble with her?

"Not here," she insisted, glancing around the café as if expecting eyes to be watching us. "It's not safe."

"Safe?" Jonah echoed, a low growl of protectiveness creeping into his tone. "We just fought our way out of a hostage situation. How much more dangerous could it get?"

"More than you know." Ava's gaze hardened, a spark igniting in her eyes. "The Raven isn't just a name. He has ties that run deeper than you can imagine. You've uncovered something bigger than you realize, and they won't let you go easily."

Her words hung heavy in the air, weighing down on us like a thick fog. A chill crawled down my spine as the implications of her statement sank in. "What do you mean 'they'?" I asked, my voice barely above a whisper.

"I can't explain everything here. Just trust me. We need to move." Ava's eyes darted to the door, her anxiety palpable. "If he finds you again... it won't just be the two of you next time. He'll come for everyone you care about."

"Isn't that a little dramatic?" Jonah challenged, but there was an undercurrent of fear in his voice. "We just took him down. How could he possibly come back?"

Ava shook her head, frustration flaring in her expression. "You don't get it! You've awakened something. They're watching, waiting. We need to go—now."

Jonah and I exchanged glances, a silent conversation passing between us. My instincts screamed for caution, yet the urgency in Ava's voice ignited a fire of concern. "Where do we go?" I finally asked, my heart racing at the prospect of stepping into the unknown once again.

"Somewhere safe," she replied. "Follow me, and keep your heads down."

Before I could respond, she turned and strode toward the exit, her figure cutting through the crowd like a beacon of hope mixed with dread. We followed, the weight of uncertainty settling in my chest. As we stepped outside, the rain began to fall heavier, each drop feeling like a harbinger of the storm that was closing in around us.

Ava led us through the streets, her pace brisk and determined, the city enveloping us in a cloak of chaos and uncertainty. "You have to understand," she said, glancing back at us, her expression grave. "You've become part of a bigger picture—a web that you didn't even know existed."

With every step, my heart pounded louder, fear and curiosity intertwining in a dance that felt both exhilarating and terrifying. The air crackled with tension as we turned down an alleyway, shadows looming large against the brick walls. Just as I opened my mouth to voice another question, a sound echoed from behind us—a familiar, chilling laugh that sent a shiver racing down my spine.

The Raven.

I turned to Jonah, panic rising in my throat as realization set in. We were being hunted, our lives once again tangled in a web of danger, and I couldn't shake the feeling that this time, the stakes were higher than they had ever been before. The chase was on, and we were caught right in the middle of it, unsure of what awaited us at the end of this dark, twisting road.

# Chapter 17: After the Storm

The soft lapping of water against the wooden dock broke the silence, creating a rhythm that soothed my frazzled nerves. I nestled deeper into the worn couch of the lakeside cottage, Jonah's warmth beside me a constant reminder that I was not alone. The crackle of the fire filled the air with a cozy scent of burning cedar, mingling with the freshness of the morning. Outside, the lake shimmered under the soft golden light, a deceptive calm in the wake of turmoil that had settled in our hearts.

"Do you think it will ever feel normal again?" I asked, my voice barely above a whisper, as if the very act of speaking might shatter the fragile peace we had found. The question hung in the air, heavy with unspoken fears. Jonah shifted slightly, his brow furrowing in thought.

"I don't know," he admitted, staring into the flames as if they held the answers. "Normal feels like a distant memory now, doesn't it? Almost like a fairytale." His tone was tinged with a wry humor that felt both comforting and poignant, a delicate balance that reflected the man sitting beside me. He had a way of finding light in the darkest corners, and I was grateful for it.

We fell into a contemplative silence, the crackling of the fire punctuating the moment. I wrapped my fingers around a steaming mug of coffee, the warmth radiating through me, grounding me in the present. I watched Jonah as he absently traced the scars on his forearm, remnants of past battles etched into his skin like badges of honor. Each mark told a story of resilience, and I admired him for it. I had witnessed his strength, but I had also seen the cracks in his facade, the vulnerability he kept tucked away.

"Do you think we'll ever go back to who we were before?" I asked, more to myself than to him. The thought lingered in the back of my mind like an uninvited guest, refusing to leave. There was a comfort in the idea of returning to a simpler time, yet I wondered if that was even possible now.

"Maybe we're not meant to go back," he replied, finally meeting my gaze. His eyes were intense, filled with an understanding that made my heart skip. "Maybe we're meant to become something new." His words resonated deep within me, sparking a flicker of hope I had thought extinguished.

"Something new?" I echoed, raising an eyebrow. "Like a new species of... what? Survivor?" I tried to lighten the mood, but the weight of his words settled heavily between us.

"Something like that," he said, a smirk dancing on his lips. "I mean, if we keep encountering death and destruction, we might evolve into something with scales or extra limbs. Who knows?"

His jest brought a laugh bubbling to the surface, breaking the tension. "Great! Just what I need—scales and extra limbs. Just what every girl dreams of."

He laughed, and the sound was like music, a melody that lifted the heaviness surrounding us. "I'd still find you beautiful, no matter what you turned into," he said, his sincerity wrapping around me like a warm embrace.

"Flattery will get you everywhere, Jonah." I nudged him playfully, feeling a warmth creep up my cheeks.

"Everywhere, huh? Well, I'll keep that in mind for the next life-and-death situation we find ourselves in." He leaned back, stretching his arms out with a mischievous grin that reminded me of the boy I had once known. The boy I had almost lost.

The fire crackled, sending a shower of sparks up the chimney, and I leaned into him, savoring the moment. It was strange how a simple act could evoke such warmth—a connection forged in fire and chaos. I let my head rest on his shoulder, drawing strength from his presence.

As the sun climbed higher in the sky, I felt the tendrils of the past creeping back in, memories of the storm we had survived, the fight against The Raven that had pushed us to our limits. The air hung heavy with the taste of ash and smoke, a reminder of how close we had come to losing everything.

"What if it comes back?" I murmured, the words slipping out before I could stop them. The dread washed over me like a wave, pulling me under.

"Then we fight again," he replied without hesitation, determination lacing his voice. "We're stronger now, you and I. We know what we're fighting for."

"What are we fighting for?" I asked, suddenly curious. "What's at stake now?"

Jonah turned to face me fully, his expression earnest. "We're fighting for the life we want. A life where we can be free to love without the shadows of the past hanging over us."

I swallowed hard, the weight of his words settling deep within me. Love felt like an elusive butterfly, beautiful and fragile, fluttering just out of reach. But in that moment, as the sun streamed through the cottage window, illuminating his features, I realized that maybe, just maybe, we could catch it together.

"Okay," I said, feeling a swell of courage. "Let's fight then."

With that declaration, a new resolve filled the air, and I knew that whatever storms lay ahead, we would face them together. The fire crackled, our laughter mingled with the sound of the lake, and in that moment, I felt a flicker of hope blossom in my heart.

The quiet of the lakeside cottage was a soothing balm for my rattled nerves, the gentle sigh of the wind through the trees a reminder that life continued, even after chaos. Jonah and I lounged together, our legs entwined on the couch, a makeshift barrier against the world outside. I inhaled the heady scent of pine and woodsmoke, closing my eyes as I leaned against him, letting the warmth of the fire seep into my bones. It was strange how easily I felt safe with him, even after the shadows we'd faced.

"I think I might have a family heirloom or two I can bribe you with," Jonah said, breaking the comfortable silence. His voice had a teasing lilt, and I opened my eyes to find him grinning at me. "There's a rustic fishing rod from the 1920s that's been collecting dust in my grandfather's garage. It might not catch fish, but it definitely tells a story."

I raised an eyebrow, intrigued. "A fishing rod? You're really pulling out all the stops, aren't you? What do I get if I reel in the big one?"

"Just your undying loyalty and friendship, of course." He flashed that disarming smile, the kind that made it impossible to stay annoyed. "And the chance to say you fished with the best, obviously."

I chuckled, imagining us on the dock, attempting to catch fish while bantering back and forth like an old married couple. "Deal. But I expect at least one wild adventure in return. The type that makes us look good in our fishing gear—something that involves epic fails and maybe a few seagulls trying to steal our lunch."

"Now that's the spirit!" he exclaimed, clearly amused by my vision. "We'll become the lakeside legends, heroes of mischief, defenders of picnic baskets!"

The playfulness of our exchange felt like a lifeline, pulling me away from the darker thoughts lurking at the edges of my mind. Jonah's ability to lighten the mood was a balm, even as I felt the weight of everything we'd faced. Yet, as the sun dipped lower in the sky, painting the room in shades of orange and gold, I sensed the unease returning.

"Do you think we're safe here?" I asked, my voice barely above a whisper. The flicker of doubt gnawed at me, refusing to be ignored. "I mean, after what happened with The Raven... what if it knows where we are?"

Jonah's smile faded, his expression turning serious. "I don't know. But we'll figure it out together. That's the whole point of this, right?" He reached out, intertwining his fingers with mine, a gesture that sent a surge of warmth coursing through me.

I leaned into him, taking comfort in his strength, but the reality of our situation loomed large. The Raven was a dark specter hovering in the background of our lives, and while we might be safe for now, I couldn't shake the feeling that it was just waiting for the perfect moment to strike again.

A sudden noise outside shattered my thoughts, a series of sharp cracks followed by the rustle of leaves. I straightened, a chill racing down my spine. "Did you hear that?"

Jonah's gaze sharpened, his body tense beside me. "I did. Probably just the wind or a deer." He paused, studying my expression. "Or it could be the town bringing us a surprise—our very own welcoming committee."

"Right. Because who wouldn't want to celebrate our return with an impromptu visit from a rogue band of deer?" I tried to inject some humor into the moment, but the tremor in my voice betrayed my anxiety.

He squeezed my hand gently. "Stay here. I'll check it out."

"No way. I'm coming with you." The defiance in my voice surprised even me, but the thought of being left alone in the cottage, surrounded by shadows and uncertainty, was far worse than facing whatever lurked outside.

With a resigned nod, Jonah stood and led the way to the door. The sun had dipped below the horizon, leaving a twilight glow that cast eerie shadows across the landscape. Each step felt like a step into a nightmare, and I could feel the adrenaline coursing through me. The air was thick with anticipation as we stepped outside, the coolness biting at our skin.

The stillness was deafening. As we crept toward the edge of the dock, the water lapping gently against the wood, I squinted into the darkness, searching for any signs of movement. The cottage creaked behind us, but it was just the house settling, or so I told myself.

"What do you see?" I whispered, not wanting to break the fragile peace but needing to know.

"Nothing yet," Jonah murmured, his voice low as he scanned the surroundings. "Just the lake and the trees."

A flash of movement caught my eye, and I turned my head sharply. "There!" I pointed towards the treeline where a figure was partially obscured by the shadows. The silhouette was lean and tall, a jarring contrast against the backdrop of nature.

Jonah's grip tightened on my hand, and I felt a rush of adrenaline. "Stay behind me," he said, a protective instinct flaring in his eyes.

Before I could respond, the figure stepped into the pale light of the moon. It was a woman, her hair wild and unkempt, and she wore a long coat that looked like it had seen better days. As she approached, the tension in my chest tightened, coiling like a spring ready to snap.

"Is this where the lost souls come to hide?" she asked, her voice eerily calm. Her eyes glinted with a strange intensity, and I shivered as an unexpected chill swept through me.

"Who are you?" Jonah demanded, stepping in front of me, his body poised like a shield.

She chuckled softly, the sound like wind chimes in a storm. "Just a friend seeking refuge, much like you. But it seems you're not alone in your little hideaway."

"Why are you here?" I asked, my heart racing. Something in her demeanor felt both disarming and threatening, a juxtaposition that set my instincts on high alert.

"I heard about The Raven," she said, her gaze shifting between us. "And I wanted to warn you. It's not finished with you yet."

A chill swept over me, and I glanced at Jonah, who wore an expression of disbelief mixed with caution. "What do you know?" he pressed, his voice steady despite the undercurrents of fear.

The woman stepped closer, her presence commanding despite her seemingly fragile frame. "The Raven is just getting started. It knows where you are, and it won't stop until it has what it wants."

The weight of her words hung in the air, suffocating and profound. An unexpected twist had arrived, shifting the narrative once again, and I could feel the ground beneath us quaking, the fragile peace we'd fought for teetering on the brink of chaos.

The woman's presence loomed over us like a storm cloud threatening to break, the air around her charged with an electric tension. Her dark hair framed her face, wild and untamed, as though she'd just emerged from the depths of a forest. The way her eyes flickered with a peculiar mix of urgency and mischief set off alarm bells in my mind. I shifted slightly behind Jonah, the instinct to hide almost overwhelming, even as curiosity tugged at me.

"What do you mean, it's not finished with us?" Jonah asked, his voice steady but edged with the unease radiating from me. I could see the wheels turning in his head, evaluating the woman as if she were an equation he needed to solve before it exploded.

"The Raven feeds on fear, on despair," she replied, taking a step closer. "And you two—" she gestured between us, "—you're like a buffet laid out just for it. You've faced it once, but it knows you now. It knows your weaknesses."

A shiver ran down my spine as her words sunk in, the imagery vivid and alarming. The thought of being prey to a creature born of darkness, a predator lurking in the shadows of our lives, sent my mind spiraling into a panic.

"Why should we trust you?" I shot back, surprising even myself with the ferocity of my tone. "You just waltz in here, spill doom and gloom, and expect us to believe you?"

She tilted her head, a slight smile playing on her lips, as if I were an amusing riddle she'd yet to solve. "Fair point. Trust is earned, not given freely. But I come with a warning, and you'd be wise to heed it."

Jonah stepped forward, a protective wall between me and the stranger. "What do you want from us?" His voice held a calm authority, but I could see the tension in his shoulders.

"Just to help," she said, the sincerity in her tone cutting through the tension momentarily. "I can show you how to prepare, how to fight back. But first, you need to understand what you're up against."

"Like a survival guide?" I asked, skepticism draping my words.

"Something like that," she replied, her eyes sparkling with mischief. "But more of a handbook for the hopelessly unprepared."

Jonah relaxed slightly, though I remained wary. "What's your name?" he asked, curiosity mingling with caution.

"Call me Iris," she said, offering a small, almost playful smile. "And believe me, if you think you've seen the worst, you're in for a surprise."

The light from the cottage flickered ominously, the shadows dancing along the walls as if mocking our predicament. I glanced over my shoulder, the familiar cocoon of safety feeling increasingly fragile. "So, what do we need to do?" I asked, my voice firmer than I felt.

Iris took a breath, her expression turning serious. "First, we need to strengthen your defenses. The Raven thrives on fear, and it will use any weakness it can find. You must confront your past and face what scares you most."

"Great. Just a casual stroll down memory lane," I muttered, my heart racing at the thought. "What's next? A group therapy session?"

"Actually, that's not a bad idea," Iris countered, her tone unexpectedly light. "But let's save the couch for later. For now, we need to gather some supplies."

"Supplies?" Jonah echoed, eyebrow raised. "Like what? Bait?"

"Not quite. More like knowledge and resources." She looked back toward the trees, the fading light casting an otherworldly glow around her. "There are places nearby where you can find what you need, but time is of the essence."

The urgency in her voice sent a shiver through me. "What happens if we don't get these supplies? What does The Raven want from us?"

"Despair, my dear," she said, her expression somber. "It feeds on your darkest fears. It wants to break you. You must understand that confronting it will require more than just bravery; it will demand everything you have."

A wave of dread washed over me. My heart pounded in my chest, echoing the uncertainty swirling around us. "And what if we fail?"

"If you fail," she said, "then it will take everything you hold dear."

The weight of her words hung heavily in the air. The world around us faded momentarily, replaced by a suffocating silence that seemed to absorb my breath.

Jonah turned to me, his gaze steady and resolute. "We're not going to fail," he said, the conviction in his voice fortifying my shaky confidence. "We can't."

"I admire your optimism," Iris interjected, her tone teasing yet sincere. "But optimism alone won't save you. We need to move. Now."

With a nod, Jonah took my hand, squeezing it tightly. We followed Iris into the gathering darkness, each step feeling like a descent into a world that was increasingly unfamiliar. As we moved through the trees, the shadows thickened, enveloping us like a shroud. The air was charged with a palpable sense of urgency, and I fought the rising tide of panic.

Iris led us through a winding path, her figure flickering in and out of the dim light, a specter weaving through the encroaching night. "We're heading to a place where knowledge lingers," she said cryptically. "Where the echoes of those who've fought before us still whisper secrets."

"What kind of place?" I asked, trying to keep my voice steady.

"The kind that will make you question everything you thought you knew."

Jonah and I exchanged a glance, the weight of uncertainty pooling between us. The trees closed in, their branches reaching like skeletal fingers, and I felt the air grow colder, thicker.

"I can feel it," I murmured, almost to myself. "Something's out there."

"Stay close," Jonah instructed, his voice a low rumble, the tension between us palpable.

Iris paused, turning to face us. "Remember, what lies ahead is only as powerful as you allow it to be. Fear can be a weapon, but so can courage."

Before I could respond, a distant rustle shattered the stillness, drawing our attention. My heart raced as the shadows seemed to thicken, swirling with an energy that felt alive.

"What was that?" Jonah whispered, his grip tightening on my hand.

"I don't know," I replied, dread pooling in my stomach. The noise grew louder, a cascade of movement that sent a jolt of fear through me.

Then, without warning, a figure lunged from the darkness—a swift motion, a shadow that materialized into a nightmare. My breath caught in my throat as the world around us warped, and in that moment, I realized we weren't just facing The Raven anymore; we were about to confront the very embodiment of our fears.

Jonah stepped in front of me, a protective instinct burning in his eyes, but as the figure drew closer, I could see that it wasn't just a phantom. It was something more, something sinister—and it was coming for us.

# Chapter 18: Shadows Resurface

The afternoon sun dipped low on the horizon, casting long shadows across the polished floors of my art studio. It was a sanctuary of creativity, with canvases leaning against the walls, their vibrant colors whispering stories of beauty and chaos. Each stroke of paint felt like an echo of my own tumultuous journey, a dance of colors mirroring the turmoil and triumphs I had endured. I inhaled deeply, letting the scent of turpentine and fresh paint wrap around me like a warm embrace. This was my refuge, my haven, and for a fleeting moment, it felt untouched by the dark tendrils of the past that had begun to creep back into my life.

But just as I began to breathe a little easier, the first message arrived. It appeared on my phone as if conjured from thin air, a simple text that sent a shiver down my spine. "The Raven is watching." My heart raced, an old fear reawakening from its slumber. I stared at the screen, the words blurring into an ominous haze. Jonah, my steadfast anchor in the storm, sensed my tension before I could voice it. He stood by the door, arms crossed, his brow furrowed in that way that always made me feel both secure and vulnerable at the same time.

"Is it him?" Jonah asked, stepping closer, his voice a low rumble that reverberated through the quiet room.

I turned to meet his gaze, the weight of my silence pressing heavily between us. "It's just a message," I replied, attempting to keep my tone light, but the tremor in my voice betrayed me. "I don't want to jump to conclusions."

Jonah's expression hardened, his protective instincts flaring like a fire igniting in dry brush. "You don't jump. You fly, and you don't need a warning to know when the air turns electric." His eyes glinted with that fierce determination I had grown to love. He always had a way of cutting through my indecision, grounding me when I felt the world tilt on its axis.

As the sun melted into a canvas of oranges and purples outside, we settled at my worn oak table, cluttered with brushes and half-finished projects. Jonah pulled up a chair, leaning over my phone as if it contained the answers we desperately sought. With each new message that flashed across the screen, my pulse quickened—"You think you're safe? Think again." "Art is just the beginning." They were taunts, like arrows shot from the dark, each one piercing through my fragile sense of security.

"Let's not hide," Jonah said, his voice low and steady, igniting a flame of resolve within me. "We can't let him control us. We need to find out what he wants." His fierce loyalty was intoxicating, and it propelled me into action. No longer was I a passive recipient of fear; I was ready to confront it.

We began to sift through the messages, attempting to decipher their meaning like a puzzle waiting to be solved. As we delved deeper, a pattern emerged—a breadcrumb trail leading us toward an underground auction, a sinister affair where stolen art pieces were traded in the shadows. My heart raced at the thought. The excitement of the chase intertwined with the dread of what lurked beneath the surface. I could feel the adrenaline coursing through me, a heady mix of fear and exhilaration.

"Are you sure you want to do this?" Jonah asked, his brow creased in concern. "It could get dangerous."

"I've faced danger before," I replied, determination flooding my voice. "And I won't let fear dictate my life. Not now, not ever." I reached for his hand, squeezing it tightly, feeling the warmth of his skin against mine. "We're in this together."

A small smile broke through his worry, and for a moment, we were just two partners on a thrilling quest. "Together," he echoed, his voice a comforting balm that soothed my frayed nerves.

As night fell, we donned our disguises—black leather jackets, beanies pulled low over our brows, and a sense of purpose that electrified the air around us. We parked Jonah's motorcycle a few blocks from the venue, the engine's rumble still vibrating in my chest as we walked the dimly lit streets. The city, usually alive with noise, felt eerily quiet, the kind of silence that makes your skin prickle.

The auction was nestled in the basement of a seemingly abandoned warehouse, a façade that cleverly masked the activities within. We approached, heartbeats synchronized in a rhythm of anticipation and fear. A group of figures hovered near the entrance, their voices a low murmur, punctuated by the occasional burst of laughter. Each laugh sent a ripple of dread through me; the shadows from my past were not merely specters—they were flesh and blood.

"Stick close to me," Jonah murmured, and I nodded, pulling my jacket tighter around me, a flimsy armor against the encroaching darkness. As we slipped inside, the atmosphere shifted dramatically. The air was thick with tension, mingled with the scent of expensive cigars and the metallic tang of adrenaline. Art pieces adorned the walls, stolen treasures glinting under dim lighting—each one a story of loss, a tale of betrayal.

In that moment, I felt both exhilarated and terrified, an intoxicating blend that heightened my senses. My eyes darted around, absorbing every detail—the flickering lights, the whispers that danced through the air, and the sharp, calculating gazes of the bidders. We were in their world now, and the thrill of danger wrapped around me like a lover's embrace.

Jonah caught my eye, a silent communication passing between us. The game was on, and as the first bid rang out like a gunshot, I knew we had crossed an invisible line into a realm where shadows held dominion, and the thrill of the chase was just beginning.

The auction room buzzed with a chaotic energy that thrummed through the air, electrifying every nerve in my body. As I stood beside Jonah, the flickering overhead lights cast a surreal glow on the art that surrounded us, illuminating pieces that had been ripped from the very fabric of their creators' souls. Each painting, sculpture, and artifact was a testament to the beauty that had been stolen, echoing the pain that resonated in the hearts of the artists who had lost them. My fingers itched to reach out, to touch the textured canvases that felt like a lifeline to another world, but I held back. This wasn't a sanctuary; it was a battleground.

"Are we really doing this?" I whispered to Jonah, keeping my voice low amidst the din of hushed conversations and the rustle of expensive suits. I felt both exhilarated and terrified, a cocktail of emotions swirling within me. The stakes had never felt higher.

Jonah glanced around, his eyes sharp as he surveyed the room. "We're not here to admire the decor," he replied, a hint of mischief creeping into his tone, despite the seriousness of our mission. "We're here to find answers. And maybe—just maybe—give The Raven a reason to rethink his choices."

A chuckle bubbled up from my throat, surprising me. "You make it sound like we're in some kind of action movie. What's next, a dramatic slow-motion walk across the room?"

"Only if you promise to wear shades," he quipped back, the corner of his mouth curling into that lopsided grin that always made my heart race.

Before I could respond, an imposing figure stepped onto a small platform at the front of the room, commanding immediate attention. The crowd hushed, eyes turning toward the auctioneer—a sleek man in a tailored suit, his demeanor as sharp as the cufflinks glinting on his wrists. "Ladies and gentlemen," he began, his voice smooth like silk, "welcome to our exclusive event this evening. We have a selection of extraordinary pieces, each with its own rich history."

I leaned closer to Jonah, my curiosity piqued. "Do you think he knows the backstories of these pieces? Or is he just here to sell the secrets?"

"Probably the latter," Jonah said, scanning the crowd for any familiar faces. "But secrets have a way of unraveling when you pull the right threads."

The auctioneer continued, unveiling a stunning painting that glimmered under the dim lights. "Our first piece is a modern masterpiece—stolen, as many of you know, from the prestigious gallery on Fifth Avenue. The artist's vision, though lost to us for now, remains eternally vibrant in this work."

My breath caught in my throat. The piece he held was familiar; it had graced the walls of my own gallery not long before its disappearance. My heart raced, a mixture of indignation and outrage fueling my resolve. "Jonah, that's—"

"I know," he interrupted, his eyes narrowing as he watched the auctioneer closely. "We need to play this smart. Wait for the right moment."

I nodded, the adrenaline coursing through me like wildfire, igniting every thought and feeling. As the bidding began, I forced myself to focus, my gaze flitting between the auctioneer and the buyers in the crowd. Each bid escalated the tension, the stakes climbing higher with every offer shouted across the room. I could feel Jonah's presence beside me, a steady anchor in the storm of emotions that threatened to pull me under.

Then, as the bids soared into the thousands, a sudden commotion erupted at the back of the room. A woman, impeccably dressed in a crimson gown, pushed through the crowd, her face a mask of determination. "This is wrong! You're selling stolen property!" she shouted, her voice ringing out like a clarion call.

The auctioneer's calm demeanor faltered, eyes flashing with annoyance. "Ma'am, I assure you, all transactions are legal—"

"Legal? Are you serious?" She pointed an accusatory finger. "You know exactly what you're doing! You can't profit from someone else's misfortune."

Gasps rippled through the crowd, and for a moment, I caught Jonah's eyes, a shared understanding passing between us. This was our chance. While the auctioneer scrambled to regain control, Jonah leaned closer. "We need to find a way to use this chaos to our advantage."

"I'm on it," I whispered, already formulating a plan. With the attention diverted, I slipped into the crowd, moving toward the back of the room where the woman had just emerged. She was a force of nature, and I needed to know her story.

"Excuse me," I called out, catching up with her just as she reached a corner. "Are you alright?"

She turned, her fiery spirit undiminished even in this moment of distress. "Do I look alright?" she snapped, brushing a stray hair from her face. "I just tried to expose a den of thieves, and nobody cares!"

"I care," I assured her, taking a deep breath. "My name is—"

"Ravenna," she cut me off, her eyes darting over my shoulder to ensure no one was listening. "You're not with them, are you?"

"Not at all," I replied quickly. "I'm here to find out more about these stolen pieces. I think we might have a common enemy."

She narrowed her eyes, studying me, then nodded slightly, a flicker of trust sparking between us. "Then you need to know this—The Raven is not just some faceless villain. He's a collector with a taste for destruction. He thinks he can control the art world, and it's time someone stood up to him."

Her words ignited a fire within me. "We can't let him continue this. But how do we fight back?"

Ravenna stepped closer, her voice dropping to a conspiratorial whisper. "There's a network of us, artists and advocates, ready to take him down. But we need solid evidence of his dealings, something more than just hearsay."

Just then, a loud crash echoed through the room, yanking both of our attentions back to the auction. One of the sculptures had toppled, sending shards of marble splintering across the floor. The auctioneer cursed loudly, and the crowd erupted into chaos as people scrambled to avoid the debris.

"Now's our chance," I urged Ravenna, a mix of adrenaline and determination surging through me. "Let's find what we need before the whole place descends into madness."

We slipped away from the fray, moving deeper into the shadows of the warehouse, hearts racing in sync as we stepped into the unknown. The thrill of the hunt pulsed through my veins, and in that moment, surrounded by chaos and uncertainty, I felt more alive than I had in ages. Together, we would confront the darkness, unravel the secrets that bound us to The Raven, and perhaps, in doing so, reclaim not just the art but the pieces of ourselves that had been lost along the way.

The warehouse was a maze of half-lit corners and flickering shadows, each step we took echoing like a heartbeat in the chaos of the auction. Ravenna and I moved swiftly, our senses sharpened by the palpable tension that hung in the air like the scent of smoke after a fire. My pulse quickened, the thrill of discovery mingling with the dread of what we might find. Art was a passion of mine, a lifeline, and now it felt like a double-edged sword, cutting through both beauty and darkness.

"Which way?" Ravenna whispered, urgency edging her voice. The sounds of the crowd had faded, swallowed by the cavernous space around us.

"Let's head toward the back," I suggested, gesturing toward a narrow passage shrouded in shadows. "There might be a storage area or an office—somewhere they keep records."

With a shared nod, we pressed forward, the dim lighting casting elongated shadows that danced along the walls. The deeper we went, the more the atmosphere shifted from chaotic energy to a sinister silence, as if we were slipping into another world entirely.

"Do you think they keep everything here?" Ravenna asked, her brow furrowed. "I mean, if this is truly an underground operation, they must have some serious secrets."

"Somewhere," I replied, my voice steady despite the anxious flutter in my stomach. "Let's find those secrets. They might lead us right to The Raven."

As we rounded a corner, we stumbled upon a small room, the door slightly ajar. Peering inside, I could see shelves lined with canvases wrapped in dust and dark cloths, their identities hidden from view. My heart raced. This was it.

"Let's check it out," I murmured, pushing the door open wider. It creaked ominously, revealing a trove of treasures tucked away, their very presence a testament to the corruption festering in the art world.

I stepped inside, my fingers itching to uncover the hidden stories that lay beneath the fabric. The room felt thick with secrets, and I could almost hear the echoes of artists' souls crying out for justice. Ravenna joined me, her eyes wide as she scanned the space, the weight of our mission hanging heavily in the air.

"Help me with this," I said, tugging at a canvas covered in a heavy, moth-eaten cloth. As it fell away, the vibrant colors burst forth like fireworks—an exquisite piece, an artist I recognized but whose work had been shrouded in mystery since its disappearance. "This...this is incredible!"

"Look at the condition of it," Ravenna said, moving closer to inspect the painting. "If it's here, what else is?"

We began pulling away cloth after cloth, revealing stolen masterpieces, each one whispering its tale of theft and loss. Time slipped away as we became engrossed in the beauty and pain captured on each canvas. But amid the wonder, I could feel a growing unease. This felt too easy, too perfect, as if we had walked into a trap disguised as an art gallery.

Suddenly, a loud crash echoed from the main room, jolting us from our reverie. "What was that?" I whispered, my heart racing anew.

"I don't know, but it doesn't sound good," Ravenna replied, her eyes darting toward the door. "We should get out of here."

Before we could move, the door swung open, and a tall figure stepped inside. The light from the hallway cast a stark shadow across his face, but I could see the unmistakable glint of recognition in his eyes. It was the auctioneer, the very man who had led the event we had infiltrated.

"Ah, I see we have some uninvited guests," he said, a chilling smile creeping across his lips. "How lovely of you to join the party."

I took a step back, heart pounding against my ribs. "What do you want?" I demanded, trying to sound braver than I felt.

He chuckled softly, a sound devoid of warmth. "What do I want? I want what everyone wants—power and control. But it seems you two have stumbled upon something far beyond your understanding."

"What do you mean?" Ravenna shot back, her tone fierce. "You're selling stolen art! You think we're just going to stand by and let this happen?"

"Oh, but my dear, you misunderstand. This isn't just about art. It's about influence. Connections. Money. You see, I'm not merely an auctioneer; I'm a curator of power. Every piece here has its place in a much larger game."

"What game?" I pressed, my voice rising as panic began to creep in. "And what do you plan to do with us?"

His smile widened, and the shadows behind him seemed to grow darker, enveloping the room like a shroud. "That depends on how cooperative you decide to be."

Before I could react, the sound of heavy footsteps echoed outside the room, closing in on us. My heart dropped as the door creaked further open, revealing two more figures, menacing and dressed in dark suits that screamed danger. The air thickened with tension, the realization hitting me that we were cornered.

"Raven," I whispered urgently, "we need to find a way out. Now."

The auctioneer's expression turned predatory, and he leaned closer, his voice a silky whisper. "I'm afraid there's no escape. You've wandered into the lion's den, and now, my dear, it's time to play."

Ravenna and I exchanged a frantic glance, the weight of our situation crashing down like a tidal wave. The pieces of art around us, once a beacon of hope, now felt like the final frame of a horror film. We were caught in a web, each thread tightening around us, leaving no room for escape.

Just as I felt the air grow thick with despair, I caught sight of a window at the far end of the room, its frame dusty but ajar. Hope flared within me, fierce and bright. "Raven, follow my lead!"

As the men advanced, I dashed toward the window, adrenaline coursing through my veins, my heart pounding like a war drum. "We might just have a chance!" I shouted over my shoulder, the urgency of the moment igniting my every instinct.

But just as I reached for the window, the auctioneer's voice echoed behind me, cutting through the chaos. "You think you can run? You're not just escaping from me. You're stepping into a world that you don't understand. And trust me, you will regret it."

Ignoring his words, I pushed the window open, the cool night air washing over me like a refreshing tide. But as I prepared to climb through, a hand gripped my shoulder, yanking me back. The world spun as I was pulled away from the only escape I could see.

In that heartbeat, as I fought against the grip that threatened to pull me into darkness, I realized that the shadows weren't just resurfacing; they were closing in, and with them, the very essence of danger I had tried so desperately to outrun.

# Chapter 19: The Heart of Darkness

The air pulsed with an electric anticipation, wrapping around me like the layers of silk in my gown. Each step I took echoed against the creaking wooden floorboards of the dilapidated mansion, a once-grand estate now suffocating beneath years of neglect. Shadows clung to the corners, eager to swallow the secrets whispered among the wealthiest bidders in the city. Laughter mingled with the sharp clinks of crystal glasses, an intoxicating blend that belied the undercurrent of tension. My heart raced, but I wore my confidence like armor, a carefully curated mask that shielded my vulnerability.

Jonah stood beside me, exuding an effortless charm that seemed to cut through the thick atmosphere. His tailored suit, a deep navy that complemented my gown, emphasized the rugged angles of his jaw. He flashed me a quick smile, the kind that could melt glaciers and embolden the timid. "Ready for this?" he asked, his voice low and warm, barely rising above the din. I nodded, gripping the small clutch that held our plan, each breath filled with the weight of what lay ahead.

The room was a kaleidoscope of opulence and desperation, the flickering candlelight revealing glints of gold and the sparkle of diamonds worn like badges of honor. A group of art dealers huddled near a makeshift bar, their voices a blend of haughty bravado and concealed eagerness. I recognized a few of them from previous encounters, their faces etched with a mixture of greed and ambition. They were more than mere participants; they were players in a dangerous game where the stakes were not just wealth, but lives.

With a deep breath, I let the allure of the art world wash over me, the promise of beauty mingling with the tension that crackled in the air. I had spent months piecing together clues, following the trail of The Raven, the elusive figure behind this underground auction. Rumors whispered of a stolen masterpiece—one that could rewrite history. If we secured it, it would not only be a personal victory but a triumph against the forces that threatened to consume us.

As we edged closer to the front of the room, my eyes caught sight of the prize. It hung on the wall, partially obscured by a heavy velvet curtain, its frame adorned with intricate carvings that hinted at a past filled with grandeur. My pulse quickened as I studied the canvas, the brushstrokes a riot of colors promising untold stories hidden within its depths. The description we had deciphered hinted at its value, both monetary and historical. This was it—the moment I had waited for.

"Let's make our move," Jonah whispered, his breath warm against my ear. With a nod, we shifted toward the painting, weaving through the crowd, our movements fluid, as if we were part of an elaborate dance choreographed by fate. Just as we reached the curtain, a sudden commotion erupted nearby. Voices raised in anger and confusion punctuated the air, drawing every eye toward the disturbance.

A tall man, his suit crisp and out of place amidst the elegant chaos, stood with a piece of art in hand, waving it like a flag of rebellion. "This isn't just a painting; it's a crime scene!" he shouted, his voice laced with indignation. Whispers rippled through the crowd, curiosity mingling with dread. The dealer's words hung heavy, each syllable a lead weight in my stomach. I exchanged a quick glance with Jonah, the unspoken tension between us palpable.

"Stay close," he murmured, slipping his hand into mine, fingers intertwining as we edged back into the shadows. The crowd was shifting, the excited energy morphing into something more volatile, and I could feel the pulse of danger thrumming beneath the surface. It was a dance of predators, and we were teetering on the edge, caught between the thrill of the hunt and the risk of being exposed.

The art dealer's voice rose again, cutting through the chatter, "This painting is stolen! The Raven thinks he can outsmart us, but he's made a grave mistake." Gasps punctuated the room, and I felt the collective intake of breath as people began to comprehend the implications of his declaration. The stakes had escalated beyond mere bidding; this was a challenge to authority, a rebellion that could unravel the carefully woven threads of deception.

Jonah squeezed my hand, his grip firm and reassuring. "We need to get that painting before anyone else does," he said, urgency sharpening his tone. I could see the determination in his eyes, a fire ignited by the chaos unfolding around us. I nodded, a flicker of resolve igniting in my own chest. We had come too far to turn back now.

With deft movements, we slipped through the throng, each step bringing us closer to our goal, the stolen painting almost within reach. The crowd began to break apart, people scrambling in different directions, drawn either to the drama unfolding or away from the threat of exposure. We maneuvered through the chaos, adrenaline surging as we approached the curtain that held our prize.

Just as I reached for the fabric, a hand shot out from the crowd, gripping my wrist tightly. I turned, ready to fight, my heart pounding as I met the sharp gaze of a familiar face—one that sent a chill spiraling through my veins. The tension in the air thickened as recognition dawned. This was not just a random encounter; it was a confrontation with my past, and the stakes had never felt higher.

My gaze locked onto the familiar face that gripped my wrist with a force that felt all too familiar, sending a shiver of recognition coursing through me. A sly smile twisted across the lips of Marco, a ghost from my past who had a penchant for stirring trouble like it was his favorite cocktail. His presence in this volatile moment felt as unexpected as a summer storm. I had spent years weaving a tapestry of careful decisions to distance myself from his chaotic energy, and here he was, materializing from the shadows just as I was about to seize the most critical piece in my quest.

"Fancy seeing you here," he drawled, a hint of mockery in his tone, eyes glinting with mischief. The room around us continued to swirl with drama, but in this moment, it felt as if we were encased in our own little bubble, suspended in time. "Are you here to bid, or have you graduated to thievery?"

"Funny, I was just about to say the same about you," I retorted, forcing a smirk to mask my unease. Marco always had a way of unsettling me, as if he could peer into the depths of my carefully constructed armor and expose the soft underbelly within. "Last I checked, you weren't invited to this exclusive soirée."

"Neither were you, darling," he shot back, his voice laced with that insufferable confidence that made my skin crawl. "But here we are, two uninvited guests crashing the party. You must really be desperate if you're willing to get your hands dirty."

"Desperation is an interesting word," I replied, forcing my tone to remain light even as my pulse quickened. "You should know all about that, considering how you claw your way into every room with your charming personality." My eyes darted around, searching for Jonah, hoping he hadn't gotten caught up in the throng of bidders or the escalating tension surrounding us.

Marco chuckled, the sound smooth yet tinged with a hint of danger. "You think you can play this game without me? I've seen how far you've come, but you're still a step behind. The Raven isn't just some art thief; he's a mastermind. And here you are, trying to match wits with the best of them." His grip on my wrist tightened, a physical reminder that our fates were now entwined in this chaotic web.

I had always known Marco was dangerous, a seductive force that could turn even the most calculated plans into a whirlwind of chaos. "Let go of me," I said, forcing the words out through gritted teeth, determination fueling my voice. "I don't need your help, and I certainly don't need you dragging me down."

He released me with a flick of his wrist, a devil-may-care attitude that made my blood boil. "You're mistaken if you think you can do this alone. This isn't just about the painting anymore; it's about survival. The Raven has eyes everywhere, and trust me, he's not above playing dirty."

As the room buzzed with newfound tension, I felt the edges of panic begin to unfurl like a tattered banner. If Marco was here, that could only mean trouble. "What do you know about him?" I asked, trying to regain some control over the spiraling situation. "How do you fit into all of this?"

His expression shifted, seriousness replacing the playful banter. "Let's just say I have my own reasons for wanting to find The Raven. The stakes are higher than you realize, and you're not the only one searching for answers." His eyes flickered toward the crowd, scanning for unseen threats. "If you want to walk away from this alive, we might have to consider an alliance."

"An alliance with you? Really?" My skepticism was palpable, and I crossed my arms defensively. "You're not exactly known for your loyalty, Marco. You'll stab anyone in the back if it means getting ahead."

"True," he conceded, a wry smile curving his lips. "But I also have my limits. And right now, we share a common goal. You want that painting, and I want The Raven. So, what do you say? Team up for the time being, at least until we both get what we want?"

Before I could respond, the crowd erupted again, a wave of chaos surging through the room. The art dealer who had earlier raised the alarm was now shouting something about a bidding war, and people began to jostle for position, their eyes glimmering with ambition. Marco and I exchanged a look—one that spoke of reluctant understanding. We had no choice but to navigate this storm together.

"Alright," I said, my voice steady despite the turmoil around us. "But if you try anything funny, I won't hesitate to throw you to the wolves."

"Sweetheart, I wouldn't dream of it," he replied, his tone dripping with mock sincerity. "Now, let's get that painting."

We slipped into the throng, moving with purpose as the crowd surged toward the raised platform where the auctioneer stood. A beautiful woman draped in emerald satin took center stage, her voice smooth as silk, coaxing the bidders to offer higher and higher. "Ladies and gentlemen, tonight we unveil a masterpiece that has eluded many, a piece of art that carries with it a legacy shrouded in mystery. I present to you—The Night's Embrace."

The painting was revealed, a vibrant canvas bursting with swirling colors and haunting figures, each brushstroke steeped in an otherworldly allure. Gasps swept through the crowd, the atmosphere thickening with desire and ambition. I felt Jonah's presence beside me, his focus unwavering as he locked eyes with me. There was a shared understanding that we needed to act quickly.

As the bidding began, I felt Marco's gaze shift, calculating and observant. "Let me take the lead," he said, a hint of mischief dancing in his eyes. "Trust me; I know how to play these sharks."

"Fine, but don't you dare embarrass me," I shot back, watching as the numbers began to soar. Marco moved into action, engaging the other bidders with a confidence that turned heads. I marveled at how effortlessly he slipped into this world, his charm cutting through the tension like a knife. He made it look easy, and I felt a begrudging respect creep in, even as I reminded myself of the danger lurking beneath his polished exterior.

The auctioneer called for bids, her voice echoing against the walls, and Marco leaned in closer, his breath warm against my ear. "Get ready. I'll start high, but you need to be prepared to back me up. If we want this, we have to outsmart everyone in this room."

"I'm ready," I said, my resolve solidifying. As Marco raised his hand, signaling our bid, I could sense the shift in the atmosphere. The other bidders turned their attention toward us, and for the first time, I felt the thrill of competition racing through my veins. The stakes were higher than I ever imagined, but with Marco by my side, the fire ignited within me—our shared ambition would either lead to triumph or ruin.

The moment the auctioneer's gavel descended, the air thickened with palpable tension, a drumroll of anticipation echoing through the room. Marco had successfully stirred the waters, drawing eyes toward us, and with each bid we made, I could feel the weight of scrutiny bearing down. The bids climbed higher, a cacophony of numbers swirling around us like confetti in a whirlwind, and I struggled to keep pace with the stakes escalating before our eyes. The other bidders, a collection of glittering suits and jeweled dresses, mirrored the greed and ambition that coursed through my veins, a potent mix that made my heart race.

"Twenty-five thousand," Marco called out, his voice steady and commanding. I felt a rush of adrenaline at the audacity of it all. I had seen his bravado before, but this was something else entirely—a dance on the edge of a razor, a tightrope walk between danger and desire.

A murmur swept through the crowd, whispers of shock mingling with admiration. I glanced sideways at Marco, noting how effortlessly he navigated this treacherous landscape. It was a skill I admired, even if it was tinged with a twinge of jealousy. "What's the plan if they counter?" I asked, the weight of uncertainty settling in my stomach.

"Leave the counters to me," he replied, a grin tugging at his lips. "Just stay ready to back me up. I've got a few tricks up my sleeve."

As the auctioneer raised her gavel again, my heart pounded in rhythm with her next call. "Do I hear thirty thousand?" The room held its breath, the air thick with possibility. I could almost taste the tension, sharp and metallic. A hand shot up across the room, a rival bidder whose face I didn't recognize, his expression unreadable beneath the flickering candlelight.

"Thirty-five," he said, his voice dripping with confidence.

Marco's smile faded slightly, but his resolve remained unbroken. "Forty!" The word shot out like a cannon, and the crowd responded with an impressed ripple.

My breath caught as I realized just how high we were reaching. "We're playing with fire here," I murmured, my unease creeping back in. "What if we draw too much attention?"

"Attention is the name of the game," Marco said, his eyes glinting with a fervor that made my pulse quicken. "Besides, what's a little heat without some fireworks?"·

As the bidding continued, I kept a watchful eye on the crowd, my instincts honed from years of navigating treacherous waters. I spotted Jonah across the room, his gaze locked onto me, a subtle nod of encouragement sending a wave of calm through me. We were in this together, even if I was now tethered to Marco in ways I couldn't quite comprehend.

"Forty-five thousand," I called out, feeling the thrill of the gamble invigorate me. I had never been one for high stakes, but here I was, immersed in a world that felt electric and alive.

The auctioneer's gavel raised once more, and she scanned the room, her voice slicing through the tension. "Fifty thousand! Going once, going twice..." The countdown began, and I felt a surge of triumph as I caught the glimmer of a potential victory on the horizon.

Before she could finish, a figure emerged from the shadows, gliding toward the front with an air of undeniable authority. It was a woman dressed in a striking crimson gown, her hair cascading like liquid rubies around her shoulders. The crowd parted for her as if she were a force of nature. Her presence demanded attention, and even the auctioneer paused, momentarily caught off guard.

"I'm afraid you'll have to do better than that," she purred, her voice smooth as silk. "You see, I have my eyes set on The Night's Embrace, and I'm willing to offer seventy thousand."

Gasps echoed around the room, and I felt my heart plummet. This woman was not just a player; she was a formidable opponent, one whose reputation hung in the air like a dark cloud.

"Seventy-five," Marco retorted quickly, his confidence undeterred.

"Eighty," the woman shot back, her eyes sparkling with mischief. The tension crackled, a high-stakes poker game where every player held their cards close to their chests, and I was struck by the realization that we were now tangled in a web much larger than our own ambitions.

"Let me handle this," Marco whispered, leaning closer, his breath warm against my ear. "Trust me."

My stomach churned with apprehension, but I nodded, forcing myself to remain calm. The stakes had escalated beyond our control, and I could see Jonah moving through the crowd, drawing closer, the expression on his face a mix of concern and determination.

"Eighty-five," Marco called out, raising his hand like a general preparing for battle.

"Are we really going to let her waltz in here and take what we want?" I asked, my voice tight with frustration.

"Relax, darling," Marco replied, his tone teasing. "I've got this. Just stay close."

But the woman didn't flinch; her gaze remained steady and unwavering, a predator sizing up her prey. "You'll need more than charm to win this one," she taunted, her smile like a snake ready to strike. "Let's see what you're really made of."

The crowd's excitement swelled, energy pulsing like a heartbeat. "Ninety," I declared, unable to hold back, propelled by a mix of desperation and defiance.

"Ninety-five," Marco countered smoothly, a twinkle in his eye.

"Going once," the auctioneer said, the atmosphere teetering on the brink of chaos, "going twice...?"

Just then, the lights flickered ominously, a stutter that sent a shiver of apprehension through the room. Gasps erupted as a loud crash echoed from the back of the mansion, a commotion that cut through the bidding frenzy like a knife. The chandelier swayed, its crystals clattering against one another, and a sense of dread settled over the crowd.

"What was that?" I whispered, adrenaline coursing through my veins, the thrill of the auction now tainted with the taste of danger.

Before anyone could respond, the front doors burst open, revealing a cadre of men clad in black, their expressions grim, eyes scanning the room with a calculated intensity. "Everyone stay calm!" one of them shouted, a commanding presence that commanded immediate attention. "We have reason to believe this auction is under surveillance. Everyone here is now a suspect."

The tension shifted into a whirlwind of confusion, as whispers erupted among the bidders, uncertainty gripping the atmosphere like a vise. Marco turned to me, urgency flashing in his eyes. "We need to get out of here. Now."

But before I could respond, the auctioneer stepped forward, her bravado faltering for the first time. "What do you mean surveillance? We're just here to bid!"

The man in black stepped closer, his voice low but firm. "I suggest you all keep your heads down and listen. We need to find The Raven, and we need to do it fast. Anyone who gets in our way... well, let's just say it won't end well."

With that, chaos erupted, a mass exodus of wealthy bidders scrambling for the exits, the tension morphing into sheer panic. I grasped Marco's arm, my heart racing as adrenaline surged. "What do we do?"

But even as I asked, the answer hung in the air, uncertain and precarious. I glanced back toward Jonah, only to see him caught in the throng, a look of alarm on his face as the reality of the moment crashed down around us.

"Stick with me," Marco said, pulling me toward a side door, his grip tight and unwavering.

But just as we made our move, a piercing scream shattered the chaos, echoing through the mansion like a death knell. The floor beneath us trembled, and I turned to see the crimson-dressed woman standing defiantly at the center of the room, her eyes ablaze with fury and a hint of something darker, her laughter rising above the panic.

"Let the games begin!" she called, her voice a siren's song that sent chills down my spine.

And in that moment, everything changed. The night had morphed into something I could never have anticipated, a storm of betrayal, ambition, and danger that promised to engulf us all.

# Chapter 20: The Web Tightens

The air thrummed with tension as the auctioneer's gavel slammed down, echoing through the grand hall like a battle cry. I stood at the edge of a sprawling crowd, a sea of elegant evening wear and shining accessories, yet the beauty of it all felt suffocating, a gilded cage hiding a monstrous predator. Each shout of a bid, each clang of that gavel sent ripples of anxiety coursing through me. The opulent chandeliers overhead swayed slightly, casting flickering shadows that danced around the room, making every face I saw seem vaguely sinister. The Raven had orchestrated this chaos with a maestro's precision, and I was caught in the web, struggling to escape.

Jonah had been at my side, a steadying presence amidst the swirling uncertainty. His warm brown eyes, which usually held a spark of mischief, were now clouded with concern. I remember the way he brushed a loose strand of hair behind my ear, whispering words of comfort that felt like a lifeline in the storm of our lives. But now, in this frantic frenzy, he was gone, swallowed by the crowd, and my heart lurched in my chest. Panic surged, forcing my pulse to quicken as I wove through the throng, each face a blur of exquisite dresses and tailored suits, all too absorbed in their own ambitions to notice the danger lurking just beneath the surface.

"Excuse me! Pardon me!" I squeaked, elbows at the ready, each shove creating more distance between me and Jonah. The laughter of wealthy bidders rang hollow in my ears, an unsettling counterpoint to the urgency pulsing within me. It felt absurd to be at an auction where fortunes were being made while our lives hung by a thread, yet here we were—bids skyrocketing as if the items being sold were worth more than the very souls fighting for their safety.

It was in the far corner of the room, amidst the flickering light and shadows, that I spotted him. Jonah stood rigid, his back pressed against a marble column, facing a group of men whose crisp suits could do nothing to mask the menace in their eyes. Their laughter was low and threatening, a guttural sound that twisted my stomach into knots. As I watched, one of the henchmen leaned in closer, his lips curling into a grin that sent a jolt of fear racing through me.

"Let him go!" The words erupted from my mouth before I even had time to think, adrenaline igniting every nerve in my body. I pushed my way forward, hands clenched into fists, ready to fight for the man who meant everything to me.

"Ah, the little bird has come to play," one of them mocked, turning to face me. His voice was slick, a rich layer of honey laced with malice, and I felt a chill race down my spine. The others laughed, their mirth sending ripples of dread through the crowd, but I pressed on, fueled by love and desperation.

"Leave him alone," I demanded, forcing my voice to steady as I stepped closer. My heart was a wild beast, clawing against my ribs, but I stood my ground, refusing to let fear drown me. "He's done nothing wrong."

Jonah's eyes widened as he caught sight of me, and for a fleeting moment, the chaos fell away. I could see the turmoil behind his gaze, the silent plea that begged me to retreat. But retreat was not an option. Not now, not ever.

"Isn't it adorable?" the lead henchman sneered, his posture relaxed as if he were merely observing a play. "But you really should have stayed in the nest, little dove. This is no place for you."

With each word, I felt my resolve harden. "If you think I'm going to just stand by and watch you threaten him, you've underestimated me," I shot back, my voice sharper than I intended but dripping with defiance. The crowd around us continued their mindless chatter, blissfully unaware of the danger lurking just inches away.

"You're feisty," he replied, amusement dancing in his eyes. "But this is bigger than you. The Raven doesn't take kindly to interference."

A surge of fear gripped me. The Raven. The name alone felt like a curse, echoing with the weight of our shared history, of shadows that had loomed over us for far too long. This was no ordinary confrontation; this was a reckoning, and I wouldn't let Jonah face it alone.

"Get away from him," I repeated, stepping forward, every fiber of my being screaming to protect what was mine. I could see Jonah shifting slightly, a mix of worry and admiration crossing his face, urging me silently to be cautious. But what did caution matter when the stakes were this high?

"Brave little bird," the henchman said, a hint of mockery threading through his tone. "But bravery can be so easily extinguished." With that, he motioned to his companions, and the world around me shifted once more.

Before I could react, they surged forward, their intent clear. The air crackled with tension, and time seemed to stretch as my instincts kicked in. I lunged for Jonah, determined to pull him out of harm's way, but as I reached him, a fist collided with my stomach, knocking the breath from my lungs. Pain exploded within me, a sharp reminder of the danger we were in, but I refused to crumble.

"Run!" I gasped, forcing the command through gritted teeth as I regained my footing, eyes blazing with fury. The laughter of the henchmen filled the space, echoing against the elegant walls, but I focused on Jonah, my resolve unwavering. This was our fight, and I wouldn't let the darkness swallow us whole.

Adrenaline surged through me as I felt the sting of the henchman's fist against my stomach, but I refused to let it deter me. I steadied myself, focusing on Jonah, who had shifted slightly, panic flashing in his eyes. "Run!" I gasped again, each word a challenge thrown into the tempest of chaos that surrounded us. It was a command born of desperation, a plea steeped in the urgency of the moment. But Jonah didn't budge, and that stubbornness—his unwavering loyalty—only fueled my fire.

The lead henchman chuckled, an unsettling sound that grated against the frantic rhythm of my heart. "You think you can just waltz in here and save the day? How quaint." He stepped closer, a predatory glint in his eye that made my skin crawl. It was a game to him, a dance of power, and in his mind, I was nothing but a pawn.

"Quaint? Is that what we're calling it?" I shot back, raising my chin defiantly. "I was aiming for spectacular, but you know, I guess I'm just setting the bar low for you."

The other henchmen laughed, but their amusement was hollow. Jonah, still trapped but desperately trying to keep his cool, managed a small smile, a spark of light in this shadowy nightmare. "You know, this would be a lot easier if you just let me go," he suggested, his voice steady despite the tension wrapping around us like a noose.

"Charming," the lead henchman sneered. "But I think we'd prefer to keep you both. You're far more valuable as hostages." His grin widened, and he gestured behind me. "Take her."

Instinct kicked in, and I spun around just as two of his companions lunged at me. My body reacted on its own, an uncoiling spring of motion. I ducked and rolled, my mind racing, heart pounding. It was a gamble, but in moments like this, it was all about the odds. I found my feet, adrenaline sharpening my senses, and saw Jonah push away from the column, his eyes fierce with determination.

"Get out!" he shouted, his voice cutting through the chaos. "I'll find a way to distract them!"

"Like hell!" I retorted, moving to his side, the two of us forming a barrier against the encroaching threat. "We do this together. It's our fight, remember?"

"Two birds, one stone!" he quipped, forcing a lightheartedness I could only admire amidst the looming peril. I shot him a look, half-annoyed, half-grateful for his humor. I appreciated the attempt, even as the laughter from the crowd continued to morph into an unsettling chorus that hummed with dark anticipation.

With a swift motion, I grabbed Jonah's hand, feeling the warmth and strength radiating from him, and we made a break for it, shoving through the mass of spectators who remained blissfully unaware of the storm brewing at their feet. The crowd, enraptured by the high-stakes auction, provided an unexpected barrier, a cover as we twisted and turned, dodging the grasping hands of the henchmen.

"Keep moving! Don't look back!" Jonah urged, his voice a steady anchor amidst the turmoil. I could sense the urgency in his tone, the unspoken fear that loomed just beneath the surface. I squeezed his hand tighter, our fingers interlocked like a promise, a vow that we wouldn't let the shadows take us down without a fight.

We darted into a narrow corridor that led to the back of the hall, where the luxurious ambiance gave way to stark, cold walls. The din of the auction faded, replaced by the echo of our hurried footsteps and ragged breaths. "Where now?" Jonah asked, glancing over his shoulder, the tension etched in every line of his face.

"I have no idea," I admitted, forcing a smirk despite the fear clawing at my insides. "But I have a gut feeling we need to find a way out. Fast."

As we navigated the dimly lit corridor, I could hear the distant shouts of the henchmen, their anger palpable. They were closing in, and with each echoing footfall, I felt the walls close tighter around us, the air thickening with impending doom. "You know, if we survive this, I'm definitely adding 'ran from henchmen at a fancy auction' to my résumé," I quipped, hoping to lighten the mood.

"Good luck finding a job that lists that as a skill," Jonah shot back, his eyes twinkling even in the face of danger. It was that flicker of light that kept me grounded, reminding me that we were in this together.

Just ahead, a heavy wooden door loomed, its surface worn but sturdy. Without hesitation, I pushed against it, and to my surprise, it creaked open with a reluctant groan. "This is it!" I exclaimed, practically dragging Jonah through the opening.

We stumbled into a darkened room, the air cool and still, filled with an odd mix of mustiness and something floral, as if the space had been neglected for far too long. Shadows danced around us, and I could hear the faint thrum of the auction still resonating outside, oblivious to our plight.

"Where are we?" Jonah whispered, glancing around, his senses on high alert.

"Beats me," I replied, trying to suppress the rising tide of panic. "But I'm pretty sure we're about to find out."

As I turned to survey the room, something glinted in the corner of my eye. It was a series of boxes stacked haphazardly against the wall, each one adorned with ribbons and delicate floral arrangements. The sight was incongruous, a bizarre juxtaposition to the urgency we were facing. "Look at these," I said, moving closer to inspect them.

Jonah stepped beside me, his brow furrowing. "What do you think they are?"

"Gifts? Decorations? I have no idea," I mused, lifting the lid of one box to reveal a cascade of silk scarves, vibrant and luxurious. The fabric shimmered under the dim light, and an idea sparked within me. "We could use these!"

"Scarves? How?" he asked, skepticism tinging his voice.

I didn't have time to explain, so I simply grabbed a couple of the silk scarves, their coolness slipping through my fingers like water. "Distract them, create a diversion, confuse their senses—whatever it takes."

Jonah raised an eyebrow, a smile tugging at his lips. "You really think we can distract a group of trained henchmen with some pretty scarves?"

"It's worth a shot!" I countered, quickly wrapping one around my waist and tossing another over his shoulder. "We need to improvise, and this is better than nothing!"

He chuckled, the tension easing just a fraction. "I never thought I'd find myself dressing up for a hostage situation. But here we are."

With that, we both slipped into the shadows of the room, cloaked not just by the darkness but by the absurdity of our makeshift disguises. The noise outside had grown louder, punctuated by angry shouts that threatened to slice through the air like a knife. But with Jonah by my side, I felt a strange sense of confidence.

"Ready?" I whispered, meeting his gaze, the gravity of our situation settling between us.

"Let's do this," he replied, and together, we took a deep breath and prepared to face the storm that awaited us beyond that door. The world outside was chaotic, but within that chaos, we were determined to carve our own path.

The door creaked ominously as we edged back into the fray, the soft rustle of silk brushing against my skin reminding me that we were still dressed for an auction, not a battle. With each step into the blinding light, I felt a rush of uncertainty course through me, but Jonah squeezed my hand, grounding me amidst the chaos. His confidence was infectious, a spark that ignited my own courage, and as we stepped through the doorway, I steeled myself for whatever awaited us.

The auction hall loomed larger than life, a vast expanse of opulence and desperation. The rhythmic thump of raised bids seemed to pulse through the air like a heartbeat, and the crowd continued its frenzied dance, oblivious to the storm gathering around us. Just beyond the thrumming noise, I could hear the shouts of The Raven's henchmen, their anger and frustration spurring them into action. They would be on us in seconds, and the tightness in my chest threatened to constrict my ability to think clearly.

"Stick close," I murmured to Jonah, my voice barely above a whisper as I scanned the hall for a way out. A flurry of bodies surged around us, each person fixated on the luxurious items on display, blissfully ignorant of the chaos threatening to engulf us. The glint of jewelry sparkled under the lights, tempting bids higher and higher, but all I could think about was how to escape this glittering trap.

"Do you see any exits?" Jonah asked, his brow furrowing as he kept his gaze on the writhing mass of attendees.

"Over there!" I pointed toward a pair of heavy wooden doors at the far end of the hall, partially obscured by the throng. "We can make it if we push through!"

"Right behind you," he replied, determination etching every line of his face.

With renewed purpose, we maneuvered through the crowd, ducking and weaving, our makeshift scarves fluttering behind us like banners of defiance. As we drew closer to the exit, I felt the adrenaline crackling beneath my skin, a rush that was both exhilarating and terrifying. The air thickened with tension, each shout from the henchmen amplifying my anxiety.

Then, just as we reached the threshold, a thunderous voice boomed behind us. "Stop right there!"

I spun around, heart racing as I caught sight of the lead henchman barreling through the crowd, his face twisted into a mask of fury. "You think you can escape?" His voice echoed through the hall, a warning wrapped in menace.

"Time to move!" I hissed, dragging Jonah with me as we burst through the doors, the cool air hitting us like a wave of relief. We stumbled into a narrow alley, dimly lit by flickering streetlamps. The sounds of the auction faded behind us, but the looming threat was far from gone.

"What now?" Jonah asked, breathless as we pressed our backs against the brick wall, the dampness seeping into our clothes.

"Let's create a diversion," I suggested, glancing around for anything we could use. "If we can distract them long enough, we might buy ourselves a little time."

Jonah's eyes lit up with mischief, that familiar spark I loved shining through even in the direst of moments. "What are you thinking? A dance-off? I'm pretty sure I could take them with my killer moves."

"Funny," I shot back, stifling a laugh. "How about we make a ruckus instead? There's bound to be something around here we can use."

As if on cue, a series of loud crashes erupted from a nearby dumpster, the sound echoing through the alley like a gunshot. Jonah raised an eyebrow, and I could see the wheels turning in his mind. "Or we could just find a few more things to throw," he said, a grin spreading across his face. "I like that idea."

"Great minds think alike!" I replied, feeling the tension ease just a fraction. We approached the dumpster, tossing aside empty cans and discarded boxes until we unearthed a few glass bottles. I held them up triumphantly, their necks glinting like small weapons in the dim light. "This should do the trick."

"On three?" Jonah suggested, a mischievous glint in his eyes.

"On three," I agreed, adrenaline coursing through my veins as I readied myself. "One... two... three!"

With a coordinated throw, we sent the bottles crashing against the pavement, the shattering glass creating a cacophony that echoed off the walls. The sound reverberated through the alley, and I could almost feel the shift in the atmosphere as the henchmen's voices fell silent, confusion replacing their anger.

"Now's our chance!" I exclaimed, grabbing Jonah's hand once more. We took off down the alley, our footsteps muffled by the chaos we had just unleashed. The adrenaline fueled our escape, each heartbeat ringing in my ears as we turned corners and ducked into side streets.

Just when I thought we might make it, a dark shadow loomed ahead, blocking our path. My stomach dropped as I recognized the silhouette—the lead henchman, flanked by two of his associates, their expressions a blend of amusement and frustration. "Did you really think you could outsmart us?" he taunted, stepping closer, his voice dripping with mockery.

"Let me guess," I shot back, my voice steady despite the fear creeping in. "You've got a degree in 'how to be a menacing jerk.'"

"Clever girl," he replied, his smile widening. "But this little game of yours ends here."

"Time to change the game!" Jonah suddenly shouted, lunging for the nearest trash can and tipping it over. The contents spilled onto the ground—rotten food and scraps tumbling out in a putrid avalanche. The henchmen recoiled, their faces twisting in disgust, giving us a split second to react.

"Go!" I yelled, dragging Jonah with me as we slipped past the stunned figures. We dashed into the street, but just as hope surged within me, I heard a growl from behind, the unmistakable sound of pursuit.

"Stop them!" The lead henchman's voice boomed, the command slicing through the air. Panic coursed through me as I felt Jonah's grip on my hand tighten.

"Which way?" he panted, glancing over his shoulder.

I looked around frantically, spotting a narrow alley to our left, a potential refuge that promised escape. "That way!" I pointed, leading him into the shadows.

We raced down the alley, the distant shouts of the henchmen echoing behind us, growing ever closer. Just as I thought we had gained some distance, a searing pain shot through my ankle, and I stumbled, crashing to the ground.

"Julia!" Jonah shouted, turning back to me, concern flooding his features. "Are you okay?"

I grimaced, forcing myself to sit up, the sharp throb in my ankle making my head spin. "I'll be fine," I gasped, but even as the words left my lips, I could see the realization dawning in Jonah's eyes.

"Go!" I urged, my voice breaking. "You need to keep moving!"

"No way," he replied, his jaw set in stubborn defiance. "We're getting out of this together."

Before I could argue, he took a step closer, but it was too late. The henchmen were upon us, their figures emerging from the shadows like nightmares made flesh. My heart raced as I looked up at Jonah, our eyes locking in that brief moment before everything changed.

"Run!" I shouted, my voice cracking under the weight of our reality. But as I struggled to rise, the lead henchman lunged, his hand outstretched, and I realized with chilling clarity that our web was tightening.

# Chapter 21: A Desperate Escape

The air was thick with the scent of damp earth and blooming nightshade as Jonah and I slipped through the narrow doorway, the old wood creaking in protest. I felt the weight of the mansion behind us, its secrets whispering in the shadows. We had been running for what felt like hours, each frantic heartbeat resonating against the cobblestone paths that twisted like veins through the garden. The moon hung high, a silver sentinel illuminating our escape while simultaneously draping the night in an unsettling glow.

"Keep going!" Jonah urged, his voice low and urgent, barely above a whisper, but it thrummed with energy. I could see the tension etched in his jaw, the way his brows knitted together as he scanned the surroundings. His concern only fueled my determination. We were in this together, and failure wasn't an option.

The garden sprawled before us, a labyrinth of overgrown hedges and twisting vines. I caught glimpses of roses, their petals like whispered promises in the night, each one heavy with the scent of desperation and danger. The iron gates loomed ahead, glimmering like a distant dream, a promise of freedom. Yet, my mind raced with thoughts of The Raven—the enigma wrapped in a shroud of darkness, the specter of our pursuer who seemed to always be one step ahead.

"Do you think we lost them?" I asked, my voice trembling with a mix of adrenaline and exhaustion. I could feel the pulse of fear quickening my veins, a treacherous companion that urged me to look back, to glance over my shoulder at the darkened windows of the mansion. Each flicker of shadow seemed to pulse with menace.

"For now," Jonah replied, his gaze steady, though I could see the flicker of worry behind his eyes. "But we can't slow down. They won't stop until they find us." He grabbed my hand, his grip firm, grounding me amidst the chaos swirling in my mind. The warmth of his palm against mine sent a bolt of strength through me.

We dashed through the garden, dodging branches that snagged at our clothes like fingers grasping at escape. The ground beneath our feet was uneven, the cobblestones slick with dew, but I barely noticed as I focused on the sensation of the cool night air against my skin and the pounding rhythm of our footfalls echoing the frantic beat of my heart.

Suddenly, the sound of footsteps echoed behind us, the heavy thud of boots against the earth breaking through the cocoon of silence that enveloped us. My stomach twisted, panic clawing its way up my throat. "They're coming!" I gasped, glancing back to see the dark silhouette of a figure materializing in the moonlight, eyes gleaming with a predatory glint.

"Run!" Jonah's voice was fierce, a command that surged through me like electricity. We bolted forward, the sound of our breath mingling with the cacophony of our racing hearts, drowning out the impending footsteps. I could feel the adrenaline coursing through my body, propelling me onward, each stride a promise of survival.

As we neared the gate, I realized it was locked. My heart sank as the reality of our situation crashed over me like a wave. "Jonah, the gate!" I shouted, pointing frantically at the iron bars that felt like a cruel reminder of our imprisonment.

"Let me see." He rushed to the gate, tugging at the latch, cursing under his breath as it resisted his efforts. Desperation clawed at my insides; the footsteps grew louder, a relentless reminder that our time was running out.

"Do you have a key?" I pleaded, glancing back at the approaching figure, my mind racing through options, weighing our dwindling chances.

"No," Jonah said, frustration evident in his voice. "But we can climb over!"

"Are you serious? It's—" Before I could finish, he grabbed my waist, lifting me effortlessly as if I weighed nothing. I gasped, both from shock and the sudden surge of warmth that spread through me. "Jonah!" I protested, half-excited, half-terrified.

"Just trust me!" He hoisted me higher, and I scrambled, grasping the cold iron of the gate. The moonlight illuminated his features—determined, fierce, and impossibly handsome, even in this frantic moment. I couldn't help but steal a glance at him as I clambered onto the gate, momentarily mesmerized by the way his hair caught the light, tousled and wild.

"Now, you!" I called down, heart racing as I teetered precariously. The figure behind us drew closer, their shadow stretching across the ground like a harbinger of doom. Jonah was right behind me, his hands finding the bars as he began to climb.

I felt the gate shudder beneath us, a harsh reminder that time was not on our side. "Come on!" I urged, my voice a sharp edge against the night. I barely had time to catch my breath before he reached the top, pulling himself over with an effortless grace that made my heart flip.

With a final heave, he was beside me, the two of us perched on the brink of freedom. But just as we prepared to leap down, a voice sliced through the air like glass shattering. "You think you can escape me that easily?"

A shiver danced down my spine as I recognized The Raven's voice, rich and dangerous. My heart thudded in my chest, a warning bell clanging in the dark. I glanced down, the ground rushing up to meet us, the world narrowing to that one, pivotal moment.

"Now!" Jonah shouted, and we jumped together, hearts synchronized in their desperate leap toward freedom.

We landed on the damp earth with a soft thud, the cool night air enveloping us like a thick blanket. A chill ran through my bones as I glanced back at the looming mansion, its silhouette dark and foreboding against the starlit sky. The Raven's voice echoed in my mind, a chilling reminder that our troubles were far from over. Jonah and I stumbled into a patch of wildflowers, the sweet scent of honeysuckle mingling with the earthy aroma of freshly turned soil, providing a stark contrast to the adrenaline thrumming through my veins.

"Did you see the look on his face?" Jonah chuckled, shaking off the tension that clung to him like the remnants of a nightmare. I couldn't help but smile at his attempt to lighten the mood. It was a small comfort, a flicker of warmth amid the chaos swirling around us.

"Honestly, I was too busy trying not to die," I shot back, trying to sound lighthearted, though the fear simmered just beneath the surface. "But you did look heroic, like some sort of dashing knight."

"More like a desperate fool, but I'll take the compliment." He flashed a grin, and for a moment, the weight of the night lifted. But reality clawed back at me, a heavy hand pressing down as I remembered our predicament. "What's the plan now?" I asked, my voice barely above a whisper, as if speaking too loudly would summon the darkness that chased us.

Jonah paused, his expression shifting from playful to serious. "We need to find a way to put some distance between us and that place. There's a path through the woods," he gestured towards the looming trees, their branches twisting like gnarled fingers reaching for the sky. "We can cut through there and find a road. If we can get to the nearest town, we'll figure out the rest."

"Great, because running through a dark forest sounds like a splendid idea," I replied, rolling my eyes, though I felt a shiver of excitement course through me. The woods were thick and alive with the rustle of leaves, a living entity that felt both enchanting and menacing.

"Trust me, it's better than being caught," he said, and I could see the fire in his eyes. He turned, leading the way, and I followed, my heart racing not just from fear but from the thrill of the unknown.

The underbrush crunched beneath our feet, and the air thickened with the scent of damp moss and wild ferns. Shadows danced around us as we delved deeper, the moonlight filtering through the canopy overhead, casting patterns on the ground that flickered like memories. Every sound seemed amplified—the distant hoot of an owl, the rustle of unseen creatures in the bushes, and our own breathing, ragged and urgent.

"Do you think he'll follow us?" I asked, glancing over my shoulder. The darkness felt oppressive, as if the very trees were watching us with bated breath.

"If he does, he'll regret it," Jonah replied, his tone resolute. "I won't let him take us again."

We pressed on, adrenaline fueling our steps, but the deeper we went, the more I felt the shadows encroaching, a palpable sense of dread wrapping around me. I couldn't shake the feeling that we weren't alone, that something sinister lurked just out of sight, waiting to pounce.

"Do you ever think about what you'll do when this is all over?" Jonah asked suddenly, breaking the silence, his voice thoughtful and calm against the eerie stillness of the woods.

"What, aside from enjoying a good cup of coffee and catching up on all the Netflix I've missed?" I shot back, trying to inject some levity into the conversation, but it fell flat, the weight of our reality pressing in.

"No, I mean really," he insisted, his tone serious. "Once we're out of this, what's next for you?"

I paused, caught off guard by the question. "I guess I never thought about it much. Just... getting through this feels like enough of a goal right now," I admitted, my voice trailing off. The truth was, I had never envisioned a life beyond this chaos. All I knew was survival.

"Fair enough." He nodded, though I could see the wheels turning in his mind. "But once we're free, you should think about what you want. You deserve to live your life without this hanging over you."

"Jonah," I said, feeling a surge of warmth toward him, "you're one to talk. You've been swept into this mess, too."

"I can handle it," he said, his voice steady, but I caught the flicker of doubt in his eyes. "But I want you to be safe. I want you to have the chance to be happy."

Before I could respond, a rustling in the underbrush startled us. My heart leaped into my throat, and I turned, scanning the darkness. "Did you hear that?" I whispered, the panic returning, a cold shiver tracing my spine.

"Yeah, I did," Jonah said, his voice tense. "Stay close."

We moved cautiously, hearts pounding, straining to hear above the cacophony of the night. The rustling intensified, branches snapping like bones, and out of the shadows emerged a figure—a tall silhouette with a menacing presence that sent a jolt of fear through me.

"Who's there?" Jonah shouted, stepping protectively in front of me. I could see the outline of the figure, the glint of something metallic reflecting the moonlight.

"Relax, it's just me," a familiar voice called out, and I recognized it immediately, a rush of relief washing over me.

"Charlie?" I exclaimed, stepping out from behind Jonah. My heart raced with a mix of surprise and confusion. "What are you doing here?"

Charlie, our quirky friend with a penchant for bad jokes, stepped into the moonlight, a backpack slung over one shoulder and an odd grin plastered on his face. "I figured you two might need a getaway car, or at least a snack," he said, pulling out a granola bar and waving it like a white flag.

"Not exactly what we had in mind for escape gear," I replied, still trying to process the sight of him, but relief bubbled beneath my anxiety. "How did you find us?"

"I have my ways," he shrugged, eyes sparkling with mischief. "I saw the commotion at the mansion. You really know how to throw a party, don't you?"

"Party? More like a nightmare," Jonah interjected, his brow furrowing in disbelief. "You shouldn't be here, Charlie. It's dangerous!"

"Dangerous? Pfft." Charlie waved his hand dismissively, unfazed. "Danger is my middle name. Well, it's not, but it should be. Now, are you going to stand here chatting, or are we going to make a run for it?"

"Charlie, we need to—" Jonah began, but I interrupted, sensing the urgency in the air, and the pull of adventure flickered to life within me.

"Let's go! If you're here, we might just stand a chance."

"Finally, some enthusiasm!" Charlie beamed, and without another word, he led the way deeper into the woods, the trees closing in around us, the shadows shifting with every step. I glanced at Jonah, his expression a mixture of disbelief and determination, and I knew we had crossed a line—into the heart of something unpredictable, where danger lurked and hope flickered like a candle in the wind.

The woods enveloped us, the treetops twisting overhead like ancient sentinels guarding secrets long forgotten. Charlie led the way, a bright beacon of audacity and humor in a world that had turned ominously dark. I kept close to Jonah, my heart racing not only from fear but also from an inexplicable thrill that coursed through me. With every step, I felt as if we were stepping deeper into an adventure that had been waiting for us to stumble into it, unbidden yet tantalizingly real.

"Charlie, do you have a plan or are we just running blindly into the wild?" I asked, my breath coming in quick bursts as we wove through the underbrush.

"A plan? Please, those are for people who think ahead," he shot back with a grin that lit up the shadows. "I figured we'd just keep moving until the bad guys get bored. Works for me."

"Right, because boredom is a killer in the world of organized crime," Jonah muttered, his voice low but laced with exasperation. I couldn't help but chuckle despite the urgency of our situation.

"Hey, laughter is the best medicine! That's what they say, right?" Charlie replied, and even in the chaos, I admired his ability to lighten the mood.

A loud crack echoed behind us, the sound of a branch snapping, and my heart dropped. "We're not alone!" I hissed, my voice trembling. I turned to see Jonah's jaw clenched, the fierce determination in his eyes replaced by a flicker of concern.

"Keep moving," he urged, quickening his pace. The forest seemed to close in around us, shadows shifting with every rustle, every whisper of the wind. The weight of our situation pressed heavily on my chest, a reminder that danger was hot on our heels.

"Are we sure Charlie's not just leading us into a bear den or something?" I whispered, trying to maintain some semblance of humor even as my heart raced in response to the growing sense of dread.

"Oh, please. I wouldn't lead you into a bear den without a good backup plan," Charlie retorted, his playful tone only partially masking the tension in his stance. "Besides, I have snacks."

"Great, because that's the kind of emergency rations I need right now," I shot back, forcing a smile as we navigated the tangled roots and creeping vines that threatened to trip us.

The path wound deeper into the woods, and the air thickened with humidity, clinging to our skin like a second layer. I was acutely aware of the wild, untamed beauty surrounding us—the way the moonlight filtered through the branches, illuminating the soft glows of bioluminescent mushrooms peeking from the undergrowth. It was a bizarre juxtaposition against the danger lurking behind us.

"Okay, so what's the plan if we run into The Raven?" I asked, glancing at Jonah. "Do we just throw snacks at him until he goes away?"

"Definitely my first choice," Jonah replied, a flicker of amusement dancing in his eyes despite the gravity of our situation. "But I'd prefer to use a different tactic—like running away faster than him."

"I thought that was the plan already," I said, raising an eyebrow.

"Plans evolve," he said with a slight smirk, but then his expression turned serious again. "In all honesty, we need to find a place to hide, gather our thoughts, and come up with a real strategy."

"Sounds brilliant," Charlie chimed in. "I'm all for a solid hiding spot that doesn't involve me wrestling with foliage like some sort of woodland creature."

Just as the banter lightened the mood, another loud snap echoed behind us, closer this time. My stomach dropped. The shadows deepened, the darkness felt thicker, and an icy shiver crept down my spine.

"Run!" Jonah shouted, breaking into a sprint. I followed suit, adrenaline surging through me as we dashed deeper into the forest.

We didn't stop to think, our instincts taking over as we navigated the underbrush, our hearts pounding in unison. The rush of blood in my ears drowned out everything else—the rustle of leaves, the soft thump of our feet, and even Charlie's jovial commentary turned urgent as he kept pace beside us.

"Left! There's a clearing up ahead!" he shouted, veering off the path. I followed, my feet barely touching the ground, propelled by sheer adrenaline and the desperate need to escape.

As we burst into the clearing, the moonlight bathed us in a silvery glow, revealing a small, dilapidated cabin nestled among the trees, its wooden frame weathered and worn, but standing defiantly against the night.

"Is that even safe?" I gasped, still breathless from our flight.

"Better than out here in the open," Jonah replied, glancing over his shoulder. "We can barricade ourselves inside until we figure out what to do next."

"Fantastic," Charlie said, eyeing the cabin with a mix of skepticism and curiosity. "Looks like the perfect place to set up camp for the night, assuming it doesn't collapse on us first."

"Come on," Jonah urged, moving toward the door. He pushed it open with a creak that echoed like a groan of the weary structure, and we slipped inside.

The air inside was musty and stale, a far cry from the fresh scent of the forest, but it felt like sanctuary. I quickly scanned the small room, taking in the rotting floorboards and cobwebs strung across the corners. A single window framed our view of the darkened woods, and I stepped closer, pressing my palms against the cool glass.

"Let's make sure we're secure," Jonah said, moving to the door and checking the lock. He frowned, glancing at the deteriorating wood. "This might not hold for long, so we need to stay alert."

"What's the plan now, Captain?" Charlie asked, dropping his backpack to the floor and rummaging through it, pulling out a flashlight and a pack of granola bars.

"We wait," Jonah said, his voice low. "We need to catch our breath and figure out our next move. There's no point in panicking when we can plan."

Charlie chuckled as he tossed me a granola bar. "At least we'll have something to eat while we're hiding. I'm all about priorities."

"Great," I replied, taking a bite and feeling the crunchy texture dissolve on my tongue. "Survival snacks in the middle of a horror movie scenario."

Just as we settled into a tentative calm, a loud crash echoed outside the cabin, the sound jolting me upright. My heart raced as I turned, staring at the door as if it might burst open at any moment.

"What was that?" I whispered, my voice barely audible.

Jonah moved to the window, peering through the grime. "I don't know, but it didn't sound good," he replied, his voice taut. "Stay quiet."

The night felt alive with danger, a palpable tension that gripped me as I held my breath, straining to hear through the wall of silence that enveloped us. I exchanged glances with Charlie, whose eyes mirrored my own fear and confusion.

"Do you think it's The Raven?" I murmured, every instinct telling me we weren't safe yet.

"I can't tell," Jonah whispered back, his gaze fixed outside. "But we need to be ready for anything."

The silence stretched, oppressive and thick, and just as I thought we might have a moment of peace, the unmistakable sound of footsteps crunched on the leaves outside, steady and deliberate.

"They're here," Jonah breathed, tension radiating from him.

Suddenly, the door rattled violently, as if someone was trying to force their way in. My heart dropped, and I instinctively moved closer to Jonah, the instinct to flee battling the need to stay and fight.

"Hold on!" Charlie said, backing away toward the far corner, his eyes wide with a mix of excitement and fear. "Maybe they'll just get bored and leave."

A low, chilling laugh echoed outside, slicing through the air like a blade, sending chills racing down my spine. "You can't hide from me forever!" The Raven's voice taunted, smooth and velvety, carrying a sinister promise that made the hair on my arms stand on end.

The door creaked ominously as something heavy pressed against it, and I exchanged a frantic glance with Jonah. This was it—the moment we had feared was finally here.

With a surge of courage, Jonah took a step forward, determination etched on his face. "We're not going down without a fight," he said, his voice steady, and I felt that familiar spark of hope igniting within me once more.

As the door buckled, the air filled with tension, an electric charge that hinted at the chaos to come. The world outside was waiting for us, but so was our fate, hanging in the balance like a pendulum about to swing.

# Chapter 22: Confronting the Past

The cottage stood quietly by the lake, its weathered boards soaked in the memories of summers long past. Each creak of the floorboards echoed like a whisper of forgotten laughter, and the faint scent of pine mingled with the crisp, cool air that wrapped around us like a comforting shawl. I could feel the gentle sway of the trees outside, their leaves rustling in a low, conspiratorial murmur, as if they too were part of our unfolding drama. I drew a deep breath, inhaling the mingled scents of woodsmoke and damp earth, an earthy promise that hinted at renewal amidst the turmoil we faced.

Jonah sat hunched at the old wooden table, his fingers tapping nervously against the grain. His usually bright eyes were clouded with shadows, the kind that linger when old ghosts refuse to be exorcised. It was as if the walls themselves absorbed his unease, exuding it back into the room. The sunlight spilled through the window, casting a warm glow across the faded photographs on the mantle—smiling faces, sun-kissed summers, carefree days that now felt like distant fairy tales.

"Jonah, we need to talk about The Raven," I said, my voice steady despite the tremor in my heart. The urgency of the moment thrummed in the air between us, a taut string waiting for the right touch to snap. His gaze met mine, and in that moment, I saw a flicker of vulnerability, a glimpse of the man beneath the layers of hurt and secrecy.

He sighed, the sound heavy with unspoken burdens. "You don't understand," he began, his voice low, almost a whisper. "This goes back farther than I can explain. My family..." He hesitated, the words tangling like the roots of the towering trees outside. "We thought we buried it all, but The Raven is digging it up, piece by piece."

The way he spoke made my skin prickle. It was like listening to a gripping tale, yet I was fully aware that this was our reality—a dark narrative that threatened to consume us. "You need to tell me everything," I urged, my pulse quickening with the weight of his words. "If we're going to confront this, we have to understand what we're up against."

He ran a hand through his tousled hair, frustration flashing across his face. "It's not just about us. It's about my father and a betrayal that tore our family apart." His voice cracked slightly, and I could see the emotions swirling within him—a tempest of regret, anger, and sorrow. "The Raven wasn't just a name to us; it was a ghost that haunted our lives. It's why we moved here in the first place."

"What happened?" The question slipped from my lips, weighted with anticipation.

Jonah leaned back in his chair, his gaze distant as he wove the tale. "When I was a kid, my father had a partner—an ambitious man, ruthless in business, but he was also like a second father to me. He taught me everything about the family business. But one day, he vanished. My father always said it was a business deal gone wrong, but I later found out he was framed for embezzlement. He lost everything—his reputation, our home, our lives."

"Why didn't you tell me this before?" I pressed, frustration rising. "We could have faced this sooner."

"Because," he snapped, the tension snapping like a twig underfoot, "I thought I could protect you from it. I thought if I kept it buried, we could start fresh, away from the shadow of my family's mistakes. But The Raven isn't going to let us go that easily."

The silence hung heavy in the air, charged with the electricity of our shared fears and unspoken hopes. I could see the weight of the past pulling at him, twisting the corners of his mouth downward as he grappled with the enormity of his revelation. "So The Raven is after your family's business?" I asked, piecing the puzzle together in my mind, each new revelation fitting together like jagged shards of glass.

"It's more than that," he said, his voice low. "The Raven believes we owe him. For the betrayal. For the downfall of my father's partner. For the sins of the past that my family tried to erase." His eyes met mine, and I felt the chill of his words seep into my bones. "He's not just a shadow from my past; he's a vendetta brought to life."

An uneasy silence enveloped us, the gravity of his words settling over me like a shroud. I could feel the fear creeping into the corners of my mind, but I pushed it aside. "Then we have to confront him together. We can't let him dictate our lives any longer."

Jonah nodded, a flicker of determination igniting in his eyes. "You're right. It's time we stop running. But it won't be easy. The Raven knows our every move."

"Then we need to be smarter. We need to gather information, find out what he knows, and turn the tables." I could feel the fire of resolve kindling within me, a fierce determination that drowned out the gnawing doubt.

He reached across the table, taking my hand in his, the warmth of his touch grounding me. "You make it sound so easy," he murmured, a hint of a smile breaking through his earlier tension. "But I don't want to drag you into this mess."

"I'm already in it, Jonah," I countered, squeezing his hand. "We're in this together, remember? You're not alone in this fight."

He gazed at me, his expression softening, the shadows lifting just enough to reveal the glimmer of hope that lay beneath. "I don't deserve you," he said, his voice barely above a whisper.

"No one's perfect, Jonah. But together, we might just be able to find a way through this." As we sat there, hands clasped, the weight of the world seemed just a little lighter, the path ahead a little clearer. The lake outside shimmered under the midday sun, a mirror reflecting not just our fears but also the possibility of a future unburdened by the chains of the past. And with that thought, I felt a flicker of something more—something like hope, stirring within me.

The air in the cottage was thick with unspoken thoughts, a palpable tension that lingered like the wisps of fog hovering over the lake. As we sat together, hands still clasped, the reality of what lay ahead began to sink in. Each breath felt like a silent promise, a commitment to face whatever darkness loomed beyond the gentle lapping of the water against the shore. I could hear the faint rustle of leaves outside, a reminder that nature was indifferent to our troubles, yet I longed to lose myself in its tranquil embrace.

"Okay, so what's our plan?" I asked, drawing back to look Jonah in the eye. The sunlight cast a golden hue across his features, illuminating the worry lines etched deep on his brow. He was handsome in that rugged way, the kind that made you want to reach out and smooth away the tension with gentle fingertips. But right now, he was too preoccupied with the specter of The Raven to notice the way his presence filled the space around us with warmth.

Jonah leaned back, the chair creaking beneath him. "We need to figure out where The Raven is operating. He's smart, and he won't reveal himself unless he has a reason to."

"And we'll have to lure him out," I added, a spark of mischief dancing in my chest. "What's a little danger without a touch of theatrics?"

He chuckled softly, the sound a balm to my nerves. "You're enjoying this way too much."

"Of course! Nothing like a little suspense to spice up a weekend at the cottage." I grinned, but his serious demeanor pulled me back. "But really, Jonah, do you have any leads?"

He nodded, raking a hand through his hair, sending his curls into delightful disarray. "There's a local bar in town, The Soggy Pine. It's where people go to drown their sorrows and share secrets. If The Raven is still lurking around here, he might show up there."

"A bar? How very classic villain," I quipped, raising an eyebrow. "You think he'll be twirling a mustache too?"

Jonah smirked, the tension breaking for just a moment. "You're not wrong about the clichés. But I'll take any advantage we can get."

We made a plan, our conversation shifting from fears to strategies, each suggestion punctuated with laughter that felt both necessary and terrifying. It was as if we were crafting our own little rebellion against the shadow that loomed over us. The cabin was becoming a fortress of sorts, one built on secrets and survival, but also on a fierce, growing bond that tied us together.

With the sun sinking low in the sky, casting vibrant hues of orange and pink across the lake, we decided to make our way to The Soggy Pine. The air outside was crisp, carrying the scent of damp earth and pine needles, a reminder of the wild beauty surrounding us. As we walked, I felt the weight of Jonah's past beside me, and I wondered if we could ever truly escape it.

The bar was tucked away at the end of a narrow lane, the kind of place where the flickering neon sign felt like an invitation to a different world—a world filled with laughter, tears, and stories half-remembered. Inside, the dim lighting cast shadows on the walls, and the murmur of voices created a comforting hum. My heart raced as we crossed the threshold, a heady mix of excitement and anxiety washing over me.

We found a corner booth, the vinyl seats sticky and cracked, but it felt right. I ordered a drink—something fruity to mask the taste of tension—and Jonah opted for a beer. The waitress was a no-nonsense type, her eyes sharp as she jotted down our order. "First time here?" she asked, glancing between us.

"Something like that," I replied with a smile, hoping to exude an air of confidence that I didn't quite feel.

"Better brace yourselves. The locals can be a bit... passionate about their drinks," she said with a knowing smirk before sauntering off.

"Passionate is one word for it," Jonah murmured, his gaze sweeping over the room. "We'll blend in, keep our ears open. The Raven will reveal himself if he thinks we're not a threat."

Time slipped by, our drinks arriving and the conversations around us weaving together into a tapestry of laughter and shared stories. I leaned in close to Jonah, lowering my voice. "Do you think anyone here knows anything?"

He shrugged, his expression contemplative. "If they do, they're keeping it close. But everyone has a secret. We just need to find the right person willing to share theirs."

The night wore on, the bar filling with a motley crew of patrons. Laughter erupted in one corner, a couple sharing a passionate kiss in another, while a group of friends debated the merits of their favorite sports teams. I found myself drawn into the energy, the carefree ambiance momentarily allowing me to forget the shadows lurking in the corners of my mind.

But then, I noticed a figure leaning against the bar, his back turned to us. He had an air of confidence that felt dangerously familiar. "Jonah," I whispered, nudging him gently. "Look at that guy."

Jonah's gaze followed mine, and his expression hardened. "That's Malachai. He was my father's partner's right-hand man. If anyone knows something, it's him."

"Then let's get his attention," I said, a spark of mischief returning to my voice. "How about a little game of charm?"

Jonah raised an eyebrow, a mix of skepticism and amusement flitting across his face. "You think charm is going to work on him?"

I grinned, my heart pounding with adrenaline. "Trust me. I've got a few tricks up my sleeve."

With that, I stood up, smoothing down my shirt and making my way toward Malachai. The bar hummed around me, the noise fading into a blur as I focused on my target. I could feel Jonah's gaze burning into my back, a mixture of worry and hope.

"Excuse me," I said, flashing a bright smile as I approached him. "Mind if I steal a moment of your time?"

Malachai turned, his eyes narrowing as he sized me up. "Depends on what you want," he replied, his voice gruff but edged with curiosity.

"Just a friendly chat," I said, leaning slightly against the bar. "I hear you're quite the well-connected guy in these parts."

He smirked, a hint of challenge in his gaze. "And who's asking?"

"Just a girl looking for answers," I replied, allowing a playful lilt to enter my tone. "You'd be surprised at what secrets can be found in a bar like this."

Jonah watched from a distance, tension coiling in his shoulders as he waited for the outcome of my gamble. I felt the weight of his gaze, a steady reminder that we were in this together, but for now, I was on my own. I leaned in closer, the atmosphere crackling with potential as I prepared to pull the thread that might unravel the mystery of The Raven.

The tension between Malachai and me crackled like static electricity in the air, his eyes narrowing in that way that suggested he was sizing up more than just my words. I could almost hear the gears in his mind turning, weighing my intentions against the possibility that I might actually be a threat. I leaned in slightly, letting my smile widen, hoping to project an air of confidence that masked the nervous fluttering in my stomach.

"You must be the local legend," I said, injecting a playful lilt into my voice. "Malachai, right? I hear you're the go-to guy for all things... interesting."

His brow quirked, a flash of amusement breaking through his initial suspicion. "Interesting, huh? That's one way to put it. What's it to you?"

"Let's just say I'm a curious soul." I shrugged, adopting an air of nonchalance. "I'm in town for a little adventure and thought I might pick the brain of the most connected man in the room."

A flicker of interest danced in his eyes, though he still held his cards close to his chest. "Adventure's a risky game. You sure you want to play?"

"Risky games are my specialty." I laughed lightly, the sound buoying my spirits as I tried to navigate this precarious dance. "I've come to realize that sometimes the most dangerous adventures lead to the most rewarding outcomes. Don't you agree?"

He chuckled, a deep rumble that resonated through the air like the sound of distant thunder. "You've got guts, I'll give you that. But guts without sense will only get you into trouble."

"Trouble is what I'm trying to avoid," I replied, meeting his gaze with unyielding determination. "I'm looking for information, something that might help me piece together a puzzle that's been haunting me. You wouldn't happen to know anything about a certain shadowy figure known as The Raven, would you?"

At the mention of the name, the color drained from his face, and for a brief moment, I thought I'd hit the jackpot. "That's a name best left unspoken," he said, his voice low and heavy, as if the very syllables weighed down the air around us. "You should tread lightly, girl. You don't want to get mixed up in that mess."

"I've already waded knee-deep into the muck, Malachai," I shot back, my heart racing as I leaned closer, my voice barely above a whisper. "I'm not here for idle gossip; I need to know what he wants, why he's after Jonah's family. You must know something."

For a heartbeat, I thought I saw a flicker of recognition in his eyes, a connection to Jonah's past that he was grappling with. "You don't understand the danger," he warned, his tone shifting from one of challenge to genuine concern. "The Raven is a vengeful spirit. He doesn't just play games; he makes examples out of those who cross him."

I straightened, the gravity of his words settling over me like a cold fog. "Then you know what we're up against. You've got to help us. We can't do this alone."

Malachai studied me, his expression shifting as he weighed his options. The air around us was thick with tension, and I could sense the imminent decision lingering between us. "You want help? You'd better be ready to pay the price," he finally said, his voice a low growl.

"Name it," I replied, meeting his fierce gaze with resolve.

"First, you need to understand that getting involved with The Raven means stepping into a world where trust is a luxury you can't afford. You want answers, you'll need to get your hands dirty." He leaned closer, his eyes boring into mine. "Are you willing to do that?"

"I'm in," I declared, the weight of my choice settling over me like a shroud. "I'm ready to do whatever it takes."

"Good. We'll need to make some noise to lure him out," Malachai said, a wicked grin spreading across his face. "You're going to need a plan—and I might have a few tricks that could help."

As the details began to spill from his lips, my heart raced with a mix of excitement and dread. I could almost hear the ticking clock in the back of my mind, each moment taking us deeper into a labyrinth that could either lead to salvation or doom.

Meanwhile, Jonah remained at the table, his eyes fixed on us, tension etched into every line of his face. He watched as I engaged with Malachai, the weight of his past seemingly heavier with every passing second. I shot him a reassuring glance, silently communicating that I was still firmly in our corner, even if I was straying slightly into the unknown.

"Meet me back here tomorrow night," Malachai said, pulling me back from the dizzying swirl of thoughts. "I'll have a plan, and you'll need to bring your friend. We'll need all the hands we can get."

"Tomorrow night," I confirmed, feeling a thrill of anticipation mingle with apprehension. "I'll be here."

As I turned to head back to Jonah, a sudden commotion erupted at the entrance. The door swung open with a bang, and a gust of wind swept through the bar, momentarily dimming the flickering lights. A tall figure stepped inside, his silhouette sharp against the dim glow of neon. There was something about him that felt like a slap of cold water—a shiver racing down my spine as he surveyed the room with piercing eyes.

The moment he stepped into the light, my heart plummeted. It was The Raven, or at least someone who looked all too familiar. Dressed in dark clothes that clung to him like a shadow, he carried an air of danger that sent chills spiraling through the bar. The murmur of conversations faded to a hush, and I could feel the collective breath of the patrons held tight, their gazes fixated on the new arrival.

"Jonah!" I hissed, urgency bleeding into my voice as I gestured toward the door, panic rising within me. "We need to go. Now."

But Jonah was already on his feet, his expression a mixture of determination and fear. "Stay close," he ordered, scanning the room as if expecting a storm to break loose at any moment.

The Raven moved with a predatory grace, his eyes glinting with a chilling knowingness as he made his way deeper into the bar, completely unaware of the fraying nerves surrounding him. My heart raced as I grabbed Jonah's hand, urging him to move toward the back exit, where the shadows lingered and the noise faded.

Just as we turned to make our escape, the Raven's voice cut through the air like a knife. "I've been looking for you, Jonah."

Time froze. The atmosphere shifted, charged with a tension so thick it felt like a physical presence. I could feel Jonah's grip tighten around my hand, a mix of defiance and fear radiating from him as he faced the man who had become the embodiment of our nightmares.

And in that moment, standing on the precipice of chaos, I realized we had stepped beyond the point of no return. The night had just begun, and the storm was about to break.

# Chapter 23: The Final Showdown

The warehouse loomed like a forgotten sentinel, its weathered façade casting long shadows in the twilight. Abandoned crates lay strewn about, a graveyard of stories that whispered to anyone brave enough to listen. Each creak of the floorboards beneath my feet echoed with the weight of our resolve, the determination to confront The Raven, that shadowy figure whose presence had haunted our every step. I pressed my back against the cool steel wall, the gritty surface grounding me as I exchanged a glance with Jonah. His blue eyes were stormy, flickering with a mixture of fear and fierce determination, much like the sea on a tempestuous night.

"Are you sure about this?" he murmured, the tension in his voice crackling like static electricity. He reached out, brushing a strand of hair behind my ear, his touch both comforting and electric. I could feel the heartbeat of the world around us, a rhythm synchronized with our own.

"It's now or never," I replied, summoning the bravado I desperately wished to feel. "If we don't stand up to him, who will?" I took a deep breath, the musty scent of the warehouse mixing with the faintest hint of rust, a reminder of the battles we had fought and the sacrifices made along the way. Memories swirled around me like a wraith, each one anchoring my resolve.

The plan we had crafted was both daring and reckless, a tightrope walk between bravery and insanity. We had gathered every scrap of information about The Raven, piecing together his twisted motives and tangled history, but knowledge alone wouldn't be enough. As we stood in the hollow silence, the dim light from a flickering bulb above us cast eerie shadows that danced along the walls, and I couldn't help but wonder if this was truly the end of our journey or merely the beginning of a darker chapter.

"Remember what we talked about?" Jonah's voice broke through my reverie, a gentle reminder that pierced through the fog of anxiety. I nodded, the corners of my mouth tugging up in a ghost of a smile. It was a dangerous game we were playing, one that could shatter the fragile peace we had fought so hard to maintain. Yet there was something invigorating about the impending confrontation, a spark that ignited the fire in my veins.

Time stretched, the moments suspended in a thick haze of anticipation. Every scrape of a rat's claws on the floor echoed through the cavernous space, reminding me of our vulnerability. A shiver danced down my spine, but I straightened my shoulders, inhaling deeply, determined to remain steady. "We can't back down now. Not after everything."

Jonah clenched his jaw, his expression hardening with a mix of resolve and fear. "I know. I just... I can't shake the feeling that he knows we're here."

As if summoned by our whispered fears, the sound of footsteps reverberated through the warehouse, heavy and deliberate. I exchanged a glance with Jonah, our hearts beating in synchrony, adrenaline coursing through us like wildfire. The atmosphere crackled, a tension so thick I could almost taste it on my tongue.

Then he appeared, The Raven, cloaked in darkness as if he had emerged from the very shadows themselves. His presence felt suffocating, the air around him charged with a palpable malevolence. His eyes glinted with a predatory hunger, a wolf among sheep, and I could feel my heart race, pounding like a war drum.

"Ah, the little moths have decided to dance into the flame," he purred, his voice silky smooth, wrapping around me like a noose. "How quaint."

Jonah stepped forward, his posture defensive. "This ends tonight, Raven. You've terrorized enough lives." His voice was steady, unwavering, but I could see the tension in his clenched fists, the quiver in his jaw.

The Raven's lips curled into a sinister smile, revealing teeth that glinted like knives. "Oh, how noble of you. But you seem to forget, I thrive in the darkness." With a flick of his wrist, the shadows deepened around him, swirling like smoke, and I felt a wave of despair wash over me.

"No!" I shouted, stepping into the fray, fueled by desperation. "We're not afraid of you!" My voice was stronger than I felt, each word a shield against the creeping dread. "You've tried to break us, but look at us! We're still here!"

For a heartbeat, silence enveloped us, as if the world itself paused to listen. The Raven's expression shifted, confusion flickering across his features, and I seized the moment, drawing upon the strength of our bond.

"Jonah, remember our promise?" I turned to him, meeting his eyes, the warmth of our shared memories flooding my mind. "We're not alone in this. We have each other."

The words ignited something deep within him. Jonah's stance shifted, determination filling his gaze. "You're right. We're stronger together."

The air thickened with tension, a precarious balance of power hanging between us. The Raven seemed to falter, just for a moment, as if our combined strength had momentarily unsettled him. I could almost see the cracks forming in his dark façade, the edges of his control fraying.

With renewed vigor, I stepped closer to Jonah, our hands intertwining, a solid anchor against the tempest swirling around us. "We're not here to be your prey, Raven. We're taking back what's ours."

His laughter filled the warehouse, chilling yet intrigued, the sound echoing against the walls like thunder. "How delightfully naïve. But very well, let's see if your resolve holds when faced with true darkness."

Suddenly, the shadows surged, swirling violently around him, and I braced myself, the adrenaline surging in my veins like wildfire. We had come too far to back down now, too far to let fear dictate our fate. This was our moment, a culmination of everything we had fought for, and I would not let it slip away.

The shadows pulsed, undulating with a life of their own, as The Raven loomed larger in the dim light, his smile a snake's hiss, devoid of warmth. A chill crawled up my spine, but I forced myself to stand firm. Jonah's grip tightened around my hand, a lifeline anchoring me to reality. The air felt electric, charged with our collective resolve, a moment suspended in time. I had never anticipated that fear could feel this much like exhilaration.

"Let's not play games," I challenged, my voice cutting through the tension like a knife. "You may thrive in darkness, but we're done being shadows on your wall."

The Raven's laughter echoed in the vast emptiness of the warehouse, a sound that sent shivers down my spine. "Spoken like true children of light, but your bravery is a naive cloak, easily torn."

He stepped forward, the shadows coiling around him like smoke, and for a fleeting moment, I felt the weight of hopelessness trying to creep in, whispering that we might not emerge from this confrontation unscathed. But the flicker of fear was snuffed out by the heat of our bond, a flame that burned bright in the darkest corners of our souls.

"Maybe you've forgotten," Jonah interjected, his voice steady and resolute. "Light isn't easily extinguished." The confidence in his tone stirred something deep within me, a shared understanding of our unyielding spirit.

"Is that so?" The Raven's eyes gleamed with malicious delight as he took another step closer, his gaze darting between us. "Then let's see how much light you can muster when faced with your own fears."

In that instant, shadows erupted around him, swirling violently, threatening to consume everything in their path. It was as if he were summoning the very essence of our deepest anxieties, each wisp a tendril of doubt reaching out to ensnare us. I could feel my heart race, the echo of panic reverberating within me.

"Jonah!" I called, urgency lacing my tone. "We need to stand together!" The shadows crept closer, almost tangible in their menace, but I willed myself to take a step forward, feeling Jonah's unwavering presence beside me.

"We're not afraid of you!" Jonah shouted, and his defiance sparked something within me, igniting the fire of our determination. The shadows retreated momentarily, recoiling from our combined light, a flicker of uncertainty crossing The Raven's features.

"Your resolve is admirable," he said, the bravado in his voice wavering slightly. "But futile. You cannot escape your own truths."

"Try us," I said, stepping into the fray, emboldened by the shared strength we had cultivated. "You think you know our fears, but you've underestimated the power of what we've built together. Love isn't a weakness; it's our greatest weapon."

In that moment, the shadows faltered, as if reconsidering their assault, drawn back by the light that radiated from us. I could almost hear the whispers of hope woven into the fabric of our connection, rising to challenge the darkness.

The Raven's expression shifted, and in that flicker of vulnerability, I saw an opportunity. "You're nothing without the power you think you wield. Let's put that to the test. Come at us with everything you have!"

He hesitated, perhaps for the first time, and I seized the moment. "Together, we can face anything," I said, squeezing Jonah's hand, feeling the warmth radiate between us. "You've built your empire on fear, but love will dismantle it brick by brick."

The Raven's laughter faltered, caught off guard by our resolve. He extended his arms, the shadows swirling more intensely around him, a tempest threatening to unleash. "You believe you can defeat me with mere words? Let me show you true darkness!"

The shadows lashed out, forming tendrils that reached for us, twisting through the air like serpents. Instinct kicked in, and I pulled Jonah close, our bodies intertwining, the warmth of his presence warding off the chill. "Stay close!" I shouted, a blend of fear and determination fueling my voice.

In that moment, the world narrowed down to us and the swirling darkness. I could feel the fear trying to claw its way back, a whisper of doubt lingering at the edges of my mind. But I pushed it down, focusing instead on the strength we shared.

"Jonah, think about what we've fought for!" I urged, recalling the laughter, the quiet moments spent together, the dreams we had woven into our future. "We are not defined by what he wants us to be!"

"Right!" Jonah agreed, his voice strong and unwavering. "He can't take that from us."

As if our words had woven a shield against the encroaching darkness, the shadows recoiled, losing their grip on reality. A surge of warmth enveloped us, igniting every part of my being with courage. "We are more than what you see, Raven!" I declared.

With a howl, The Raven surged forward, a dark storm intent on shattering our bond. But as he moved, something unexpected happened. The shadows that had once felt so oppressive began to fragment, scattering like leaves caught in a gust of wind.

It was as if our shared resolve had turned the tide, breaking the spell he had cast over us. I could feel the air shift, a sudden clarity cutting through the darkness. "Now, Jonah!"

Together, we stepped into the void, our combined light pushing back against the storm. The shadows hissed and writhed, their power dimming against the brilliance of our unity. The Raven's expression shifted from confident amusement to outright fury, and in that moment, I saw the fear lurking beneath the surface of his malevolence.

"You think you can defeat me? You're merely two moths drawn to the flame!"

"Maybe," I countered, determination surging through me. "But moths can dance in the dark, and we've brought our own light."

With that, the warehouse erupted in a blaze of brilliance as we unleashed everything we had—the love, the shared dreams, the promises that had anchored us. In a flash, the shadows shattered, leaving behind a whisper of defeat that clung to the air like smoke. The Raven staggered back, confusion etching lines across his face as he struggled to regain his footing in the chaos we had unleashed.

This was our moment, a point of no return. Together, we faced the remnants of his darkness, ready to reclaim what he had tried to take from us. The light surged brighter, and we stood as one, unyielding and fierce, prepared to finally end this fight on our terms.

The light surged like a tidal wave, breaking through the remnants of The Raven's darkness, casting him in a stark glow that highlighted the turmoil etched on his face. For a brief moment, uncertainty flickered in his eyes, a crack in the armor of confidence that had cloaked him throughout our ordeal. Jonah and I stood shoulder to shoulder, the heat of our shared determination radiating between us.

"Looks like the shadows can't hold you forever," Jonah taunted, his voice dripping with bravado as he took a step forward. The air hummed with energy, almost vibrating with the promise of victory. I felt the corners of my mouth twitch into a smile, buoyed by our unyielding connection, even as The Raven clenched his fists, frustration evident in the set of his jaw.

"You think this is a victory?" he sneered, a flicker of his former arrogance trying to reclaim its place. "You're merely stalling the inevitable. Darkness doesn't die; it evolves."

"Sounds like someone's afraid of a little light," I shot back, matching his intensity with a bravado I barely felt. The audacity of our exchange felt surreal, almost ridiculous in the face of the chaos swirling around us, but I was done letting fear dictate my life.

"Clever, little moth," The Raven replied, his voice low and dangerous. "But I assure you, your light is dim. I've seen brighter flames extinguished with a single breath." With a sudden motion, he raised his hands, and the shadows around us coalesced, forming a thick veil that wrapped around him like a cloak.

I felt a wave of panic wash over me. "Jonah, we need to hold this together," I urged, my heart racing. The shadows began to pulse with a life of their own, undulating in a way that felt almost sentient.

"I'm not going anywhere," Jonah assured me, his voice steady, though I could hear the strain beneath it. We tightened our grip on each other, grounding ourselves in the reality of our shared strength. The shadows, however, were relentless, whispering dark promises that crawled under my skin, sowing seeds of doubt.

With a deep breath, I pushed through the fear. "What do you think this is, a horror movie? You're not going to scare us into submission!" I shouted, the conviction in my voice surprising even me. "You're a coward hiding behind these tricks."

The Raven's laughter rang out, sharp and mocking. "Oh, sweet child, how naive you are! You think you can defy me? You have no idea what's at stake."

I took a step forward, daring the shadows to close in. "No, we know exactly what's at stake. We've lost enough to you. We're not going to lose ourselves."

With that declaration, a fierce determination surged through me. A light flared inside my chest, bright and unwavering, illuminating the darkest corners of my mind. I could almost see the shadows recoil, hesitant in the face of our conviction. "Jonah, now!" I commanded, and we advanced together, our united front pressing against the darkness.

We drew upon the strength of our bond, feeling the warmth of shared memories and dreams envelop us like armor. "You may thrive in the darkness, but you're outnumbered," Jonah said, his voice calm and steady. "We will not back down."

The Raven hesitated, his expression shifting from amusement to something darker—perhaps desperation. The shadows quivered, oscillating in rhythm with his fluctuating control. "You think you can defeat me with mere words? This is a fight for your very souls."

"Then let's make it a fair fight," I challenged, adrenaline surging through my veins. "Show us what you've got!"

With a roar, The Raven released a wave of darkness, a rush that swept over us, icy and suffocating. I felt the shadows wrap around me, trying to snuff out the light we had built. "Jonah!" I gasped, the cold creeping in.

"Hold on!" His voice rang out like a beacon, a lifeline that pulled me back from the brink. We had faced too much to let fear win now. "Together!"

I closed my eyes for a moment, reaching deep within myself, searching for that flicker of light. "Together!" I echoed, and as our voices melded, something extraordinary happened. The shadows began to fragment, splintering like glass shattering under immense pressure.

"Impossible!" The Raven shouted, disbelief etching itself into his features. But there was no room for doubt; we surged forward, our light slicing through the darkness like a knife.

In the chaos, I felt a sudden rush of energy, an overwhelming power coursing through me. It was as if the very essence of our connection—the love, the trust, the defiance—had manifested into something tangible, something we could wield against him.

"Let's finish this," I declared, and with a determined breath, I focused that energy into a single point, channeling every ounce of our shared strength. The light blazed, brighter than I ever thought possible, illuminating the warehouse with a brilliance that made the shadows hiss in retreat.

But just as it seemed victory was within our grasp, The Raven threw his head back, a wild, desperate laugh erupting from his lips. "You fools! You have no idea what you're unleashing!"

In an instant, the ground beneath us began to tremble. The warehouse, our battleground, shuddered as if the very foundation was rebelling against the power we had summoned. "What's happening?" I shouted, the fear clawing back into my throat as the walls groaned ominously.

"Stay strong!" Jonah shouted, trying to maintain focus amidst the chaos. But just then, the roof above us began to crack, long fissures snaking through the wood and metal.

"Get out!" I yelled, adrenaline flooding my veins as I pulled Jonah toward the exit. But the shadows surged once more, swirling violently, a desperate attempt to reclaim their dominion.

Suddenly, a blinding light erupted from the shadows, and I felt the force of it push us back, knocking the breath from my lungs. I struggled to regain my footing, but as I looked up, my heart dropped. The Raven was no longer just a man cloaked in darkness; he was transforming, becoming something more—a monstrous figure wreathed in shadows and fury, a storm unleashed.

"This is just the beginning!" he roared, and with one final sweep of his hand, the shadows surged toward us, a tidal wave of darkness ready to swallow everything whole.

As we stood on the precipice of despair, I realized we had unwittingly awoken something far more powerful than we had anticipated. I reached for Jonah, our hands clasping tightly, hearts pounding in sync, ready to face the unknown together.

"Jonah!" I screamed, but the shadows rushed forward, and in that final moment, the world dissolved around us. The darkness engulfed us, swallowing our cries, leaving only silence.

In the void, my mind raced, racing to grasp at the thread of hope that had guided us this far. What had we unleashed, and was it too late to reclaim our light?

# Chapter 24: New Beginnings

The air buzzed with a crackling energy as we stepped out of the subway station, the familiar scent of roasted chestnuts wafting through the crisp autumn air. People brushed past us, each wrapped up in their own little world—lovers laughing, children darting between the legs of their parents, the occasional street performer strumming a catchy tune on a guitar. It was the kind of scene that would make anyone feel alive, yet it contrasted sharply with the dark cloud of uncertainty that had followed us for too long. But now, the weight of our shared ordeal—the threat of The Raven—had begun to dissipate like morning fog, revealing a world reborn.

Jonah's hand was warm in mine, grounding me amid the delightful chaos. I turned to him, his face alive with that boyish enthusiasm I had come to adore. "What do you think?" he asked, a teasing glint in his deep-set eyes as he gestured to a nearby art installation, a chaotic whirlwind of color and texture that seemed to dance with the wind. "Can you believe it? They've already started replacing the art that The Raven defaced."

I laughed, the sound bubbling up from somewhere deep within, a sound that felt foreign yet liberating. "Only in this city could they turn chaos into something so... extravagant." It was a bold and unapologetic statement of resilience, much like the artists who thrived here.

With a playful shove, Jonah pushed me toward the vibrant display, its colors swirling like a painter's palette gone wild. "I dare you to try to describe it without using the word 'chaotic,'" he challenged, a smirk dancing on his lips.

"Oh, please!" I countered, crossing my arms. "You know that's practically impossible. It's a beautiful mess." I leaned closer, inhaling the tang of fresh paint mingled with the aroma of sizzling street food. "Like a firework show gone slightly off the rails."

"Ah, but don't you see?" he replied, stepping up beside me and lowering his voice as if sharing a secret. "That's life, isn't it? A beautiful mess."

There was something intoxicating about the way he saw the world—his perspective shone a light on every shadowy corner, illuminating the beauty in imperfection. I found myself smiling, buoyed by the rhythm of the city and the unexpected spark that lit our conversations. It was a different kind of dance, one that flowed through words and laughter instead of music.

As we ambled down the cobblestone streets, I felt the first tentative stirrings of hope within me. Hope that the scars left by The Raven's chaos would fade, hope that we could rebuild not just our lives but the vibrant threads of our community. I turned to Jonah, the corners of my mouth curving upward. "So, where to next? The art show at The Curiosity Gallery or the bookshop with the enchanting name?"

He pretended to mull it over, tapping his chin thoughtfully. "Both sound delightful, but I know you—your heart lies with the stories. You need a good tale to spin."

I chuckled, my cheeks warming at the truth in his words. "And you're always my favorite storyteller."

With that, we veered toward the bookshop, its charming exterior adorned with vines that clung like eager fans to the aging brick walls. The bell above the door chimed softly as we entered, the familiar musty scent of paper and ink enveloping us. Rows of books towered over us, whispering their secrets, while an array of mismatched armchairs beckoned in cozy corners.

"Look!" I exclaimed, pointing to a shelf filled with dusty tomes. "It's like a treasure trove just waiting to be discovered. Think we could camp out here for a week?"

Jonah snorted, pretending to adjust an imaginary pair of glasses. "Sure, just give me a blanket and a few cups of that overly sweetened tea you love. We'll make it a literary holiday."

"Only if we can swap tales of epic romances while devouring pastries." I winked, imagining us ensconced in our own little world amid the chaos outside.

We lost ourselves in the aisles, flipping through pages filled with adventures, poetry, and heartbreak. I paused to admire a vintage edition of my favorite classic, its leather cover worn and soft, like a beloved companion. Jonah wandered over, his eyes dancing with mischief. "You know, if we ever want to start a book club, I'll happily join as long as the snacks are included."

"Deal! I'll bring the pastries, you bring the questionable opinions." I grinned, then turned serious, my thoughts drifting to the darker times we'd faced. "Do you think we'll ever really be free of The Raven's shadow?"

Jonah's smile faltered for just a heartbeat. "I think shadows linger to remind us of what we've overcome," he said quietly, his voice steady. "But they don't define us."

The warmth of his words enveloped me like a blanket against the chill of lingering fear. He was right—our scars were stories, battle wounds from a fight we hadn't chosen but had survived together. I looked around at the colorful covers lining the shelves, each a testament to resilience and rebirth. "Then let's write our own story," I declared, determination sparking in my chest.

"Absolutely." His gaze met mine, and in that shared moment, a world of unspoken promises hung between us—a commitment to embrace the future together, to fill the pages of our lives with joy and laughter, and to seek out the adventures waiting just beyond the horizon.

As we stepped out into the afternoon light, the city pulsed with life, vibrant and loud, reminding us that amidst chaos, beauty thrived. Hand in hand, we plunged into the bustling streets, ready to chase down new beginnings, armed with hope and a determination to forge our own path. The story was ours to write, one word at a time.

The light danced through the tall windows of the bookshop, casting a warm glow over the pages of countless stories, each waiting for someone to breathe life into them. Jonah and I had settled into one of the inviting armchairs, the kind that hugged you like an old friend, and while I rifled through a collection of poetry, he perused a hefty volume on local artists. The atmosphere was a blend of hushed whispers and the soft rustle of turning pages, punctuated by the distant clink of tea cups from the café at the back.

"Listen to this," I said, reading aloud a passage that spoke of love as a transformative force. "It says here that love doesn't just make us better; it reveals our true selves." I glanced up, catching the glimmer of curiosity in Jonah's eyes. "What do you think? Is love a mirror or a magnifying glass?"

Jonah leaned back, his expression thoughtful. "Definitely a mirror. It shows you who you really are, sometimes in ways you'd rather not see." He paused, a half-smile creeping onto his lips. "But it can also amplify the best parts, like a perfect Instagram filter. You know, the one that makes you look less like a potato."

I laughed, shaking my head. "Only you would relate love to social media aesthetics." But his words hung in the air, a reminder of how we had both grown in the wake of our shared trials. Our relationship was now an intricate tapestry woven from trust, vulnerability, and a healthy dose of sarcasm.

"Speaking of amplifying," Jonah said, turning serious as he shifted closer, "I think we should have a little chat about what's next for us—like, really next." The teasing spark in his eyes dimmed, replaced by a flicker of concern.

"What do you mean?" I asked, the sudden gravity in his tone making my stomach flip.

"I know we've been through a lot, and I don't want to rush into anything, but we should talk about where we're headed." He glanced at the floor, then back at me, sincerity etched across his face. "I just don't want to end up in the same place we were before, with secrets and uncertainty hanging over us."

A rush of warmth enveloped me. Jonah was right; we needed to lay a foundation built on honesty, not just shared experiences. "I've been thinking about that too," I admitted, my voice softer now. "This last chapter—our fight against The Raven—made me realize how important it is to be open about our dreams."

"Then let's start there." Jonah leaned forward, his elbows resting on his knees, a signal that this was more than just idle chit-chat. "What do you want? What does this new beginning look like for you?"

I took a deep breath, the sweet scent of old books filling my lungs. "I want to create something meaningful, something that resonates. I've always loved art, and being around it again has reignited that spark." I glanced at him, gauging his reaction. "But I also want to build a life that feels whole—together."

His eyes softened, the warmth returning. "And I want to support you in that. I've been considering starting a gallery—something that showcases local artists, gives them a voice. What if we partnered up? Art and storytelling, a true reflection of what we love."

A flutter of excitement coursed through me. "You'd really do that? Partner with me in something like that?"

"Why not?" he replied, a playful glimmer returning. "You've got the vision, and I've got the charm. Together, we'd be unstoppable."

"Oh, so you're charming now?" I shot back, my laughter mingling with the joy swelling in my chest.

"Charming enough to woo you, right?"

"Touché," I conceded, warmth creeping into my cheeks. "Okay, so we'll start dreaming up our gallery. What about the practical stuff? Financing, location, all the boring but necessary details?"

"We'll figure it out together," he said confidently. "Let's make a list, brainstorm ideas, and just see where it takes us."

As we tossed ideas back and forth, the possibilities began to bloom like the vibrant autumn leaves outside. We envisioned cozy exhibition spaces adorned with works that spoke to the heart, workshops where aspiring artists could learn and share, and community events that would draw people together.

With each idea, I felt a surge of enthusiasm, a tangible excitement thrumming in the air. I grabbed a nearby napkin and started scribbling notes, my pen racing to keep up with the flood of creativity flowing between us. "And we'll definitely have to have an opening night with a killer playlist," I said, my fingers almost dancing on the paper. "Something that gets people vibing."

"Absolutely, but you know I'm in charge of the music," Jonah shot back, feigning a serious expression. "Your taste in music is questionable at best."

I gasped, clutching the napkin to my chest. "How dare you! I'll have you know my playlists are legendary!"

Jonah raised an eyebrow, a smile tugging at the corner of his mouth. "Legendary in the same way that a train wreck is entertaining—everyone stares, but no one wants to be a part of it."

"Fine, I'll allow you to curate the music," I relented, laughing as I rolled my eyes. "But only if you promise to include at least one of my songs."

"Deal," he replied, grinning. "This is going to be amazing, you know that, right?"

With a renewed sense of purpose, we left the bookshop, hand in hand, the world outside bursting with color and life. The trees stood adorned in fiery reds and oranges, and the sun dipped low, casting long shadows that danced at our feet. There was an energy in the air, a promise that whispered of adventure and new beginnings, and as we walked, our laughter mingled with the vibrant pulse of the city.

That's when the unexpected happened. Just as we rounded the corner, a familiar face appeared—a fleeting shadow from the past. My heart raced, a jolt of apprehension spiraling through me. It was a figure I recognized, a remnant of The Raven's chaotic legacy.

"Isn't that..." I whispered, my voice catching in my throat.

Jonah followed my gaze, his brow furrowing in concern. "Yeah, it is."

And just like that, the promise of new beginnings clashed with the unsettling echo of unresolved tensions, reminding us that while we were ready to paint a bright future, the shadows of our past still loomed just out of sight.

My heart raced as I locked eyes with the figure across the street, a fleeting shadow of the past that I hadn't expected to see again. A rush of adrenaline surged through me, flooding my senses with the bitter taste of fear and uncertainty. Jonah's grip tightened around my hand, his body tensing as he followed my gaze.

"There's no way..." I breathed, half in disbelief, half in dread. The figure stood at the corner, partially obscured by the shadows of a nearby café, but the familiar silhouette was unmistakable. The unmistakable chill of recognition crept down my spine. "Is that—?"

"Yes, it is," Jonah confirmed, his voice low, an edge of caution lacing his words.

"What's he doing here?" I asked, the question bursting forth before I could filter it through a web of rational thought.

"I don't know, but we should—"

But before Jonah could finish, the figure turned. A sharp gasp escaped my lips as I took in the face that had haunted my dreams and loomed in the corners of my memories. It was Nico, the one who had once been a confidant, now an enigma wrapped in layers of betrayal.

I could feel my heart thundering in my chest, the streets buzzing around us, oblivious to the chaos swirling in my mind. I wanted to turn and run, to escape the past, but the fear of turning my back on the person who had once been an ally kept me rooted to the spot. "We need to go," I whispered urgently, my voice barely rising above the din of the bustling street.

But Jonah didn't move. "Wait. Let's see what he's up to."

"What? Are you crazy?" I shot back, the panic rising in my throat. "You think he's here for a friendly chat?"

"I'm just saying that we shouldn't jump to conclusions." He stepped closer to the edge of the sidewalk, determination flickering in his eyes. "We need to know if he's a threat."

Nico took a step forward, his expression inscrutable, caught in the amber glow of the streetlights. A slow smile spread across his face, a smile that sent a cold shiver racing down my spine. "Fancy seeing you two here," he called, his voice smooth and mocking, as if he relished the tension hanging between us.

"Not so fancy for us," Jonah retorted, his protective instincts surging. "What do you want, Nico?"

"Straight to the point. I see you've lost none of your charm," Nico replied, casually adjusting the collar of his leather jacket, as if we were simply meeting for drinks rather than standing on the precipice of old grudges. "I come bearing news."

"News?" I echoed, skepticism dripping from my tone. "What could you possibly say that we'd care about?"

"Oh, you'd care," he said, leaning in, his voice dropping to a conspiratorial whisper. "You see, The Raven may have been apprehended, but the game is far from over. There are still pieces in play—pieces that could change everything."

Jonah took a step forward, his brow furrowing. "What are you talking about? What game?"

Nico's eyes sparkled with a mischievous gleam. "You're not as naïve as I thought, Jonah. There's a bigger picture here—one you both failed to see." He leaned back against the lamppost, a satisfied smirk dancing on his lips as if he were enjoying our confusion. "You think you're safe, but the truth is, The Raven had allies. You didn't eliminate the threat; you only made it more complicated."

A wave of dread washed over me, every instinct screaming for us to get away. "You're lying," I snapped, but doubt crept into my mind like an unwelcome visitor. Was it possible? Had we truly ended one nightmare only to tumble into another?

"Am I?" Nico raised an eyebrow, challenging me to dismiss his words. "I've come to warn you. There's a storm coming, and it's much bigger than anything you've faced before."

"Why would you care?" Jonah asked, a hint of accusation lacing his tone. "You've always been on your own side."

"True," Nico replied with a disarming shrug, "but sometimes the enemy of my enemy is... well, my enemy too. We're all connected in this chaotic web." He pointed toward the bustling streets, where laughter rang out and the city thrummed with life. "You think you can just walk away? No one walks away clean."

"I don't trust you," I said firmly, though the tremor in my voice betrayed my conviction. "You've manipulated enough lives for your own gain."

"Maybe," he said, the smirk fading for a moment as his eyes grew serious. "But I'm not the one who pulled the strings this time. You've only scratched the surface."

I glanced at Jonah, searching for answers in his steady gaze. "What do we do?" I asked, the gravity of our situation sinking in.

"We have to know more," Jonah replied, his voice calm but resolute. "If there's even a chance that The Raven has allies, we can't afford to ignore it."

Nico's gaze flickered between us, a predatory gleam igniting in his eyes. "Now you're thinking. Meet me tonight, 10 p.m., at The Gilded Lounge. I'll share everything I know. But come alone."

"Why should we believe you?" I challenged, crossing my arms defiantly.

"Because it's your only choice," he said simply, a sinister smile resurfacing. "I promise you'll want to hear what I have to say. It might just save your lives."

Before we could respond, he turned and melted into the crowd, leaving us standing there, stunned and uncertain.

"What the hell just happened?" I muttered, still trying to process the gravity of his words.

"Exactly what he wanted," Jonah replied, his expression darkening. "A threat disguised as an invitation. But he might be right. If we ignore this, we could find ourselves in a world of trouble."

I swallowed hard, the weight of our new reality pressing down on me. "So, we actually have to go."

"Yeah," Jonah agreed, his voice steady despite the turmoil in his eyes. "But we'll go prepared."

As we walked away from the corner, the laughter and warmth of the city felt like a distant memory, overshadowed by the looming darkness of uncertainty. Every step echoed with the promise of an unknown danger lurking just beyond our grasp, a reminder that the past never truly let go, and new beginnings might be built on shaky ground.

The sun dipped below the horizon, casting long shadows as we hurried home, the thrill of our plans overshadowed by a sense of foreboding. We couldn't shake the feeling that this was merely the calm before the storm, and as we reached our apartment, I glanced back at the street, a chill creeping up my spine.

Something was coming—something big. And as I closed the door behind us, the weight of the unspoken lingered in the air, wrapping around us like an unwelcome cloak. We had to face it head-on, but the question remained: would we be ready for what lay ahead?

Milton Keynes UK
Ingram Content Group UK Ltd.
UKHW030912121124
451094UK00001B/127

# BALUNGI'S GUIDE

## TO A HEALTHY PREGNANCY

## A GUIDE TO A HEALTHY PREGNANCY
## AND CHILD BIRTH

### BALUNGI FRANCIS

# TABLE OF CONTENTS

INTRODUCTION ..................................................1

CHAPTER ONE ...................................................3

When is the right time? ..........................................3

CHAPTER TWO ...................................................8

It has happened, what next? ...................................8

CHAPTER THREE ..............................................15

Traditional medicine a myth.................................15

CHAPTER FOUR.................................................19

My husband......................................................19

CHAPTER FIVE..................................................24

The infection, cure and life ...................................24

About The Author ..............................................28

CONNECT WITH BALUNGI FRANCIS...........31

# INTRODUCTION

One evening I visited my sister Ria Gorret whose baby Gogy was sick. The doctors had said that he had an infection which they couldn't examine and ascertain with accuracy. The problem here was not examining the infection but rather a question as to why a baby born so well without any problem fall sick and suddenly dies within 24hours. Why does it happen mostly to the first born? Is it caused by the father or the mother? Could it be the polluted air we breathe?

There have been instant deaths in infants all around the world. The issue I am presenting here is not about death during birth, but it is about how many die after birth. It hurts to loose someone after you have done

1

every good deed for him for the betterment of his life and future hardships to come.

Think about it this way, after carrying a baby for nine months, after taking all the medicines, after wearing loose outfits, after shopping for him and finally thereafter someone tells you the baby has died in two days. What the heck is this? Believe me or not this book is about you, it is for you the youth planning for a baby, it is for you a mother and father of a four hourly baby and lastly to you a doctor operating in the maternity ward. It is a call for you and me to do something about this infection.

In the chapters which you will go through, I present the steps that I assume led to the infection.

# CHAPTER ONE

# When is the right time?

When I was 23years old, my big aunt Mofi used to bang me with freaking questions like, when is your first child, hey I wish to see her jumping , woo… all your big buddies have heirs when is yours. My stupid answer as it may sound was, responsibility is the issue. Then she laughed at me uttering words like, responsibility is when you have a child and a wife at home, you won't get anywhere in this world without the two, I mean the baby. This touched me so much with fear. I then rushed into things without planning and guess what happened.

There is no right time for having babies as it is to marriages. Why is it that we spend a lot of time preparing for engagements and spend little or nothing on having a baby? A baby is a precious gift one can get, but what is its use when you have it in your womb for 9 months and then in your hands for only one day. I think it adds up to nothing. I recommend proper planning before having babies.

Before the right time knocks on your door, you should at least have taken proper inquiries from those who have experienced all the tough times of baby days and nights.

Age also matters. If I may ask, what is the basic age for someone to get pregnant or to impregnate? Some recommend 18years and others 24 years. There are those who even urge and shout 40years. I may then ask a question, at what age is the infection at work? This to a professional doctor is a myth. But any way we will explore the question in the coming chapters.

The age issue has been a catastrophe to law makers and implementers. While we have witnessed that even a 13 year old can give birth in some religious sectors we node our heads and proclaim liberty where there is ignorance. Birth at 13years happens but it is forced labor. I recommend willingness to do something for oneself at the right time.

Babies are innocent. Therefore whatever you do regardless of your baby most especially a baby still in her mother's womb causes death to him. We may for God sake not believe this but note carefully that, what you speak, what you eat , what you drink and what you feel in some way affects a baby in your womb. That is why I say, what your mother and father did will affect you in future. I therefore recommend total care to the unborn child. You will note in the coming chapters that the infection was you. The ignorance in you might have led to the infection.

I want you to know that having babies is your decision and not someone's as my aunt Mofi. Therefore it is your duty to do away with any forceful engagements and artworks of pregnancy at any level. Note that the right time is you and what you are going through. The age limit on the other hand is when you can handle all the responsibilities due onto you. To the women out there, birth is what you can have when you can handle it mentally not physically because what kills a baby is how you have been thinking all along. To the father out there having a son or daughter is what you have analyzed in your mind that you are ready for any responsibility that comes your way because what kills a baby is how you respond to the need of the mother on behalf of a baby.

If you qualify you can go ahead and give that lady a big B. For a lady you can go a head and carry it for nine months. Now that you have it for the first time, second or may be 20times, how are you going to care for it, are you ready to face the world.

The next chapter takes you through the mistakes most men do in the process of carrying the unborn. I encourage you to read through because you could save a life of one or two infants each day.

# CHAPTER TWO

# It has happened, what next?

A seed put in good soil will only germinate and produce good fruits only if put to good fertilizers. Of course birds and small animals will want to eat it before germination but proper protection is given with the help of a scarecrow. This also happens to pregnant women and the unborn baby to. But do not worry there is provision for every need we need only if we think our way to the highest of everything.

Many people will start giving advice on how you should care for your unborn child, I urge you to take good advice because not every advice is good for the betterment of your child. Advice is sometimes given where someone thinks that you know nothing about the situation you are going through. But I tell you, whether you are aware about the problem, the advice given should be analyzed because what kills a baby is hate and dissatisfaction.

Stylish women most especially the celebrities are faced with the problem of not showing off their pregnancy to the society. They then resort to cosmetics, whereby they smear it on the stomach to prevent the stomach from exploding. If only they knew that they were hurting the baby they would stop. Such advice given by friends, doctors and some influential people should be analyzed before taking it.

Another technique used by people in developing countries, is the one of tying the stomach with belts or a piece of a cloth to keep it in shape. This is due to peer pressure, where you find someone telling others that a big stomach is not good to show off in community or a gathering because it makes others sick. Such people are far more than primitive, do not listen to them. If only they knew what they are doing they could stop immediately.

What you eat is also important as a child carrier. We have heard of women who eat soil and dried clay. Wonder why they do this, a child feeds on what you take, as an alcoholic what do you expect from your child's behavior after birth. Think twice and change your ways. Eating clay gives your child a shape good for animals residing in the same, will he or she be able to cope up with the atmosphere you are nurturing her into.

How you feel about others is also how your baby feels unto them. People who spend time gossiping about others, spreading all the hate is dangerous to the unborn. I tell you hate kills the baby before birth. Now that you are carrying a baby you should behave differently.

There is this woman who lived a far off in Gupe town of Edenen, he was so in love with his husband to a point were he could give out her life for his sake. After a year had passed by, he was pregnant. The scan results as were analyzed by a doctor read that she was carrying a baby boy. Needless to say, in the four months of her love for a baby, the husband totally changed. He could beat her every night, no food at the table and on top of that uttering words like, "I hate to see you like that", "I think the baby isn't mine". What a mess. With all this humiliation the wife decide to go in a far off village to stay with her mother.

In many instances you find that, what we expect during the nine months is far more different than what we face during these months. As a husband you are expected to show much love than before because love does not kill. What makes you think that you will be loved by a child when all you did was cursing him? Do you even know that what you say to your wife is told to your child by the wife herself in mind and action? I can assure you that every bit of it is known by that little baby.

The peace of every unborn is the peace of his mother "the carrier". Where there is peace also love is. A day spent with your pregnant wife is a day with your infant.

When something new happens to you or when there is a change in you, people close to you seem to behave differently about you. They ask questions most of which are stressing, they look at you with a red eye and shy away, they also tend to control you and thereby advice you on how you should behave.

I have seen people who have fallen sick because of too much headache, most of which is due to many questions at the work place, in the taxi cab and in the neighborhood. These things also happen to pregnant women.

After pregnancy a lot is expected to happen. What infects the baby among many things is the question of "when are you delivering" this is when someone even at earlier periods of pregnancy asks with confidence about the actual date, time and month of delivery. Why should someone be curious about the actual date of delivery, why do we force birth when it is not ready? I care less about such issues because I know how it feels when speediness reduces on the birth rate.

What happens next after pregnancy is the question here. Let us explore the question presented to us by asking ourselves other questions like:

Will you visit the hospital together with your husband for medical checkups?

Will you take every advice from your siblings, doctors and friends about your unborn baby?

Will you feed on every diet that comes your way?

Are you ready to quit smoking?

Alcohol is harmful to your baby, are you quitting?

Will you exercise or visit gyms every day?

If you agree please tick that which you agree to and read the next chapter. Otherwise for those who disagree do not read the next chapter because you do not apply.

# CHAPTER THREE

# Traditional medicine a myth

Traditional medicine would have been good, but superstitions and the poor quality of the brand have made it difficult for most people to buy the idea.

Imagine for example, a person's belief, that water from a banana plant when taken a few minutes toward labor speeds up the birth process. Also there is belief that labor done while holding a banana plant is better than that done by a medical doctor from a renowned hospital.

Beliefs of the kind are still going on in a world were education is a threat.

Women between the ages of 21-40 years use traditional medicine. They collect the medicine from forests and bushy areas. While gathering the medicine, they refer to their grandmothers ideas about the type of the plant. The ideas perceived by people about the medicine are those collected or taught from generations to generations. These ideas seem to work for a few people in instances termed as "luck".

It has been said that, a pregnant woman who does not drink or bathe the medicine will face birth complications. The fear that comes with such instructions is great and you will find that many people resort to traditionalists in fear of losing a baby.

Because of the abundance of traditional medicine, many pregnant women have given a deaf ear to professional doctors. Even when sensitized to go for check up every week, they tend to ignore the media.

This also happens when people are called on to go for immunization.

The infection in infants is not very far, it is within us the caretakers. Many infants have died because of lack of knowledge to differentiate between what is wrong and what is right. Why should someone sacrifice life while building on ideas of our past fathers? Some of these ideas where not even tested and on top of that, there is not even a written manuscript from our ancestors that clearly indicates the procedure one is required to follow while using the medicine.

Many people have heard from their grand fathers and mothers for God sake, that, when you mix sand with avocado leaves and cook for some time, you will have a medicine good for the cure of skin diseases in babies. These things of "I have heard someone says so, that it works or my mother told me, will not work.

Remember we leave in a world of scientifically proven ideas. These ideas are tested in a laboratory and then proved to work with no harm on human life. Thing like, my mother told me, are not tested, they are just guesses taken from our ancestors with no proof to back them up.

A pregnant woman is not advised to take medicine any how, be it herbal or laboratory medicine. Medicines taken without proper advice from a professional doctor will either infect the unborn baby or led to birth complications. It is therefore the duty of a husband and a wife to visit a professional doctor on issues concerning pregnancy.

Deaths in infants occur because we fail to visit hospitals, we tend to ignore a doctor's advice on medication and also the use of traditional medicine not tested for the wellbeing of the unborn baby.

# CHAPTER FOUR

# My husband

In our tradition it is said that, during pregnancy a wife leaves his husband and goes to her mother's house for comfort. The reason behind the statement is that, the husband is brain drain of the requirements of his wife. On the tradition side of it this may be true simply because the type of medicine needed is only known by the mother.

However, I disagree with the reason as to why the wife leaves his husband for her mothers. The most evident reason is that, during times of pregnancy the behaviors of the wife change, she becomes violent and sometimes handicapped.

What most men do during these times is to do away with every bit of home responsibilities, and worst of all fornication.

I wonder sometimes why a wife who used to listen, who was kind and could take care of his husband, would change during pregnancy times and start using abusive language. The one who used to be clean and smart is now dirty and shabby. For women, if I may ask, how do you expect your man to react while seeing you in that shadow situation? I hope if he is that kind, he will kindly ask you to seek advice from a physiatrist and not send you to your mother as you think.

A peaceful mind is what is required of every pregnant woman. A mind that is peaceful is good in shaping the mind of the unborn baby. A violent woman who shouts because he earlier heard that, a pregnant woman should be violent will end up producing a foolish baby. The infection that kills our infants is us; we should be peaceful both in mind and spirit.

20

The question is what is required of the husband during pregnancy times? The question is put forward because women tend to complain, that, the husband absentees himself during times of pregnancy. During these beautiful times of expecting a baby, a husband should behave in away as if the baby is present, he should believe in his mind that the baby is in existence, perceive as if holding him. In this, you will be able to purchase every need that is required for the baby. A husband at this time is required to do all the shopping for the baby. A husband is required to show affection in inquiry for the sex of the baby. Lastly , a husband is required to take her wife to the hospital for medical checkups. All in all he should show much love ever than before for his wife, he is required to repeat the same crazy things that he did for her when they first mate.

During labor every woman would like to be in direct contact with the husband because it is at this time that the wife needs protection, which neither the doctor can provide. The protection required by the wife is the one that can only be provided by his husband. She feels secure when the husband is around taking care and most especially to act as a seal or evidence that the baby came exactly from her wife.

Sadly to say, you find few men who can stand outside the hospital or who even call. Most of them are busy on work; they do not even care about anything that happens. They know for sure they have hired a nurse and a driver to take care of that.

There is a friend of mine, a marketer of rain coats, it was a rainy day and business was booming. Her wife was taken to a family clinic not feeling well, she had labor pains. They called the husband on phone, he said, "I am busy making money, doctor take care of that I will send the money via mobile money". The wife tried to push with no results, this took a long time, I think the wife had no much power to do this, she needed an operation. But this was a clinic with no operation ward.

The doctor advised her to push or else they were to lose both the baby and the mother, to which she did and there was a beautiful baby boy. Unfortunately the baby needed some oxygen to breath well, a nurse together with the mother rushed the baby to a big hospital for help, with the mother crying they put the baby on oxygen and tried to call the father. This time he was on time because the rain coats had just got finished. He had to pay for visiting fees and some medicines, after four minutes the doctors examined the baby to which they found that he was cold meaning that he was dead. I tell you all the blame was put on the first doctor in the clinic. Guess who did the blaming, the father of course.

To this day, no one knows the infection, but from my analysis, the father in this case was the infection because he failed to take his responsibility up to the end.

# CHAPTER FIVE

# The infection, cure and life

When Ria had delivered, the maternity doctor carried out a few medical checkups on her and the baby to and thereafter sent them right away.

Ria got up went home with a baby and all was fine. Then in the evening at around 4pm, the baby cried unceasingly. Checking on the body temperature, he was very hot and had failures in breathing. They rushed her to a nearby hospital for help. The usual key word for the doctors is "this is malaria", for anybody with a high temperature that is their key word but this was serious to the extent that the baby's skin became yellowish in color.

Now the problem was not why the baby temperature was rising steadily but to why the skin of the baby was yellow, this puzzled the mother and the doctors to, until one unknown woman from a nearby word laughed with cheer saying in a "luganda" language "that is Kamuli" although Kamuli is the type of the infection, but the doctors cautioned her to not scare off the mother, to my surprise the woman went ahead to say " the only cure is to lay the baby in the morning sunrise" once he has received this little light everything will be okay. As if we were deaf , early in the morning while everybody was asleep we put the baby in the sunshine, we did this for three days but guess what? It never worked all was a lie.

The baby's condition worsened to the extent that it was difficult for him to breast feed and I hope you know what it means for the baby to not take milk, the doctors had to use a capillary to feed the little poor one with milk powder.

In this I thank the almighty Father that the more we prayed for the baby the better he became, prayers also do work in these hospitals, every morning on the hospitals radio station and television they served us with the word of God to keep us moving. They did this while encouraging us that however much the doctors work it is the lord who heals.

The doctors injected the baby with all sorts of medicine but the situation was still not fine until when they repeated the whole process with new checkups and drugs. It is at this stage that the baby was healed of the infection. It was a miracle for us that he was well since many babies in the same hospital had died of the same infection. But up to this day the infection is not known to English doctors but in our country to traditional doctors it is called "Kamuli". From my analysis I still argue that, the father was the infection since he was not

there for the baby until birth.

# About The Author

*Balungi Francis was born in Kampala, Uganda, to a single poor mother, grew up in Kawempe, and later joined Makerere Universty in 2006, graduating with a Bachelor Science degree in Land Surveying in 2010. For four years he taught in Kampala City high schools, majoring in the fields of Gravitation and Quantum Physics. His first book, "Mathematical Foundation of the Quantum theory of Gravity," won the Young Kampala Innovative Prize and was mentioned in the African Next Einstein Book Prize (ANE).*

*He has spent over 15years researching and discovering connections in physics, mathematics, geometry, cosmology, quantum mechanics, gravity, in addition to astrophysics, unified physics and geographical information systems . These studies led to his groundbreaking theories, published papers, books and patented inventions in the science of Quantum*

*Gravity, which have received worldwide recognition.*

*From these discoveries, Balungi founded the SUSP (Solutions to the Unsolved Scientific Problems) Project Foundation in 2004 - now known as the SUSP Science Foundation. As its current Director of Research, Balungi leads physicists, mathematicians and engineers in exploring Quantum Gravity principles and their implications in our world today and for future generations*

*Balungi launched the Visionary School of Quantum Gravity in 2016 in order to bring the learning and community further together. It's the first and only Quantum Gravity physics program of its kind, educating thousands of students from over 80 countries.*

*The book "Quantum Gravity in a Nutshell1", a most recommend book in quantum gravity research , was produced based on Balungi's discoveries and their potential for generations to come.*

*Balungi is currently guiding the Foundation, speaking to audiences worldwide, and continuing his groundbreaking research.*

# CONNECT WITH BALUNGI FRANCIS

*I really appreciate you reading my book*

*If you enjoyed this book or found it useful I'd be very grateful if you'd post a short review. Your support really does make a difference and I read all the reviews personally so I can get your feedback and make this book even better.*

*Thanks again for your support!*

What happens next after Birth is the question here. Let us explore the question presented to us by asking ourselves other questions like:

Will you visit the hospital together with your husband for medical checkups?

Will you take every advice from your siblings, doctors and friends about your unborn baby?

Will you feed on every diet that comes your way?

Are you ready to quit smoking?

Alcohol is harmful to your baby, are you quitting?

Will you exercise or visit gyms everyday?

If you agree please tick that which you agree to and read the next chapter. Other wise for those who disagree do not read the next chapter because you do not apply.

What happens next after Birth is the question here. Let us explore the question presented to us by asking ourselves other questions like:

Will you visit the hospital together with your husband for medical checkups?

Will you take every advice from your siblings, doctors and friends about your unborn baby?

Will you feed on every diet that comes your way?

Are you ready to quit smoking?

Alcohol is harmful to your baby, are you quitting?

Will you exercise or visit gyms everyday?

If you agree please tick that which you agree to and read the next chapter. Other wise for those who disagree do not read the next chapter because you do not apply.

What happens next after Birth is the question here. Let us explore the question presented to us by asking ourselves other questions like:

Will you visit the hospital together with your husband for medical checkups?

Will you take every advice from your siblings, doctors and friends about your unborn baby?

Will you feed on every diet that comes your way?

Are you ready to quit smoking?

Alcohol is harmful to your baby, are you quitting?

Will you exercise or visit gyms everyday?

If you agree please tick that which you agree to and read the next chapter. Other wise for those who disagree do not read the next chapter because you do not apply.

What happens next after Birth is the question here. Let us explore the question presented to us by asking ourselves other questions like:

Will you visit the hospital together with your husband for medical checkups?

Will you take every advice from your siblings, doctors and friends about your unborn baby?

Will you feed on every diet that comes your way?

Are you ready to quit smoking?

Alcohol is harmful to your baby, are you quitting?

Will you exercise or visit gyms everyday?

If you agree please tick that which you agree to and read the next chapter. Other wise for those who disagree do not read the next chapter because you do not apply.

What happens next after Birth is the question here. Let us explore the question presented to us by asking ourselves other questions like:

Will you visit the hospital together with your husband for medical checkups?

Will you take every advice from your siblings, doctors and friends about your unborn baby?

Will you feed on every diet that comes your way?

Are you ready to quit smoking?

Alcohol is harmful to your baby, are you quitting?

Will you exercise or visit gyms everyday?

If you agree please tick that which you agree to and read the next chapter. Other wise for those who disagree do not read the next chapter because you do not apply.

What happens next after Birth is the question here. Let us explore the question presented to us by asking ourselves other questions like:

Will you visit the hospital together with your husband for medical checkups?

Will you take every advice from your siblings, doctors and friends about your unborn baby?

Will you feed on every diet that comes your way?

Are you ready to quit smoking?

Alcohol is harmful to your baby, are you quitting?

Will you exercise or visit gyms everyday?

If you agree please tick that which you agree to and read the next chapter. Other wise for those who disagree do not read the next chapter because you do not apply.

What happens next after Birth is the question here. Let us explore the question presented to us by asking ourselves other questions like:

Will you visit the hospital together with your husband for medical checkups?

Will you take every advice from your siblings, doctors and friends about your unborn baby?

Will you feed on every diet that comes your way?

Are you ready to quit smoking?

Alcohol is harmful to your baby, are you quitting?

Will you exercise or visit gyms everyday?

If you agree please tick that which you agree to and read the next chapter. Other wise for those who disagree do not read the next chapter because you do not apply.

What happens next after Birth is the question here. Let us explore the question presented to us by asking ourselves other questions like:

Will you visit the hospital together with your husband for medical checkups?

Will you take every advice from your siblings, doctors and friends about your unborn baby?

Will you feed on every diet that comes your way?

Are you ready to quit smoking?

Alcohol is harmful to your baby, are you quitting?

Will you exercise or visit gyms everyday?

If you agree please tick that which you agree to and read the next chapter. Other wise for those who disagree do not read the next chapter because you do not apply.

What happens next after Birth is the question here. Let us explore the question presented to us by asking ourselves other questions like:

Will you visit the hospital together with your husband for medical checkups?

Will you take every advice from your siblings, doctors and friends about your unborn baby?

Will you feed on every diet that comes your way?

Are you ready to quit smoking?

Alcohol is harmful to your baby, are you quitting?

Will you exercise or visit gyms everyday?

If you agree please tick that which you agree to and read the next chapter. Other wise for those who disagree do not read the next chapter because you do not apply.

What happens next after Birth is the question here. Let us explore the question presented to us by asking ourselves other questions like:

Will you visit the hospital together with your husband for medical checkups?

Will you take every advice from your siblings, doctors and friends about your unborn baby?

Will you feed on every diet that comes your way?

Are you ready to quit smoking?

Alcohol is harmful to your baby, are you quitting?

Will you exercise or visit gyms everyday?

 If you agree please tick that which you agree to and read the next chapter. Other wise for those who disagree do not read the next chapter because you do not apply.

What happens next after Birth is the question here. Let us explore the question presented to us by asking ourselves other questions like:

Will you visit the hospital together with your husband for medical checkups?

Will you take every advice from your siblings, doctors and friends about your unborn baby?

Will you feed on every diet that comes your way?

Are you ready to quit smoking?

Alcohol is harmful to your baby, are you quitting?

Will you exercise or visit gyms everyday?

If you agree please tick that which you agree to and read the next chapter. Other wise for those who disagree do not read the next chapter because you do not apply.

What happens next after Birth is the question here. Let us explore the question presented to us by asking ourselves other questions like:

Will you visit the hospital together with your husband for medical checkups?

Will you take every advice from your siblings, doctors and friends about your unborn baby?

Will you feed on every diet that comes your way?

Are you ready to quit smoking?

Alcohol is harmful to your baby, are you quitting?

Will you exercise or visit gyms everyday?

If you agree please tick that which you agree to and read the next chapter. Other wise for those who disagree do not read the next chapter because you do not apply.

What happens next after Birth is the question here. Let us explore the question presented to us by asking ourselves other questions like:

Will you visit the hospital together with your husband for medical checkups?

Will you take every advice from your siblings, doctors and friends about your unborn baby?

Will you feed on every diet that comes your way?

Are you ready to quit smoking?

Alcohol is harmful to your baby, are you quitting?

Will you exercise or visit gyms everyday?

If you agree please tick that which you agree to and read the next chapter. Other wise for those who disagree do not read the next chapter because you do not apply.

Lightning Source UK Ltd.
Milton Keynes UK
UKHW040106010820
367514UK00009B/153